THE HANGMAN'S HITCH

DONNA MARIA MCCARTHY

First published in 2016 by:
Britain's Next Bestseller
An imprint of Live It Publishing

27 Old Gloucester Road
London, United Kingdom.
WC1N 3AX

www.britainsnextbestseller.co.uk

Copyright © 2016 by Donna Maria McCarthy
The moral right of Donna Maria McCarthy to be identified as the author
of this work has been asserted by her in accordance with the
Copyright, Designs and Patents Act 1988.

All rights reserved.

Except as permitted under current legislation, no part of this
work may be photocopied, stored in a retrieval system,
published, performed in public, adapted, broadcast, transmitted,
recorded or reproduced in any form or by any means, without
the prior permission of the copyright owners.

All enquiries should be addressed to Britain's Next Bestseller.

Cover design by Dark Imaginarium Art & Design

ISBN 978-1-910565-71-1 PBK

Dedication

To the last of the Great Norse Women

My Mum

Without whom I would sometimes take myself too seriously

And sometimes not enough

Acknowledgements

Murielle Maupoint, David McCaffrey, Diane O'Toole,
Chris Tetreault-Blay, Ben Sawyer, Julie Timlin,
Steven Hayward, Andy Males, Rosemary Carr
and all my awesome author friends!

Prologue

Cast a future before a drowning man, be it light or dark, and he will grab it.

These moments in time slip silently past an unconscious world only apparent to those who so desperate that even the most human quality of forgiveness is lost for them.

Silenced hooves of blackened beasts carry Lucifer's generals to the one who shines so brightly. To the one who would turn back, if he could, and stands fighting alone, stands fighting himself …

For there are none who will challenge him whatever his choice, not anymore, not now he is lost …

Angels forsake for the fire too hot
One found on the road who the Devil begot
His shadow cast on victims past
Where some become witches
With poisoned hearts.

Chapter 1

'Choose your weapon.'

I chose with fingers so cold I barely knew them, the weapon so heavy it slipped from my fingers as I struggled to comprehend that which had brought me here. I was frozen, no blood coursing. Everything had escaped me, no thoughts, every sense was numbed both bodily and common, as though the trigger had already been pulled. As though I was already too late.

Was this the sound of death as it approached? On the darkest night, on ground that gave with every step, air thick, and heavy with freezing fog and suffocating earthly smells.

'Twelve paces turn and then fire!'

Was that the last I would ever hear? Almost collapsing onto heavier ground I began to pace. How many now? I wanted to scream, I have lost count! But the words would not come, mouth too dry, throat too tight. So I fell to the ground weak and exhausted, grateful to the earth that it was soft. I heard myself say,

'I do not want to do this, I cannot!'

I knew not what depraved inch of me whence these words came. I felt sick and cowardly, but also like escaping, too strong the latter I think. This was easier than I had thought!

I was as new, cunning, genius, and quite, quite enlightened.

To me very attractive, although I knew to the unenlightened I would appear the opposite. I cared not! I was damned sure I would never give somebody their satisfaction, far too costly to my meagre purse. No longer blessed with riches that would extend to charity I had felt them slip away when I fell to the ground. My honour, my standing in society, the love and respect of family and friends. If it had hurt to lose them I was too numb to feel it.

'I must, I demand satisfaction!'

Broke an indulgent contemplation.

'I am afraid not, dear friend, you shall have my ruination, surely that is enough? This is a barbarous business and I pledge this day to never make such demands of another.'

Chapter 2

'Cold, isn't it?'

Shaken by the fact that I was not alone I spluttered a nervous response, and feigned fatigue to take better stock of my assailant. He was a well-dressed fellow if not a little over, mid-thirties at a guess and his confident manner of address and cut of his jib should have quelled any worries one might have at such an assault. So wonder then that I felt a little vulnerable, perhaps was the mist that thickly smothered my view of what lay ahead, perhaps this in itself was something I should have been more guarded of. A dark glare through heavy eyes was all he afforded me as he scanned the inadequate before him, an unearthly attraction too intense to be called handsome it was unsettling. He kept a brisk pace and seemed to not have the difficulty in keeping his balance that I did, he had obviously trodden the road before. I barely had chance to reply before he was ten paces ahead and had to stop, the air was too frosty for me at least to maintain a sensible conversation. Talking and walking was best practised by silly girls as they came upon you in the street, and never had any sense to it.

I was scared, why? I could not have told you at this point and confused the emotion with surprise. One thought tickled me laced with a little bravado – does not the very Devil creep upon you in such a way with a predilection for such atmospheres? I laughed though shuddered with the chill, uncommonly cold. However, I thought, as in all such tales at least those I had secretly read in favour of the more sinister, the morning was crisp, and the air hurt to breathe it, short shallow breaths the order and concluded lack of oxygen. The human mind was so susceptible that I wondered if perhaps too many times that which was ignored and put down to a suspicious or over imaginative mind was the very instinct that might save you. Alas, it was too elusive and ethereal in nature to ever hold any gravitas, funny that people more put their faith in luck or chance rather than something that was deeply part of them.

'Well, are you coming, or not!?'

It did not feel like a question, more a taunt but the paranoia had to be put to bed.

'I beg your pardon?'

Halted by the beastly carrion, that mocked me with a twitch of its head and a glare, taking apart its prey with disinterest, I looked about for my new acquaintance, to the human eye he was barely visible, the thickening atmosphere clung to his form … But I was aware. A primitive instinct told me turn back but I felt shackled to this path and so heavy in my lungs was this godforsaken mist and so confused my eye that I ventured on. He had stopped by an aged oak and upon a buckling bough a darkened figure, a shape that looked as if it had life. He beckoned me closer, no word, the gesture was enough. I approached propelled by a need to obey. Closer I came to he and with each step the darkened figure that hung from the bough took shape. A ghastly given up soul of a man, still struggling with a noose about his neck, limbs bound, not inches from the ground to add time and torment to his death. Shaken I felt I must share the spectacle with he, though my mind and body willed me not.

'A lack of control is not unheard of in such situations.'

Highlighting the fact that I had, indeed, urinated down one side of my breeches.

'You are forgiven.'

I choked out some gibberish, some attempt to make light in response and looked upon this man who faced the tormented figure.

'Is no concern for you at this time.'

He mocked me, I was sure, and encouraged my state of growing hysteria to soar and lose its binds.

'Unless of course, you are a damned poacher too? I say this with some irony, Sir, considering your attire. And so repeat, is not your concern for this day, for we never can be sure of the future?'

Had I not been so confused by this devilish armoury I would certainly have run for was a sentence passed that day, witnessed by one giving up whatever soul he had left and that which had sent me this way. He turned, the horrified wretch, to face me.

'Here is something to see, for my sins I am obsessed with the drama!'

And he kicked him, kicked him so hard that the neck finally gave in with a thunderous crack breaking the smothering quiet of the morn. It was too much for my stomach and mind and I violently gave up my last meal.

'Unto Hades deliver me, for I am done.'

He stroked the deformed face of the departed and his own vanity with his words.

'An odd amusement?'

I managed to say,

'And you offer him no Heaven? No forgiveness?'

Ignoring me he turned the figure about again to face me.

'As you see a human is only rendered beautiful by the soul, once it has gone, gah! Ghastly! Don't you think? And as for your smart quip and observations on the last rites or lack of them, do you wonder that they are not offered up too freely? I am sure for a healthy percentage it is a waste of breath! I have many thoughts on the subject, I would impart some if you have an ear to listen? But let us walk as we do. You look in need of something less holy than an epiphany and more welcome than another cold judgement! I am right, am I not?'

Not waiting for response he continued.

'Of course you would be justified in wondering why God in the heavens thinks it wise to bless you all with a soul? More an indulgence! Or is it that he simply enjoys the sport also? What say you to that? Or do I offend and am mistaken and that you are in fact a deeply religious man!?'

'What answer can I give? I come from a society that of late shuns such things, all this as you say, you can retrieve from my attire.'

I had caught him up, not wishing to remain to see what happened to the hanging man be it spiritual or just the carrion that waited patiently at his feet.

'Tell me? You are aware of a malady you suffer? I am truly struck by it.'

'I am aware of none, Sir, would you explain?'

'Of course I shall but let us make haste unless you derive some pleasure?'

He gestured to the death that lay in our wake.

'Of course I do not! Please let us away!'

'I feel as though we have shared something here this day? Something deeply private and quite touching do you not think? A dying man's last. I wonder if he thought me merciless or merciful?'

I could not answer. I cringed at the fact that I had witnessed such things before, I cringed at the fact that I had found them amusing but found a little comfort in the fact that they had not, perhaps, been discharged so brutally.

'The malady I speak of is a propensity to attribute every lash to yourself you blatantly stole from that man with your dramatics and hysteria! And so from this I conclude, bad times?'

Grateful for the change in subject, for the change in his tone and finding myself comfortable in what appeared to be worship for this man, if he be so, I gave in a little more.

'Not the best.'

'Perfect! Come, I am glad you find a confidante in myself but we shall reserve this conversation for later.'

I did note, as we walked, the road closed in behind us and wondered how I would ever find my way back that day.

'You will stay of course? Forgive me, I am no psychic but you will have a sore neck as our friend does if you keep twitching and looking behind! As I say, there are not many who actually choose this path but then you are not so aware as others, makes it rather more exciting for all! Yes?'

'You have a strange manner of address, Sir? Do you enjoy riddles?'

I managed to speak a little trying to level the field of combat.

'I see much and nothing confuses me ever, you simply attribute your state to mine but then this is natural upon first meetings. I believe, and will allow that people like to draw similarities, but personally I find chit-chat a bore especially when there is no point!'

'Again, Sir, I would say that you speak strange and that you make promises. I almost feel threatened?'

'Ha! I would return that is you who are strange and perhaps too familiar?'

'I suppose considering what we have shared?'

'What we have shared I shared with Heaven also, man! But do not think to call the divine one a friend!'

'But I accompany you so I say surely there is no need for caution?'

'And I repeat, so does he, yet we are not similar. I do enjoy the great reveal. You shall see, all will become clear.'

His wicked smile took my breath away for was pure evil if

ever I had seen it, one last look behind but the road was gone.

'Your poor neck!' he remarked over his shoulder.

'To the inn!'

'I did not know there was one?'

The morning's events had confused my state but I was sure I had not missed an invite.

'I feel as though I ought to know you, Sir? Or is it just you who is too familiar and assumes?'

I could do little to contain a sudden explosive nervous laugh, and begged his forgiveness to which he replied with the most baronial of bows and yet another riddle.

'Know me? Why of course not! Ha, ha! Beyond ridiculous! I say you would remember me.'

It must be said, however, I was finding his more than familiar address contagious, it was striking that he had in very short verse assured himself of my company at least for the next few hours and it took no psychic power to guess that it would be at the very inn he spoke of. I had no wish to shorten the interview so left room for him to expand upon his statement. There is humiliation in a mistaken assumption and I of late had had enough of the stuff.

'There is only one reason why somebody would tread this godforsaken road on such a morn, you are not lost, your stride is too assertive for that so you must be to the inn!

Still I believe you have had enough quizzing for the present, and I note a lack of enthusiasm in your joints for venturing further, 'tis cold, is it not? Join me then. The inn I speak of is but a short walk from here and you are sure to find the company acceptable. Lots of assertive walkers who have been steered to cosier recesses such as I would you. Quick, quick man if you come, I am half-frozen!'

To be honest I knew not what I was doing on that road, or where I was going. I had decided to take the air and fear I had lost my way. Such excursions were more fitting for the huntsmen, those who seek to pot duck as they wake, and the thought of some light hearted company, a nice blaze and some Hell's fire to drink was to prove irresistible to me as was his company. The respite from the solitude of my own thoughts was refreshing and in a round about way he justified his actions, surely was mercy…

Only the door of the Inn was visible, a heavenless creature lit our way swinging his lantern through the unearthly fog.

'Elijah! Thank you, you have been here since I left?'

'Aye I have, Master, not liquor, or meat tempt me.'

He took me aside but not so private so the unfortunate might be privy.

'Elijah has attached himself to me but I fear neither Heaven nor Hell want him!'

Bleary eyed from the icy blast that seemed to expedite our short journey there, I found little to keep me from almost falling through the doors as I was beckoned within by my new acquaintance. By lucky hap we managed to find seats by the blaze and my companion, whose patronage of the place was obviously frequent from the roar that went up on his entrance, found us drinks.

It must be said that I received no such welcome, rather an uncomfortable murmur, and my smile quickly faded if it were not just a result of the freezing temperature.

Joseph that was his name … I had thought it different, it seemed too innocuous for him, though why I thought he ought be called after the school of the Devil I knew not and decided that I had been tempted from a path less comfortable and from the unknown, even though it only be a quiet country lane. How prophetic these thoughts were would become apparent too late and I would wish that I had been more conscious in this state of stupor that began to haunt.

Drinks ordered, fire found, we uttered not a word. None were needed, we were both more than happy to be there, warm from our drinks, which lit tiny fires throughout the body and brewed muzzy heady feelings.

The rabble I had heard upon entering was now taking shape, like a musical score, and one that was familiar to any that found comfort in such places. High notes and low, percussion and chorus I felt I had never heard the like. It was darkly teasing, I found it intoxicating, and as I could not decipher the gist I allowed it to confuse me, welcomed it as a good companion. I had no wish to be intellectually stretched, cold through, and exhausted with it. The conversations within were sometimes light, barely touching those who spoke, and sometimes dark, carried sombrely and received sincerely, always though relief could be seen if only because the story had ended. I barely caught a word but found this easy to surmise as most would.

Looking across at this man Joseph, a handsome man there was no doubt, features etched on the smoothest marble no natural error to them, and I would imagine a favourite of the ladies, I felt somewhat intimidated, perhaps by my own inadequacies? I knew not but I felt now in retrospect that I had had no choice but to join him; though the spirit slipped easily down and perhaps impaired my judgement. No, I would have to settle on my own short comings, I was not in the mood to entertain paranoia and he did cut a dash. An air of authority and superiority highlighted my own short comings and inferior profile that I had thought more than manly. I could not compete. I felt I would look a sickly cousin to any lady in comparison if indeed any were present. He continued to stare from the fire and then to me, if he intended to unnerve me he did so admirably, and each time his gaze fell upon me I felt myself flinch. There was no good in his face and to this I quickly added that in such cases if you could see no good then there was no good in looking. Demons danced in the fire as it flickered angrily almost whispering, nay hissing, 'Folly lies here.' I must leave, I thought, the fear was too strong in me to ignore and I was no longer enjoying the atmosphere I had found so welcoming, it became bewitching. I was indeed the subject of all who now surrounded me edging closer and daring me to object with nothing but a look or a hand upon a dagger. Whether I had a moment's clarity between sips or my senses were before numbed by the cold was of no import, desperately I thought that they had just become boisterous, infused with the spirit, and that I, being strange to them, had aroused curiosity but it would not suffice. I fought to believe it and would have gladly deceived myself as the truth filled me with despair and was too conclusive; but eyes and ears do not deceive, 'tis only the imagination, and I felt my very soul leap from me as though to find some more bearable insanity and I am sure it found it for I never felt so far from God as I did that day. Escape was beyond me and still with the desperate hope that I was mistaken I asked,

'Will you take another, friend? I see you are dry, perhaps a bottle? 'Tis a damned tasty spirit!'

Sickened to the stomach was the last thing that I wanted and spat the words out knocking over the glass as I went to call for more.

'I feel a night of it coming on! Hah! Wonderful, wonderful.'

He had sat forward in his chair not inches from me as though he wished to pass judgement on a soul that was blackened and perhaps belonged to he and I squirmed for the first time, this was truly punishment, everything that had gone before I had had a perverse liking for.

'Yet I thought you looked a little concerned before, yes, no? Tell me what do you fear? Perhaps you do not, perhaps I am too vigilant? Or perhaps Mary is less attentive than she ought! Mary! A bottle please, we are quite parched!

And now, Sir, look at you, you are not so vexed. There I am settled that you indeed were in true need of more spirit and not regretting the turn of events. I am of suspicious mind, a failing you might say but I cannot help but wonder at times why some fear me and some do not. I call them impoverished souls, though the journey most have taken in search of divine assistance has them quite the opposite. Such precipices are a favourite hunting ground for the evangelical hoping to catch them as they fall, though I pride myself in some small part for beating them to it. Take our friends here, who you see have gathered about us, note I call them friends. I say it would distress me if I thought them less than happy and would never assist those who did not wish it even if sometimes they come to me unaware. Now then, where is that blasted girl with our refreshment?'

The girl, called Mary, pushed through the spectators giving them all an earful.

'Mind, out of the way, you are like a load of bloody rats in the corn!'

'And not before time, what was you about, girl? And I suppose you shall want introducing?'

She placed the bottle before us and said,

'I'm sure there's no need after all that hollering after me! But I still like to be treated as a lady.'

'What's this Mary, heresy? You are a touch spirited this day, no matter, I must allow it. You have little more with which to recommend yourself, and of course I laugh but it might be true that you are indeed a lady! Friend, this is Mary, and be mindful to treat her with the respect she expects, especially when you pull your breeches up!'

He laughed at what was obviously impudent of her, and pulled her to a chair. She was wild in appearance though dressed in rich garb. Grubby claw like hands, more animal-like than human, and heavily marked. This said, she would have once been a very attractive girl with curly red hair and indigo eyes, but life, and the pox had ravaged her and so was never to be undone.

'She claims to be a bit of a psychic and though her predictions can be a tad ambiguous, we still like to indulge her little fantasies. Do you mind? Of course you don't! There Mary I have captured you a live one!'

He winked at me and tapped his pipe.

'How do you do, Mary, charmed I am sure.'

Quite taken aback with these new events, perhaps I had assumed too readily, and with prejudice. Surely this band of ousted devils were only so in the comical sense and that I was just this day's entertainment? Relief can be a marvellous thing, and I handsomely gestured a kiss to her hand unable to actually perform the act. Mary held her hand there, smiling, waiting. I blushed and said,

'Forgive me, I am taken in with these new fashions. I do believe the gesture is adequate, that to actually kiss a lady's hand is nowadays considered impolite?'

'So attentive and yet in danger of appearing rather more impolitic than impolite. Perhaps just in this instance you might become a risk-taker?' Joseph added, and I knew not if it a threat or smart quip. So I let the question linger for as long as I could, but with no response and Mary still waiting I said,

'You obviously have not heard of it, how ridiculous of me to presume. Please forgive me, I would never knowingly offend a lady.'

So I kissed the God-awful wretched thing. My colour rose to scarlet.

'Lord, Sir, I would not have felt slighted, I swear I wouldn't want to kiss it either!'

She laughed playfully at how she had duped me into believing her a lady, I might add assumed, as I was in no such quandary, and she delighted the patrons therein at how she had taken me in. I joined with them, though the laughter became too much almost mocking and made me uncomfortable, so much so that I would beg my absence again but somehow still felt I could not. Was this pure genius or that I was too sensible of my own vanity and did not wish to further be humiliated? Whatever it was, I remained, and the laughter abated, silence.

'You for staying then, Sir, you do not fear us then?'

She threw her arms about my neck; the smell was quite overpowering, breathtaking, and was all I could do to prevent it from showing, I nodded to the audience I was now playing to.

This was silly, I should just leave. Surely this had just been an unfortunate morning spent in equally unfortunate company?

But I felt shackled and any move to alight impossible, for sure I would have to draw my pistol. I had been there before, and at that time was unable to see it to a natural end. I did not delude myself that I was any different now. A coward, and for such a thing had acquired a habit of late courting dangerous situations that simply highlighted my true character.

Mary danced away singing and hugging herself. Struggling with what would seem an impossible situation I thought to attempt my extraction by invention; that I in fact was a wanted man, an imposter, sought by the militia, and that it would not be long before they chased me down. It was brilliant, not only would these people shy from such attentions, I was sure to find common ground with many if not all, but it was then that I felt the hand to my throat.

'What is your business?' he growled, fingers tightening around my throat, nails clawing at the flesh, blade flashing before my eyes.

Aware now of others pulling at my clothes, binding my hands, and distributing my possessions with roars of approval. Pockets emptied, they jeered and mocked me acting out the morning's events, and the man I had thought to call friend, the mastermind of all that had followed. Nothing had been chance, I had been fooled, how thick-headed to be taken in so. My situation was hopeless I had nothing left to bargain. One of the villains lifted his shirt to reveal a face painted on his rear, presumably myself, with my pipe surreptitiously placed and broke wind to roars of laughter and encores. He then sat on my lap with such a quiz on his face, but was pushed off unceremoniously by he who had bought me here. He tapped his pipe again.

'Will you smoke?'

My pipe was placed furtively under my nose by he who had used it as a prop; shaking with laughter he was knocked to the floor again. Silence descended on the rabble.

'Allow me to introduce myself properly, Joseph. Joseph Black. And you?'

Heart racing, I spluttered,

'What is this? What do you want of me?'

'Just your name please, there's a good fellow.'

I struggled to control my tongue, face contorted, it misbehaved, and I grappled with the words.

'Charles Cavendish, Sir Charles Cavendish, just Charles Cavendish.'

'Excellent! Perfect; but which is it to be? Sir Charles Cavendish or just plain old Charles Cavendish, I cannot figure how to address you. Hah! No matter I jest! Now calm yourself, nothing is going to happen to you as long as you are truthful about everything, every particular must be exact. If you choose to lie or deceive, bearing in mind we have a very talented psychic in Mary—' He winked at her and she curtseyed. 'Then I am not accountable for my actions or those of others. As you see we are more willing to believe ill of you, suspicious of you shall we say. You must convince us that your business here is benign. That you really did chance upon that road with no particular purpose.'

I could not remember the name of the house that I stayed at, I couldn't remember the landlord's name, I was struggling with the most basic. Mouth open, eyes wide, nothing came, then …

'You wouldn't be "the" Charles Cavendish of The Old Pilgrim's House, would you? Arrived there not two weeks ago under some mystery? Light luggage, always refusing company, never checking for messages, indeed none to be had. A very singular gentleman. Yes? Well if it is so man then you are the talk of the town, at least in some circles!'

'I see darkness around you! No good shall come of this day!' Mary warned.

'Yes, yes, Mary, I am sure you are right! But perhaps sometimes your psychic abilities are challenged? Yes? By say strangers doing even stranger things, and perhaps a precocious will to steal the show! You will have your chance, my sweet. Allow me to continue, strange indeed then, stranger still your arrival in town in a "fine mess" were the exact words used. Perhaps, Mary, your psychic opinion will improve on closer inspection of our new acquaintance?'

'If its money you want, all I have you can see.'

'Gambled away the rest did you, damned inconvenient!? You see, I can trace your every movement for at least the last month. Astonishing, is it not? What I can't fathom is why you left Bath? I find it intriguing to say the least. A well-to-do fellow as you appear, not lacking in looks money or society, if you do not mind me saying? I suppose we are never to know.'

He feigned a yawn.

'Do you know I heard the damnedest thing the other day, Mary, that a gentleman, just as you see before you, quite flatly refused his part in a duel! Yes! A lady's honour, such as your own Mary, had been bought into question. An absolute bounder you are to understand.'

Gasps and reproach from my audience who were growing more enlivened with every judgement.

'Well I should never want to know him! A man such as that and I dare say I speak for us all? Cut off without a penny, save his father allowed him enough to quit Bath and settle elsewhere. Now what was his name? Well I am blown, do you know it completely eludes me. For sure it will come to me in a minute. Jonathan! No, James! No still not right. Well it can't have been very memorable else I would not have forgotten it! Hah, hah, unlike yours, Sir, no your name is quite memorable almost like something you would pluck from a novel!'

I could feel my colour rising obviously undone; what did they want of me? Aware then that I had no money or connections, should I confess all? Surely he had said, nay, demanded accuracy with the truth. I felt that if I owned to all I would be relatively safe, any departure from the truth would I fear be painful. Surely amongst this band of thieves and beggars complete disclosure would render me more acceptable to their very peculiar palates.

'Yes, yes, all true I am ashamed to own it, my conduct has been reprehensible, inexcusable!'

The words flowed and for the second time in my life I attempted to extract myself from a most precarious situation, I allowed myself to hope.

'The lady's honour in question, how came you to injure it?'

'Again I am ashamed to say, but I stole a kiss and chanced further. Not forcefully you must understand, but enough to cause her humiliation. I deserve nothing less than I have already received over this act to date.'

'I agree! I am sure we all do.'

The audience marked their disapproval with ayes and growls and low hisses.

'Can you be saved, Sir? Or are you beyond salvation? I myself would want no part in it, though I may be convinced. Pray continue, is there anything else? Or should I say, is that it?' He paused. 'Good God! How boring ... Mary, be a love, and bring us some more drinks I think our friend needs one, you look quite done in man! Can't think why?

He raised his eyebrows, a gesture to the rabble.

'Do you know?'

Some went to give their full penny's worth but were stopped as he raised his hand.

'That was rhetorical and also lost on you all. Come let us have no more of this, it has been incredibly dull work, has it not?'

He confided in me.

'Goodness knows this atmosphere could do with a little ventilation, do you find it constrictive, Charles? Forgive me, you appear bound by more than just atmosphere, a bit of fun, though a tad extreme. There is nothing you could have said or done that would have shocked. I have made you my business this past few weeks.'

And he freed me of my constraints with a flick of his knife.

'There is only one thing for it, Mary, a song and a dance if you please!'

A roar of approval was followed by tables and chairs being pushed aside. Mary gathered up her skirts and sang sweetly to each and everyone, including myself. Under the circumstances it was best to keep my opinion of the show to myself, her voice owing more to a tom cat as did her too pungent aroma, had this change in my fortune not taken my breath away then she would have done admirably.

'Ha, ha, we shall have some fun! I don't mind telling you, Charles, I am rather fond of a jig!

Will you dance, Sir? I am told I am not half-bad to look at and have pretty manners to match!' he said acting the coquettish maid quite incredibly well. He dragged me to my feet and spun me around on my toes, if I could have caught my breath I do believe I would have laughed. His sense of the ridiculous was contagious, and I found that I was almost enjoying myself; I say almost, not sure what to call the emotion I was feeling but to say my fear had peaked and was now a vastly preferable thing to me would not do the emotion justice. I felt giddy, no longer cared, it was incredulous. It was adrenaline, infinitely more attractive.

I was breathing again, had no physical injuries to bemoan save my pride had took a bashing. No doubt in my mind as to what they were as a collective, but singularly I was finding them quite affable, as each took it in turn to introduce themselves. No question either as to how fortunate I had been for sure I should be dead. Wonder then at why we all seemed to be having such a famously good time in each other's company!

'I say, 'tis an odd way to forge friendships is it not, Charles?' Joseph began. 'If that be your name, complete honesty can be brutal but then you know as much of me as I would wish, nothing! And I know all I need of you, 'tis not fair but then neither am I.'

No indeed, but I knew enough to abandon hope that night, and I knew enough to make free with Mary though she had it private and informed me that she was engaged to a boy called Pike. I would not have dared it but I had never felt so intoxicated and was not purely down to the potency of the liquor. Was not memorable save perhaps her softness, the gentle hand that stroked my face and all the while I thought of nothing but the evil that brought me here. All this before me, and undressed she was truly blessed, I still felt she part of this hell-sent night. At some point my heightened state became blurred with the spirit and though no God was there that night it was truly heavenly. I remembered the whispers, curious he seemed to find me as he starred into what must have been my soul and imparted words that felt like poison.

'So easy but still I shall make it more pleasurable, you accept all with such ease yet what you are is repellent. You may wonder that one such as I should think so? You see, some are pretty and some just tired and dull, predictable. And there was I thinking I had discovered some treasure! Still, as I say, shall make something of it.'

I answered aye, but to what? Was he madman? Whatever he was I would not mock him with bewilderment. Later that night he returned to my side.

'If you accept, all will be more pleasurable for you too! I note a lack of enthusiasm to actually commit? As though you play both ends against the middle? Let me see if I cannot make your mind up for you.'

A tightening sensation in my throat I thought to trounce with some more liquid fire became unnerving, a quickening in my heartbeat, was it poison? Terrified I slumped to the ground all the while his gaze did not leave mine.

'As I say, shall enjoy myself whichever the way, even if with a trick.' He turned to face the rabble. 'Oh dear, what shall we do with him?'

None came to my side but the girl, Mary.

'Come come now, Freddy. There really is no choice, is not so bad, tell me do you see evil when you look upon me? And I am fond of you myself though I may blush at my boldness! Don't leave me now?'

Whether it was the softness of her plea that took me at my most vulnerable, or I just feigned a struggle for any angels that might look upon me, mattered not, and I began to feel easier.

'What would you have me do!?' I yelled as I struggled to my feet.

Silence fell about me but a few stifled taunts at my attempt to reach anything god-like that night.

'Yes!' Joseph yelled with equal passion and wicked laugh waving his arms to the ceiling; he grabbed the girl Mary violently by her hair. 'Never think to assist me ever!'

'I did not, I would not, Master Joseph!' she whimpered. 'I thought to aid myself.'

'Of course you did!'

He laughed and threw her to the gathering.

'Where are my manners that I do not feel it is for you to help yourself?'

Looking about for encouragement and the crowd needing none as the atmosphere was becoming fever pitched through fear of this entity and a primitive lust to taste blood.

'Somewhere more civilized I would say, somewhere polite! My fault, my fault.'

He stroked her cheek wiping his hand afterwards.

'For here is no place for such niceties! Hah! More drinks, more dancing, come we are all friends here!'

There was a touch of the insanity about him which was dangerous.

'As are all lunatics,' he remarked as I thought, and decided then that private thoughts on this matter would be better banished, not so hard when you are scared that your very breath be stolen when you feel is all you have left.

Feverish, sick and dizzy I thrust my head out of a window with violent convulsions, and had some relief but with the promise of more to come. I was ushered to bed by I know not what just that it was kindly, and though I fought sleep to prevent dizziness it came and I fell into a deep slumber.

Chapter 3

'Good God! Have a care man!'

I jumped and instinctively sought my weapon, startled by the crash of the door and the bundle thrown at me.

'Is this what you are looking for?'

Joseph dangled my pistol before my eyes.

'Take it man, though you will have no need of it. Come, if you have the stomach join me for breakfast, nay join me anyway if you do not eat out last night's poison it will rot your guts!'

Confused I tried to place myself there I relaxed, though still confused at the turn of events. I knew I had been accosted but what had brought about this change in fortune? Would I ever know? Drink and merriment had flowed freely with my erstwhile captors, rather silly I thought to call them anything more after the events of last eve. Good God, what a time I had had! I looked upon Joseph properly for perhaps the first time; a giant of a man all of six foot, with dark emotive eyes. I made up my mind then and there to never hold his gaze for fear of reading my fortune, or if I was lucky one that had passed.

I would never have entertained such a place before now, if only because they had a reputation of being lairs rather than somewhere to rest and refresh, every inch of it pointed to that fact though I had little apprehension.

Mary placed a drink before me, it smelled sweet and herby.

'Drink, it will cure that which ails you this morning.'

I caught Joseph's eye and laughed, to be honest I could find no words apart from the obvious.

'How came you to acquire my belongings? What I mean to say is, I do not understand why you have brought them here, or how you happened upon them? My landlord would surely have protested?'

'O phish, do not worry about him! I am very well respected around these parts, only mention my name, and well—'

A boy called Pike laughed into his drink, how I came to know all these names I do not recall, the drink had seen to that and aided by a secret will not to.

'I thank you kindly for this act, Joseph, but pray why have you brought them to me? I am perplexed to say the least.'

'Perplexed, now there's a fine word, aye Mary, one to put down in your journal.'

Mary signalled as if to write down.

'Aye Joseph, if I knew it, or could spell it, wouldn't that be grand!'

'Charles is perplexed, Pike, shall I remind him of a bargain struck? I say Pike, shall I remind Charles of our bargain? Ay boy! Pike! Pike! You are floundering again boy, get you gone, and see to whatever evils you are up to today.'

Pike leaped from his watch, a gangly odd-looking boy, no more than seventeen, though I am sure he would improve with age, most young men did. He kissed Mary's hand and yelled,

'I will see you later, Joseph! Oh and Charles or Frederick, whichever it is to be? Drink the drink, Mary's been in a fine fit all morning preparing it for you! She's a kind girl, but don't mistake her attentions for more than that mind, we are very much in love, isn't that right, Mary, ay? You have not eyes for any other, have you?'

He laughed boisterously whilst Mary curtseyed and scolded him with a look then bustled off into the back room. This was obviously a very liberal arrangement, though much was the case amongst these classes, some would even offer their wife or sweetheart for monetary gain and to hold them in contempt for such practices had never occurred to me. Why would I, when I no more figured their habits worthy of dissection as I did animals in the barn?

'Am I to understand, Joseph, that we have an accord?' I casually remarked, attempting disinterest woefully; after all, an accord struck with Joseph surely justified my concern and should never have been entered into half-sensed and full of spirits.

'Dear friend, do not look so fretful. Why yes, we have an understanding of sorts. Please allow me to put an end to your vexation, Sir, Freddy, or do you prefer alias? I do not know, I must tell you. You see, with your history, forgive me if I speak too boldly, it is very difficult to know whether you are excusing a foggy memory or excusing yourself entirely. Far be it from me to question a man's honour or indeed his word. I would not have it so, but humour me, I like to speculate. An agreement, it must be said, should be entered into seriously and with clarity of thought, and you were mighty free with our spirits yesterday. Even so I still have my doubts. Shall I speak plain?'

He waited for no response.

'It is just a little trifle, Freddy, I have agreed for you to lodge here and have it as your home for as long as you see fit. You have agreed to seek work and pay for your keep, though we both concurred that you in particular may find this difficult. However, there is much work to be had here if one had the inclination? You see, you have no useful qualifications to speak of, Freddy. No references other than ones that damn you. No money, friends, or family to vouch for you. For as much as you have lived a privileged life, let us take education, it would appear that you never bothered. Society, you have abused, and taken advantage of. Lineage, though this has injured you the most, cast out, and never to be known of again in the house of your father. Chance my friend, though fickle in nature, has brought you here for good or evil, I do not know which. Perhaps Mary would know?' he said with a wink. 'Frederick! You must embrace change. Principles, though I fear I speak too harshly, are for men of money, society, and standing. You, I am afraid, have abused all three, and they have deserted you. You must now seek different qualities from yourself, qualities that are, shall we say, more accessible.'

Joseph's epilogue finished as it had started, with a deal of menace, though his words spoke of hospitality and friendship. He was right; I was damned whichever way I looked. He had dealt me no harm, in fact, in cases such as this, though I can only claim cheap novels for my information, would I not be dead by now? Left to rot in a ditch somewhere? I may well have ventured too far yesterday. Perhaps these people had every right to be suspicious, and now safe in the knowledge that I had no particular purpose and it must be said a little down on my luck, had offered their hospitality. Surely then this must be construed as fortunate? And though their manners were quite rude and basic and nothing like what I was used to, they had made me jolly welcome and, as strange as they were to me, I believed I was as strange to them. Joseph had also mooted the opportunity of earning my keep, an idea that not four months ago would have been thoroughly abhorrent to me; I now thought genius. I had no money, nowhere to live, my prospects were grim and I had not been taught the survival skills necessary for such a debacle from one class to another. The money my father had so graciously bestowed upon me was with instruction to quit town, and the little of it that there was I had gambled away in a belligerent strop. A change of fortune was well overdue and now felt I must seize it. Unfortunately, what I failed to see, carried as I was by this prevailing wind, was how I would change. How my reflection in a glass would become my only reference as to who I was, and that after time even this would appear fraudulent.

'Joseph, dear friend, as I hope to call you for you are readily becoming so, I am at a loss at such kindness nay charity. I have never known the like.'

'Freddy! Freddy! Good God, man, you have quit your senses! Do not bother yourself, or I come to that with such fine words and gratitude. I am hoping that this accord will prove favourable to us both, do you follow? I do not offer charity, I have not the means, I only ask that you keep an open mind and your counsel about all that you see and hear here. You are a man of the world, are you not? This being the case you must recognize that all is not what it would seem here.'

I went to answer but Joseph continued.

'You might say that of most things in life, yes?'

I ventured no response as Joseph was waiting for none, and this was getting tiring.

'Of course you must earn your keep, one quarter of your purse once a week will more than adequately pay for food and lodging, and I do believe that tonight would be as good as any night to start.'

I waited for what seemed like an eternity then said,

'Joseph, you have only to speak and any wits or talents that I possess, though I fear these are limited, are at your disposal.'

I went to continue intrigued at the thought of this occupation but was cut off by Joseph.

'Yes, well I will expect no less! I am no fool, Freddy, but I have a penchant for hopeless causes, my counsel and guidance will cost you nothing. Follow my advice and learn from others there are no dullards to be found here.'

He paused for reflection and applause it would seem, though the inn was empty, and stroked his eyebrow with a licked finger. I wondered if he had been up all night preparing this speech. Spitefully I interrupted his reverie.

'Pray what am I to do tonight, Joseph? This all sounds rather too good to be true and I am eager to learn of this occupation.'

'If high reward for little industry sit well with you, man,

then you shall not be disappointed. I am not avoiding your question, Freddy, just the boring detail, but to summarise, one might say I offer a very particular service to an array of premises in the town. There now, that surely answers your question. As for the rest of the day – though none of us were up with the larks, ay Freddy? – the word temperance springs to mind. What say you to a ride into town? I am sure you didn't venture far from your lodgings when you were settled there? In fact, I know you did not and there is much to delight the eye in Cleveton, 'tis a pretty town. What say you then? Yes? No? Not sure?'

'No I am absolutely sure I should be delighted. A ride into town would be most refreshing! But ashamedly I have no horse and need look to your generosity once more.'

'Such obvious statements can become tiring, Freddy. Of course you have no horse! We have plenty here if you do not mind a pony a little broader in the saddle and not as pretty as you are used to, ay? What say you?'

'Lead on man!' I enthused.

'Lead on!'

Chapter 4

'You know Joseph, this really is an uncommonly attractive little place, I believe I did myself a great disservice not taking time to explore, and the journey and mount was comfort itself.'

Cleveton was colourful and alive, and not to be rushed. It grabbed you and nurtured your imagination, indeed not twenty miles from Bath, but did not suffer this poorly. The fashions and attractions diverted the attention most favourably, as did some of the ladies, and every so often the call from a paper boy, 'Cleveton Public, Cleveton Public, buy your Cleveton Public here, just a penny, Sir, if you please?'

'Wait there a moment, Freddy, would you?'

Joseph disappeared into a little establishment that groaned from its display of trinkets and curios. Its sparkle was mesmeric in the late winter sunshine and certainly commanded closer inspection. I peeped through the window and studied the scene; Joseph poured the contents of a bag onto the counter. What transpired then should surely have alerted me or at least aroused my suspicion, but alas no, I found no fault in what I saw. A rather rotund looking fellow, bearing the brilliance that only those who regularly over-indulged sported, graciously took up each piece and made notes, I believed, as to their worth. Some very fine pieces and I fleetingly wondered where they had come from and how Joseph came by them but found these thoughts irritating and foolishly pushed them aside. Joseph reappeared looking most pleased with himself – and who wouldn't be? – I eyed the purse containing the money too obviously I fear, for he said quizzically,

'I would not want to draw attention to it, Freddy. You show a keen interest in the contents of my purse. A man might displace that interest if he felt justified! It has been a while, has it not, since you saw such riches? Hungry?'

'Joseph, yes please forgive me, it has been an age that is all. I am curious not hungry, I would never covet that which wasn't my own.'

'No I just mean are you hungry? Mary's potion should have worked by now, and a good meal in your belly will keep the fire burning, we have a long night ahead of us.'

'Hah! I see now that I must accustom myself to your peculiar manner of address, dear friend! It is cryptic to say the least and I cannot keep reeling so at every comment, I am sure I feel quite dizzy.'

We shared the humour of the moment and sought out sustenance to fill our aching bellies.

The light faded in Cleveton and shadows took up residence on its dark corners and sinister recesses that magically appeared at this time of night. People became shadows, shadows became people. Joseph, I believe, sensing my trepidation, tapped my shoulder.

'Now then, Freddy, let us light a few fires, figuratively speaking of course! I noted some difficulty in following, and I would not have you believe me an arsonist! I have but one call to make, one account to settle. You will learn a salutary lesson tonight, Freddy, on the meanness of mind and spirit, prevalent in those who sup and dine on the finest meats and wines, yet do not feel the need to settle upon you that which is owed. Their pitiful attempts at exemption are tiring. Even I, Freddy, have been taken in by these machinations, but have learned my lesson – where I believed I was being kind I have been likened to an idiot. I will not have this, and I say this most sincerely, I must always have that which is owed. People will try to take liberties, yes, it is in their very nature. You must allow them to try but never to succeed. Come man, I do not wish to scare you, though this must be said, you must never return empty-handed. I will take what is owed me financially from your own purse. As for my reputation, I cannot put a price on this, I fear I should have to make an example of you. But let us not be so serious, this has never happened, and I do not believe you so very different. In fact, I do believe I spied something of myself in you, but perhaps I am too vain.'

I was about to speak, but then Joseph required no reassurance, I believed him rarely disappointed. Respect is often born out of fear and purchased with menace; though I could not place it, Joseph wielded this weapon masterfully and with the subtleness of touch that only a true genius, or perhaps should say, devil, does.

He knocked at the door of a very good and proper looking residence and an elegant lady answered shooing away her footman. A more superior looking lady I had never seen and she quickly dismissed me in favour of Joseph.

'Joseph.'

She curtseyed.

'This is most unexpected, but I see you have a companion, there really is no need. Did not Bertram speak with you last week? And did you not grant an extension of your good will, in lieu of the trust and friendship we have enjoyed these past years?'

She was blushing and becoming, her general air of confusion did her no disservice.

'Yes, he asked, I declined, there! Now will you keep me at the door, Angelica? As you say we are old friends and I am to conclude my business with your husband tonight, of that you can be sure, or does he cower in corners whilst his wife sees to his affairs!?'

Joseph pushed aside the door and entered the property, by his very address I could see no wrong in following him so I did.

'Come Bertram! Where are you man? Your lady wife is far too blessed to provide as an adequate guard.' He paused a little waiting for response. 'Do not make me seek you out then, man! I must have my dues!'

'I will settle this account with you, Joseph!'

The Lady Angelica flew at him lashing wildly with a stick, then fell back wide eyed and drained.

'Are you trying to kill me, madam!?' Joseph laughed.

'My conduct has shocked me, Joseph, I am mortified that I should lash out so. I do not, have not felt myself lately.'

'Do not be ashamed, little pet, it is still very attractive, perhaps a little uncouth? Alas made more so by your age, quite wild you look! Hair flying everywhere, some of it silvering, my dear! Though that is to be expected for soon you shall be forty, yes? But do not worry my love, you will always be precious to me.'

Joseph spoke of a friendship between them, but no, there was more to this. Some history, and it made me feel uncomfortable, so much so that I would excuse myself but was far too polite. I did not want to draw attention to the Lady Angelica's state or injure her further, as I believed Joseph's comments had.

A figure of a man appeared at the staircase; it was his fear that I first noted, he looked like he had been granted an interview with Beelzebub himself. Joseph laughed and embraced him as old friends do. How could he be so oblivious to his poor wretched state, he looked as though he would collapse if Joseph released him from his embrace? I wanted to offer assistance but felt this would undermine Joseph's command of what was passing here. After all, who was I? I knew nothing of the history. I knew not why the man looked so ghastly, or indeed why the lady seemed so attached, though I believed this to be an unfortunate alliance. If this caution was a failing in me I had never noticed it before, in fact, the truth is I had never been the type to offer assistance. A fleeting thought, were not my reservations cowardice in reality? No! That would not do, after all, I was to observe and observation, in its entirety will always make you question your perception and produce many different conclusions. In fact, the summary you alight upon is not necessarily the truth of a situation. No indeed, it is just an interpretation. There, I felt better, and did not take very long at all. Joseph broke my speculation, he was introducing me.

'Freddy! Are you alright, man? I say, this is Bertram, Bertram Toothill. I shall charge you with the administration of his account. I do believe you shall get along famously, you see he sometimes requires prompting and you are as keen as I have seen. Marvellous, marvellous, that settled then myself and he are to dine tonight at the inn. We shall escort him together but then must part company, there are delicate and pressing matters between us that you ought not be privy to, we are old, old friends.'

With much reluctance, Bertram readied for the journey, he spoke not a word, not even to comfort his wife wrought with anguish; it all seemed a little excessive, even farcical, after all no threats had been made and surely one must expect ramifications if late settling. No, Joseph had the situation right and I looked upon the two with disdain, not with sympathy as their looks begged.

The return journey was completed in relative silence, at least on Bertram's and my part. Joseph chose to expound enthusiastically on the merits of a good friendship, how subterfuge and deceit could play no part as they twisted and contorted the mind and face of those which they poisoned thus rendering them undone, in his eyes, before they had uttered a word of their treachery. Though poetic, Joseph's words were cautionary to say the least, one might interpret them as threatening if they were overly sensitive or paranoid but as I felt neither handicapped or stricken, cautionary advice I believed was the sum of his words.

I had not noticed the name of the inn until I came upon it this night, 'The Hangman's Hitch'. Nothing so remarkable in that, country inns were often called strange things, but above the door something else, something that sent me cold, these words – 'We do not judge here, we weigh your worth precisely and if you should feel lightheaded as you leave it is that you have lost it' – so I sought reassurance quickly within its walls, of Mary and Pike and the others who greeted me as only people of this class know how to. Joseph held Bertram's arm and though I had never seen a ghost, his very continence was how I might imagine one.

'Freddy, as you know my business tonight takes me from your side and to be honest man you look done in! Perhaps a night of abstinence and a warm bed, yes?'

I had to agree, the thought of sleep in the relative peace and quiet of my room was too inviting to ignore, so I said my goodnights and caught a wink from Mary, which cheered me, and I retired.

Chapter 5

'Do I amuse you all somehow this morning? You seem to delight in my presence!'

The enjoyment was plain to see and the attempted concealment was I felt deliberately amateurish. Choosing to ignore the ill-mannered lot and finding a chair by the fire, I glanced to the bar.

'Pray, who is that fellow there? I do not recall him and should very much like to pass the time of day with him, it seems an age since I spoke to someone outside, begging your pardon of course, I only mean to say that new opinions are a constant source of refreshment!'

'Pray, ask him yourself. Though I do not fancy your chances of a sensible interview, I believe you will find it rather one-sided, I cannot pry a word from him!'

Joseph tried to appear sincere but it was hopeless, this was becoming infuriating.

'I am sorry, Freddy, it's just you; you look so odd this morning.'

'I do not, man, how ridiculous of you to say so, I look very well!'

'I'd say nigh on impossible to talk with a man like that.'

A red-faced fellow name of Elijah had joined in, his face made even redder by the joke I was not privy to.

'You look like you suffer something, Elijah? Like you

would burst! Surely there is something you can take for such a peculiar condition?'

I felt I had trounced him, I could have a very authoritative air when pressed but, no, my comment just added to the general air of hysteria.

'I say you there! Sir—'

I approached the bar and sat down beside the man, he did not flinch, drink in hand, fixed stare.

It was Bertram.

'Bertram, Bertram! Do you not know me? It is I, Frederick, I accompanied you here last night. Good God man, you look like death itself, as did I last morn! The spirit here has a curse upon it, does it not!? Still let me ask Mary for one of her potions, they really do have the most miraculous effect, I will brook no resistance. Mary? Mary would you be a love, my friend here suffers, and I think a tankard of that fine brew of yours would more than likely set him right. Will you not greet me, man? I would not be as rude I am sure! Was my greeting anything other than polite? Have I not offered assistance? Bertram, come?'

I went to embrace him, but Bertram fell to the floor, quite motionless, and quite, quite dead.

'He is dead, Joseph! God save us, Bertram is dead, who has done this? Someone amongst us has done for him and violently, you see the blood on his chest?'

'Dead, how do you mean dead?'

'I mean, man, that if you look, it is plain isn't it!? Are you blind?'

Then I realized that the luxury of time and a second glance would have shown that this was not an opportunity, or good fortune, this was to be my ruination. Though had I been sensible of this history would I not still be ruined? My only hope now, and as preposterous as it seemed, was divine intervention and I clung to this fragile wisp of hope for perhaps a second but then felt the urgency of my own situation. I did not feel for this man. I had not the time for such vanities, after all it was not as though I could save him! Indeed his ridiculous expression was irritating me immensely, so I pushed him with my foot until he faced the ground.

'Poor, wretched fool!' I said, as though I could injure him further – there must be a first for everything I thought maliciously, even insulting a cadaver.

I was sure of my course now, to own this future, and would do so with my soul, money had no worth in such a contract … and if I should hesitate I too would become historic, I needed no more incentive.

'You look inconvenienced, Freddy? I do not see why you should, you have played no part in this "tragedy", shall we call it. But I have to say that I was never so put out as I was over a dead body.'

'Begging your pardon, Joseph, but bit part, I say he played bit part in this,' Elijah prodded.

'Oh trust Elijah to second guess me! But let us humour him, he has so little sense and even less propriety. Agreed then, Freddy, that you did accompany me last night and, yes, aided in the procurement of said dead person, but as for the events that followed you were of no service. In fact, so innocent were you of this situation that you even offered to buy the man a drink! Hah, oh it was too rich, Freddy, too rich! Now a court of law may interpret this all rather differently, as we all know a court of law deals purely with the facts, not fanciful ideas and pretty notions, I must confess I am guilty of both, ha! It can be a curse when offering advice in such situations, do you follow, Freddy? To clarify your position, dear friend, and part if any in this "tragedy". Approving nods from the flanks, though none of it sincere, I am sure they understood not a word of it and had learned to read Joseph by instinct.

'If say someone was to be less guarded about that which has transpired, through maybe a deep seated fear or uncertainty, fear itself not being natural to man, I believe it is a disease easily spread resulting in hysteria of epidemic proportions.'

'Can't have that, Joseph, can't have that!'

'No indeed, Elijah! For it is virtually impossible to control, as is your tongue today! No need, I really do get along very well. Now to continue, that someone suffering these doubts decides to inform certain officials in order to gain a lenient judgement for his part in this "tragedy", unable to live with the thought that he might be caught and judged as others. Let us not forget though that we have said that his part was in no way considerable, "bit part" for want of better dialogue. Now this fellow must be very clever, a singular man of endless talents, to name but one he would have to be a great illusionist, to create himself, make others believe that nothing was amiss. Now that would be an adversary worthy of my inspection; though for good or bad I can honestly say that I have never known such an animal. Perhaps then it is I that is the true illusionist?'

He gestured wildly and theatrically then continued.

'Do I create all this? But who am I to deceive? I declare I know none with wits enough to understand, save myself, and I do not wish to deceive myself! There is another I should mention, one that is never absent in any tragedy, the opportunist; not blessed with the gift of forethought he will more times than not bring himself undone at some later stage. Now of these I have known many, and fondly refer to them as my peccadilloes and must confess to some manipulation of them. Fret not then either way, Freddy, ay? What say you, Elijah?'

'I do not understand, Joseph?'

'No? It is just you have had so much to add to these proceedings I was sure you would have some fine wise words to impart, some observation that we have overlooked. No? Praise the Lord for gifting you with no more than ten words, for I can count no more! And only two of them sensible, yes, and no, Elijah! At these you are masterly, nay scholarly, old friend.'

Elijah blushed and felt complemented I am sure, as only a man of little sense would.

I cannot say that I felt harangued, this was one of his

general addresses, his words too obscure to attribute personal inflection from, but suffice to say that what he knew of me was more than I knew of myself.

'What is to be done, Joseph, with this man's body? I am in the dark as to the meaning of all this.'

Joseph smiled, though he looked irritated.

'Dear friend, it shall be disposed of as many have before it. This business of ours claims many victims, gratefully none on our part, and more oft time than not reveals the very worst in society. I cannot help but pity them, so desperate are they. In many cases these souls will resort to violence, threats, and I believe an intention to murder. I feel it a great shame that an old friend, such as Bertram, should also have harboured such thoughts, but he did and was armed and whatever insanity possessed him last night was what done for him not my pistol.'

'You are sure he meant to use his firearm, Joseph?'

Surely if I could put this incident down to a misunderstanding or misadventure it would be easier to digest than what I felt was the truth in my heart.

'Of course I am sure, you idiot!'

'I myself witnessed the man reach for his weapon, Joseph had no choice but to discharge his.'

Pike blushed with a faint smile on his lips, still amused by what had been played out there. I am sure I would have entertained the luxury of laughter too had I been aware, I almost felt jealous.

'You see, Frederick, people believe that a person such as I, a man as you see of considerable means, is in some way contemptible for this very reason. Likened to a person in trade who has earned his position in society rather than had it as birthright. I do not become vexed at this, for I see these people for what they are, desperate, shamefaced, financially impaired, and society will out them for these very reasons. Truth is they were never worthy of much if they cannot endure a little adversity. Let me tell you, I am respected, where it matters, and have been called upon and entrusted with bringing many such people to justice. I am governed by laws, Freddy, though these are forgiving, and rewarding for my endeavours. So do not think to seek reasoning behind my actions or to justify anything on my behalf, this would all be beyond your limited capabilities.

Come, man, let us not quarrel, I have had my fun with you. You have every right to be shocked, it was an ambush, Freddy, initiation enjoyed at its very ripest and I am sure you can appreciate the humour in it?'

'Yes, Joseph, but I cannot until I have drawn breath, and you must allow me some incredulity and ambivalence. I do not know whether to laugh with you or indulge a feeling to lament this loss of life. I feel somewhat vulnerable to speak plain.'

'Well as for the latter, Freddy, rest assured as I have previously pointed out I do not concern myself with you. But if you cannot naturally laugh with us at a very comical scene, then damn you, man, and go and mourn whomever you want! You will find it a solitary diversion though, and will probably last no longer than five minutes! However, if you would please me, I discover I have more to say to you, things that you may prefer to hear with a degree of privacy. These words cannot be couched in a pretty fashion.'

'I feel there must be no secrets now, Joseph, between any of us and, if you would permit, I shall have what you say right here amongst all.'

'As you wish, Frederick. Do you have the stomach for this work? I see where financial recompense is to be had, you are as clever at fetching and carrying as the smartest spaniel, but I am yet to see resolve. Can you complete transactions however is deemed fit? However I would have them so? Or am I right in what I believe I have spied in you this day, faint heart a characteristic I have come to expect in people of your society? I believe you feel embroiled, Frederick, and very uncomfortable with this, correct me if I am wrong?'

'I shall defend myself, Joseph, and I hope in thus doing so allay your fears. I have never truly been in such a situation as

I am sure is plain but this does not mean I judge you or your actions. I merely seek reassurance that all will be well and that we shall not all be to the gallows. The words you have spoken have meaning and I believe the provenance. I have no reason to doubt you and I therefore truly say that this is not so difficult for me to recover from and, as you say, I am sure I shall rally after five minutes!'

The joke was enjoyed by all and I took an odd sort of pride and some security in the fact that I had made them all laugh.

Once again and under the most dire circumstances Joseph had allayed my fears and I felt easy again. This was becoming frequent. It must be said though never beyond all reasonable doubt, and I could not help wondering if this was indeed a fake confidence I was feeling.

Wanting to divert attention away from Bertram for the jokes were becoming a little strained, I glanced at Mary, and noticed how fine she looked. The dress she wore, lavishly decorated with lace, I was ashamed to say, as Mary was a dear, was more suited to a courtier for sure she could not afford such luxury.

'Mary, may I say how lovely you look today and that dress becomes you remarkably well! I hope I do not appear impolite in asking, but how came you by such finery? Do you have a wealthy benefactor?'

'Why, Master Frederick, you are politeness itself, and I would not expect different from you. As for my finery and benefactors, as you call them, I think you mean "Dunwiths", I have much finery and as many benefactors as you have fingers and toes! They turn up unexpected, you see, and what they no longer have need of, I am not too proud to make something of.'

'In fact in the absence of relatives to call her own she finds herself quite handsomely rewarded, do you not Mary?'

'Why, yes I do, Joseph, and I thank you kindly for your charity.'

'Ah, Mary, 'tis not charity child, we each have a purpose.

Yours is an obvious charm which renders us less obvious! Hah!'

I could not see the humour in this conversation, but the sniggering told a different truth, I did not wish to discover it so announced,

'I must say you are an easily pleased lot!'

'Mary, why don't you show Freddy your chest and your treasures, go on lass you know you are eager!' somebody shouted.

Mary blushed and jumped.

'Would you enjoy that, Freddy? Lord, I would love to show you my fancies and frills and things! I have so many and never the occasion or company to appreciate them but I am sure you would, being as you are a man of society. Unlike the rest of you I might add, apart from Joseph, you all think a frill is something one of them women up in the town give you on a Saturday night! Hah, ha!'

'Well said, Mary, I couldn't have put that better myself. And I am sure I would love to, though I am not accustomed to enjoying such liberties, still I am sure there is no impropriety in doing so and, if you are sure, it would please me greatly.'

She grabbed my hand and led me into the back room and beyond again, to a little door, I hesitated, and pulled back from her.

'Mary you are quite sure? You are betrothed, are you not, and though I hate to mention it perhaps the other night we were both a little overcome, surely Pike would object if he were here?'

'Oh Pike wouldn't mind, he would be too scared to lose old Mary to speak out over such a thing, I want to enjoy myself, Freddy, he likes me to however I sees fit. Come then, Freddy, you have no need to be so polite, I have had many a beau before you at this door, with Pike fully aware, and none with a purpose as sweet as yours. You are more welcome than the whole rotten lot! I do not fear injury to my reputation for I have not one and have no money to buy one with; I may look like a fine lady today, Freddy, but it is as you see just me. You do make me laugh, Freddy! I am not fragile, bless you.'

Convinced, I followed her through the door and was as I had expected, a sweet girl's room full of all the things young ladies loved – dresses, ribbons, and other such fancies. She boasted a wardrobe one would expect a lady of society to possess though it was obvious she lacked their skill in managing such a beast. Mary's was a little outdated with no distinct theme and where a true lady's wardrobe is one of her greatest assets, Mary's looked a challenge.

'And all this from the Dunwiths? Mary, how thoughtful, they must be a very charitable lot and of good reputation I should imagine. Shall I meet with them? I only ask because a lady who would wear such garments, and even discard them must surely be young, and pretty too, I would venture, and definitely worthy of some regard. I know her only by her kind actions and elegant manner of dress but I already find myself preoccupied by her.'

Mary looked puzzled and giggled.

'Dear Freddy, you will teach the Master Joseph a thing or two about speaking in riddles I believe! But I shall play along, I am sure you will meet with many Dunwiths but I cannot give you a fixed date when I know not myself. I cannot believe you do not follow, you must be having fun with me, you do understand that these are the Dunwithses' clothes?'

'Oh absolutely, Mary, you speak uniformly plain, and I shall try to keep my address more simple for you. I assure you I do not poke fun where there is none to be had, and I agree with you that Joseph's address can be confusing at the best of times.'

'He is a puzzling one is he not, Freddy, and a true charmer, I do believe he could romance the ring off a preacher's wife's middle finger if he felt it would amuse him. But he has been a true gentleman to me. He fed me and gave me a room to rest my weary soul, so he did, when I was without hope. He showed me that the things that make your stomach groan and your eyes water can truly be yours, it's just how you get them that is different. I don't grovel anymore, Freddy, can't see a reason why a person should when there is so much treasure to be had. He also taught me how to forget, to forget my past, or at least as himself would put it, "Regret is an ugly emotion invented by the pious being a universally ugly lot!" Hah! He has such a way with words and a way of lifting me. I am truly blessed.'

'I shall not press you, Mary, but I am very fond of a good history and if you choose to, or indeed can remember any particulars, I would love to hear what made you so forlorn for such a time. Pardon me if I pry or assume, but you sound as though you would like to tell it. Come, Mary, you knew my story the very day we met, am I not deserving?'

'Very well, as you have pointed out that it may be a little unfair, I shall tell you a little of my past, though perhaps you may have gleaned some of it for yourself already noting my scarring from the pox – are not the people touched by this already living in shadows? I am sure my story will scarcely vary from others you have heard, but I shall let you be the judge. Freddy, I was once a very pretty girl, with a good job for a fine family in a grand house. I had a beau who loved me as I adored him. It was not two months before we were to be married when I took a fever which as you will guess was the pox. He kept by my side and tended me throughout the worst of it, this I treasure, and will not forget, though it is hidden well away from Joseph's stare. As I grew stronger, his visits became shorter and further apart, and when he could no longer look upon me I released him, though it broke my heart and tore out my insides to do so. I believe it was the fever still with me that took me from the house one morning never to return and I hoped against hope for as long as was sensible that my love would come find me, but it was never to be. These thoughts still hurt to think so I will stop there, Master Freddy, if you don't mind.'

'Tragic, Mary, tragic, I shall not dwell on this, as you say it is painful and I will not tell Joseph if you do not wish it. I do believe he would be annoyed as I feel he is paternal towards you.'

'Aye, let's have no more of this then, we are equal now in tragedy and I am in too good a mood today to weep.'

I did not enquire of Mary if she had been shocked or saddened by the incident that morning. She had obviously enjoyed it as much as the rest and perhaps it was not as shocking as I initially thought. The Dunwiths, whoever they were, obviously saw no gain in schooling Mary in the gentille art of being that is the well-informed young lady of today. They appeared to salve a social conscience with gifts and rather left the poor girl to chance, and I could not fault their wisdom here. This was no place for the fragile or precious and I felt they had been wise to humour the girl rather than give her airs. In praise of the girl, I thought the lack of more appropriate influences was never felt by any who knew Mary or indeed herself and here, here, to that. One small matter also had my silence over her thoughts on Bertram's death. The last thing I wanted these people to believe was that I was a latent insurgent, God forbid! I needed to assimilate myself not distinguish.

Chapter 6

Gratefully the body was gone when I returned, and ashamed though I was I felt nothing other than relief. Perhaps the humour of the situation would come to me later but as it stood I remained unaffected. I decided an interview with Joseph was well overdue, along with some timely prostration and general compliments of the day.

'Joseph, I have been thinking more on you and come to the conclusion that you are a good and righteous man, firm but fair. A man of many talents and many friends, affable and well met and even to this I must add that you are philanthropic. I feel the loss of other suitable descriptions but say I cannot find the words.'

This produced an adverse effect to which I had not bargained, a painfully long silence descended on the inn, followed by short intakes of breath, and some unchecked childish prattle.

'Good God, man, I am not dead, am I!? I will thank you to save such eulogies for your own epitaph, I have no need of them and you might do well to keep your tongue in your head! However, I may salvage something from your exaltations, I will allow that I am somewhat philanthropic, it is an elegant term and suits me well and if correctly applied will reward. I do wonder sometimes, man, if you are simple in the head. Do you not remember that this day passed I have killed a man, and thought at some point to make this your fate! And as for goodness and being righteous, both fill me with disdain, they are characteristics forged on vanity and are flawed, this being an inherent weakness. Would you proclaim me a good man again, Freddy? I would dare you to do so!'

He paused and looked about him and spied a man name of Sam.

'Sam, you seem amused by this spectacle? Do you have something to add? Perhaps something to say upon my death, something funny? You are refreshingly funny at times and I would like to know what tickles you and the others around you?'

'It be a little verse I made up, Joseph, on you dying like, it made us laugh is all at how poetic it sounded coming from the likes of me, it was only a bit of fun and I swear, Joseph, I meant no harm, or disrespect.'

'Of course you didn't! Come, man, what sort of a mentor would I be if I did not first teach you that the art of finding amusement in others is predictable? What sort of man cannot smile at himself and see where others would, let us hear it Sam?'

'Very well, I shall share it with you though I am still not sure. "Here lay Joseph, more alive than dead, so we weighed down his coffin, with two tonnes of lead!" There I have said it and I am not proud, was just a bit of fun, Joseph.'

Joseph let a faint smile flicker across his mouth; if it had been me I would not have felt as comfortable as Sam and most definitely would not have been creating verse about the man who could be misconstrued as disrespectful. In this knowledge I enjoyed the moment and begged a question to God, could he read minds? And with no deity present to answer this I made do with my own instinct and chose to be more guarded.

'O bravo Sam, bravo. Surely we would all agree that this is poetic, but mind that in your more vacant realms that you do not think it true, you might associate me with Beelzebub and I couldn't have that!'

Sam looked confused and grateful as I think he was finding sparring with Joseph exhausting. I doubt he understood a word, but Joseph's manner was jolly enough so would hopefully have felt relief.

This man had the uncommon ability to unbalance all those around him, this coupled with the magnetism to make you cling to him for a sense of equilibrium was plainly devastating. I do not know when I slipped but this I did and was now irrevocably under his control. I had hoped, fleetingly, for a commission perhaps second in command or chief advisory (I make light) but apparently I was to fall in with the ranks. I was not prepared for such a painful ascension from the most privileged in society to the most desperate, nor had I been schooled in their tongue. This being the case, conversations were small and nonsensical. I did try to single Joseph out, but to my rancour he would not abide this and treated me with contempt at each request for his society, and would quickly dispose of me with little fuss and I believe some pleasure.

Had he ever loved? I did not think so. How could such a man apply such a fragile emotion when everything he did was with broad unquivering strokes, and did not love warrant a quiver? If not at the beginning certainly on a test of fealty.

I noted that he penned a letter so my vanity sought to question him over it. At least the ability to read and write distinguished me from these reprobates.

'I notice you write there, Joseph, may I enquire of the nature? Is it a love letter? Hah, surely a man such as you are would receive many? Though I venture you would return the sentiments with much discretion and economy. I have a suspicion, Joseph, that you are never out of favour with the ladies and are the favoured topic at the whist table.'

'Very humorous, Freddy,' he said flatly. 'But my correspondence is of a more serious nature and I do not mind you knowing of its content. I am to charge you with the delivery and will expect you to wait for a reply.'

'Am I to town, Joseph, with this commission? I would

much like to take the air and did thoroughly enjoy our time there yesterday.'

'Why yes you are, Freddy. Either an informed guess, as there are no residences around here with people worthy of my penmanship, or Mary imparted some psychic ability upon you whilst you chatted? Hah, I declare I grow in wit as I do in fortune!

Now then I must instruct you, this letter is addressed to Bertram Toothill, it is a deliberate error, Freddy, I do not wish for the Lady Angelica to think that we have knowledge of the man's whereabouts, obviously. She will be distraught and waiting for news on her beloved, if indeed he was beloved. Such a small grey man, do you not think? Anyway I digress, I have devised the letter for Angelica to discover with ease that her husband left here last eve, our business concluded, and that we parted on good terms. It is simply done but then aren't all the most famous plots? I do believe that if you did not have emphatic proof to contradict my terms you would believe it yourself. Even I, as I am sat here, are almost taken in by my efforts! The new terms for the Toothill account are set out in it also, and are to be observed to the letter so forth and so on, detail, detail, detail, dull but necessary. Do not allow her to discover you and you may not elaborate on what I have said.'

'But am I truly the man for such a delicate commission, Joseph? I must ask as I know little of the particulars pertaining to it.'

'No questions, Freddy, do not ask me any and do not respond to any of the Lady Angelica's.'

He handed me the letter and dismissed me with a wave of his hand. I felt I had been dealt with as were the others, apparently, who were revelling in my discomfort.

'Joseph, dear fellow, have you forgotten I am of noble blood? Surely a more fitting task for one of these peasants? Can't you ask one of them ones to do your running for you?'

Obnoxious prattle! Jealousy and inferiority always produced such comments. I could see why for so many years I had held such classes in contempt and at a healthy distance.

'Immaculate execution, Freddy, I shall expect no less! Anything other will not bring me undone but may harass me and I am dashed uncomfortable when I am harassed. I do not worry though, Frederick, I say I spied in you a perfectionist and if it makes you feel a little less conspicuous at this time I would have charged no other with such a commission. Ay? What say you to that?'

'That is very fine and I thank you, Joseph.'

I took my leave feeling an uncommon sort of pride, one that you feel on losing everything and are told then that you had done so with dignity.

'Despot!' I announced bitterly, though more to myself than out loud.

'Despot, despot! That's rich coming from the piss pot! Freddy, Freddy, tell me honestly now, do you look to quell the wrath of this council of your peers? For it is what they have become, and if you disagree I would suggest more scrutiny of your situation. Or do you indeed have a latent appetite for humiliation? You cannot win. If you seek to trounce these animals you must first become one but never attempt to gratify yourself with me again. Such practices are irritating and I say it hurts me, Freddy, to see you flounder so. If I tell you it is beyond you then accept this, are we clear?'

'You could not speak plainer, Joseph. I did not mean to offend only to defend myself. I sometimes find the wit about this place, your company exempt, irritating.'

I excused myself and headed out into the cool fresh air. I decided that it would be no bad thing if I did not hasten a return to the inn. In fact, if Joseph had retired I would not miss his society.

Chapter 7

Rousing cheers and an informal circle was hosting some type of event as I stepped from within the inn and I decided, as I was in no rush, to take closer inspection. Gadzooks! But this was a cockfight and I was thrilled to find it! But surely this was a sport for gentlemen and these were not gentlemen even from a distance, but still this was excellent!

'Come closer with you, Freddy.'

Joshua beckoned with his old crooked hand. His doubled-over exhausted frame, made him unmistakeable and I found that many times I would seek out his company as opposed to that of others, as either time, or misfortune had made him more genteel.

'That one there is my rooster. You see how I fashioned for myself his spurs? From cat bones would you believe and if you will wager on him he will not disappoint. He's already seen to three others! Did you ever keep sporting birds, Freddy?'

'Why yes to both questions, Joshua. I would dearly love to have some sport with your bird, he looks a fine beast, and this is a most excellent diversion! A good cock fight is not to be surpassed, but truly I have no money, though if you were to accept a note of promise?'

'I will lend you a shilling, Freddy, but only if you will make it half your winnings on top then I shall be a rich man! You are sure to see profit on that one!'

'Thank you kindly, Joshua, I shall place my bet forthwith. And may I say you are to be congratulated on those spurs, they really are most exemplary.'

I placed my wager, then took a place beside Joshua. The atmosphere was convivial and I was heartened enough to feel some sort of comradeship.

'Dear Joshua, you enquired as to whether I kept fighting birds, let me tell you that I have many along with one or two handsome hounds, or perhaps I should say did have. My greatest hope is that they have been cared for in my absence, though I have dread, Joshua. The acrimonious nature of my departure from that society leads me to be reconciled to the belief that they are disposed of. But let us talk of other things, the subject vexes me greatly and I am so enjoying our sport. Joshua, I would ask something of you and if you see fit to respond I shall be most gratified.'

'Do you mind to speak simpler, Freddy? You are a good and kindly gent and all that, but I am blown if half the things you say are clear beyond me. If you ask me the company you kept before this was of ladies not lords or maybe ladylike lords? I would not be so fussy with my words round here, it will do you no favours and win you no friends, we are but simple folk.'

'Of course, of course, absolutely Joshua, well said, and duly noted. I shall refrain from this manner of speech if it is tiring. To put plain that which I would ask you, how do I come about gratuity for my efforts on Joseph's behalf? I am yet to receive any and I will say that a florin or two in my purse would see me more whole again.'

'Well "one" as you say must do a little more than "one" already has if his wish is to be a little richer, is that plain? But this said, if you have a mind to learn something off an old man, then he might not mind teaching you something?'

'This I would greatly appreciate, Joshua. The gift of knowledge is always acceptable and if in conclusion it proves lucrative then I say I am most eager. I promise, Joshua, to you this day, that for singling me out to bestow great kindness on and wisdom too, a small fortune shall be yours when I am better equipped to make so.'

'Prone to exaggeration are you, Freddy! Hah! I won't hold you to the fortune, I might be dead before you make it, but I shall speak plain with you now. You see, Freddy, how we gets by here is by lifting other gents' bits 'n' pieces, their purses and watches and stuff, gents such as you were, Freddy. We sell what we can to Joseph for fair price and that which he won't take we sell where we can. I see no point in hiding things from you, Freddy, you will witness no worse than that which you already have. What say you to this then, are you with us?'

At this point in the conversation I had a greater audience than the harassed cocks, but I was not hesitant; if I had a mind to object to their terms I would surely die and I had no wish to, after all I was no preacher and hardly righteous. So then accept this I would and, peculiarly, with relief.

'I am not shy of such an occupation, Joshua. Or do I grieve the man I once was? I am ready to receive instruction and shall apply your teachings as soon as you feel I am capable.'

'Good ole Freddy! Then you will be one of us, won't you? I will wager you will not be so quick to look down your nose or to excuse yourself from our company!'

This came from the crowd and though it was anonymous, I knew it was the general feeling.

'Very well then, Freddy, but do not be so ready to take your eye off sport you have a wager on, I believe you have some winnings there and if I wasn't such an honest man, ay Freddy!'

Joshua reminded me that at such events you must always keenly observe the combatants, as they changed very quickly and were often very similar.

'O most excellent news, Joshua! Perhaps I might spend some of my winnings in town as I am to there, I have a commission from Joseph, here take your dues I pay them gladly, I believe you have made a bad day good. Perhaps on my return we shall begin my lessons?'

'Of course, Freddy, though it is not as scholarly as you make it sound! But I can see there is nought I can teach you about that pretty tongue of yours, though it may favour you. I wouldn't suspect you anyway.'

We laughed together and I was very aware of what I was to be about but cared not, let the society that had ousted me so cruelly experience some misfortune in reward.

Joshua had remarked casually to me that treasure could be met in the simplest of places and men, and that the simpler met the greater the treasure to behold. This small gift of wisdom that Joshua would bestow was in effect priceless, and how I would apply this wisdom to everyday life, though criminal, was of no consequence to me considering my circumstances.

I left for town gladdened and excited, good sport will always do this, but then so will new beginnings.

Chapter 8

'Hold up there, Freddy! You are riding like you got a wasp up your ass!'

'Joshua! Will! And the young Tom! I say well met! Pray tell me what are you about?'

'Well seeing as you were so eager to learn of our ways, and us not being so shy, we thought we'd join you, see if you got the talent. Sides, I'm a bit light as I was betting against my own bird. Hah, fancied another, and that old capon never turned a good penny in its life before today! Made us laugh so it did.'

'You mean the tale you told of your rooster was a complete falsehood! Joshua, you surprise me, but still is that not sport? Come I have no hard feelings, how could I? I am a richer man than I was five minutes ago.'

'You are at that, and if we prosper today you will be a deal more so.'

'Av you ever filched "anything", Freddy? No matter if you never had the need, it's not the need with people of your class, it's the greed.'

Tom's appraisal of me was intuitive. There had been times in my life when the allure of chance had led me to take that which was not mine; as Tom had so succinctly put it, not through need, through greed. And though it was a rarity, I have to say that I was not half-bad at it.

'I say, Tom, why yes I have filched before and I think you shall all be pleasantly surprised as to just how proficient I am at this. 'Tis not an occupation purely for those in need, as you so eloquently put, young Sir. It certainly holds a fascination for me even though it is depraved, I am no novice.'

'Praise the Lord then, for a greener man might have seen us in a pickle. Begging your pardon, Freddy, but I am not protective of you and have I not sworn allegiance? You would have been on your own if you had been nabbed and I'm not sure how Joseph would have taken to that, can never tell with that man, gives nought away. He's a dark one alright.'

Tom, I suppose being simple, alluded to Joseph's verbal prowess and perhaps his stature. Less equipped people often called the 'well educated' dark or mysterious, simply because they did not comprehend. But for myself, though I abhorred such terminology, I had to agree with Tom. There was a deepness to Joseph that was profound and I did not relish plundering it, no indeed, for it was quite fearsome.

Tales of villainy and high times filled our journey, and by the time we reached Cleveton we were parched and I insisted on standing for a round of drinks. Only when refreshed would we attempt an assault on the town's unsuspecting populous.

Several drinks later and my sobriety in question we were joined by some ladies of a rather bold nature. To say that charm and elegance of address would not be necessary in order to woo these ladies was accurate enough description. Such as they were these creatures would often take on an unfortunate masculinity but in my cups this was opaque. Thankfully I was in my cups! One was taking a particular, rather clumsy interest in myself and having the effect of repulsion and irritation. So often was the case that one would take such a creature to satisfy friends and to have the business over and done with, never through a natural desire. A ritual I believe, observed by most classes, though on this night I believe my companions found them more physically appeasing than I certainly.

'Don't bother yourself with him my lovely, old Joshua will

sort you out. His type like to keep intact till they wed if you know what I mean. You leave that which comes natural to us folk, Freddy. I'm sure conjugal rights will be as pleasantly surprising to you as they will to your chosen one. I just hope you know where to put it. Myself, I could not be so patient, 'tis not manly and it's not natural, old as I am I still maintains this and I rarely pay, especially here. I am quite proud of that I don't mind telling you.'

'Oh no, he never pays, does he, precious?'

The harpy who haunted me turned to a rather sweet young-looking thing, in dire need of a wash.

'No, Leeny,' replied the girl.

'You cannot charge a man for falling asleep now, can you? Hah! And 'tis not the only thing that needs propping up, is it now Joshua?'

Joshua grabbed at the younger girl and told her that if she was willing he would teach her a thing or two, and that Eileen or Leeny as she called her could not even raise half a penny for the King's taxes on what she had to offer.

'Allow me in the first instance to correct you on something, Joshua. I am not intact and I wish you would refrain from such unsolicited opinions, and also to reaffirm my position as a blade, I shall not be damned by your words. Young lady, do you not discover a healthy and red-blooded male before you? I do believe you must else your attention would be diverted elsewhere. You and I both know, do we not, that I am more than capable of bringing a smile to those pretty lips?'

This was not a vicious attack, it was in good humour and had us all about our feet, especially so on my remarking on Eileen's lips as pretty and that she was young. A greater falsehood I believe had never been told the woman who was truly unfortunate and Tom added to this that anyone purchasing her for the night would need a priest to come blessing and that he would fetch one.

'I must say that this is a damned fine way to spend an evening, I would not be sorry if we enjoyed several such times in one week, in fact I defy you all to refuse me this!'

As drink will only exaggerate one's feelings and although I sounded overly generous due to this, I still meant the sentiment and would gladly endorse it the following morning, happy to find friendship in a most unsuspected place.

I heard his name before I saw him.

'Joseph! This is a fine surprise, ay boys!'

Joshua, obviously pleased to see him; something I did not readily share, more dread.

'Joshua, Will, Tom, and is that Freddy I spy beneath that pile of pig dung? Why yes I do believe it is, allow me to rescue you, Sir.'

'Joseph! It is good to see you, man, I fear we parted on less amicable terms than I would wish and would like to repair this, allow me to offer you some refreshment.'

'Why you continually promote yourself to such a lofty position, Freddy, is beyond me. Do not fret so, I do not consider you a threat or an equal therefore such tantrums are to be expected and are of little consequence. One must always allow his subordinates a voice, it is natural to them. Though I would relish some refreshment, I really am quite dry.'

Undeterred by another stinging put down, I continued.

'May I ask, do you seek an interview with me?'

'No not particularly, Freddy, I thought I smelled the local catch but I see I was mistaken, just rotten fish. What do you want, you filthy old hag!?'

Eileen was obviously unaware of who it was she molested and he grabbed her wrists until she screamed, though top marks for the woman's persistence, she remained undeterred.

'It's not what old Eileen wants, Master, more like what you wants. We are yet to sample each other I believe and you will not taste better this side of Somerset.'

'Yes, well considering we are not five miles from the coast it does not leave us much scope to speculate. I must say though the bright red moustache and glowing nostrils are appealing, one cannot help but venture up them, it is their bold placement! Still I must drag myself away as I have business to attend to, and, Freddy, take care not to stay too long, I do not make light of what you are about tonight.'

'Of course, Joseph, I shall be away very soon, with the fading light I counted on a more private interview with the lady.'

'I am heartened by your forethought, Freddy! And leave you comforted by this.'

He drank his drink and left with little ceremony, he needed none, enough to be but Joseph Black.

Tom clambered from his drunken repose to the table and after demanding his audience, recited,

'There was a young fox called Fred,

Who could not wait till he Wed,

So he paid with a guinea,

And made the nags whinny

Well met down the old King's Head!'

'Bravo Tom! Bravo! Surely a more talented poet was never known! Gentleman this has been exceptional. I am saddened to say that I must away, but do so I must before I am without senses. One thing does strike me, Joshua, did we not have a particular purpose for this evening? Though allow me to allay your fears, as I have said I am no novice and shall provide for myself most adequately; however, I thank you for opening my eyes, until the morrow then my friends. I left theatrically, bowing and waving my handkerchief, in excellent mood. Oblivious, as was becoming me regularly, to what was to play out on this most infamous of evenings.

Chapter 9

The Lady Angelica answered the door; she was pale, and once again, wild in appearance. I found this slightly irritating and could not help but remark as I passed her the letter. Later, and regrettably, I would think that perhaps I would have been less vociferous if I had not disposed of so much drink.

'Is not a lady of your stature strictly taught never to neglect her toilet madam, no matter the circumstance? And do not try to harry me or trick me into relating particulars of last eve, I have been warned of this and contrary to appearance do still have my wits about me.'

Though my confidence in this statement was waning as the fresh air took hold and the call to be sensible was intoxicating me further.

'Trick you? Why should I wish to trick you? Surely this letter is proof that neither you, I, or Joseph have knowledge of my beloved's whereabouts.'

Her sobs were catching in her throat and, as I was already struggling to comprehend, I found her address confusing and irritating.

'Lady, your fortitude is impressive if not a little extreme. I must say what I feel and it is obvious to me that yours was not a love match. I am a little influenced by hearsay but the evidence is there, madam. You are a very handsome woman, and, well, Bertram, what can I say of the man? I think I speak generously if I say he was a nonsense! Forgive my boldness but the man was a fool!'

'Oh, you are politeness itself, Freddy. I cannot formally address you as Joseph saw no need and I do not feel an urge to know you more intimately. As for grieving Bertram, Sir, I have little else to do and I do not feel inconvenienced by it. Neither is it fakery or vanity as you seem to think. You are quite right though, I am not prone to the pitfalls that true love must endure but I have a great fondness for my husband and even greater need. I should not want to face this world without him. Forgive me, but I am suddenly struck by your manner of address, you speak of Bertram in the past tense as though he is not here anymore?' I thought she would faint as she steadied herself on a chair. 'It would appear that I have all the information that I need, or am I mistaken? Bertram shall not be returning to me, he is gone!'

She was shrieking and the situation was becoming more pressing, I had to try to address this and calm her.

'You go too far, madam! I have said nothing of this, please keep your wild assumptions to yourself and I really ought to add, with what evidence do you deduce this? You have nothing from me! I will not be quizzed whilst I am full of spirit, my mind is a little foggy, and I shall not feel repercussions because of your lack of understanding! It is true I am a little intoxicated but you have no such excuse and should be ashamed!'

'Yet you are not so drunk that I do not fully comprehend what you omit to say, Sir! I shall not stand for this! I promise you one thing you and those that aided you shall hang for this deed; you cannot truly believe that you shall not!'

Her hysterics made me feel justified in the action that I took. What if someone were to be alerted to her state? It was too much to bear, so I hit her, and when she did not fall I hit her until she did. I dragged her to my horse with the light favouring me, and never was I so glad of a cold winter's eve when no soul in their wits would be about and no window ajar. The atmosphere of secrecy that this night afforded enveloped me and dulled the sense of fear that was about me. Desperate for the relative sanctuary of the inn away I rode, so hard that my mount wheezed and cringed with every strike of my whip and for sure wanted an end to this journey as much as I.

I had felt her break beneath my hand, it sickened me; please be dead, I thought, Lord I beg you do not wake; I do not think you could recover from such an attack. Had I not already been party to the destruction of that which you held so dear? Perhaps this attack, if you survived, would not seem so unbearable. But life is so fragile and subject to many horrors, we are lucky if we can guard against a handful of these. Still I say that if you still live then I would have you know that I preferred your hell to mine, surely the place itself was full of such as I. Though I do truly hope that there is an in-between for those who go unaware.

I stopped short of the inn for although the hour was late I still spied some activity, and dragged this poor woman's body across the scrub and into the back room of the inn, where Mary stirred a pot. She came to my side and eyed Angelica with what I believed to be shock but would very soon discover as avarice.

'Do not be shocked, sweet Mary, she is dead I believe, I had no other course than to bring her here.'

'Poor Freddy, I'm not, I am more than used to such goings on in my kitchen. Though you seem mighty fretful, poor lamb, do not be so, you have done no wrong, not that I can see anyway.'

'But I must worry, Mary, I must. I am full of dread for I cannot gauge Joseph's reaction. Surely I ought to feel something for this, some guilt, though I say I cannot feel owt but my own fear! Am I lost Mary, or am I discovered? Is this where I was always bound?'

'Oh Freddy! If you stayed up later you might realize that this is not so unusual, we are none of us innocent, and this being your first you are bound to be anxious. As for damnation, well most of us already know of it and it's all we can do to stay the course! You can leave this one to me, but let me fetch Joseph first, you will see he will not chastise you.'

She kissed my cheek and handed me a bottle of absinthe and whispered to me,

'She's a fancy one, isn't she Freddy?'

Humming sweetly to herself she disappeared; I wondered how one with such pretty dispositions could deliver such an objective, and offer me oblivion in a bottle so perfectly. Her soft femininity and the absinthe was a potent combination, like witchery, and I could not resist.

Joseph entered, his expression was of bewilderment though this was fakery, and he made this obvious.

'Joseph, let me repair this situation, if you can tell me how?'

'And how would you do that, Freddy, correct me if I am wrong but surely this is even beyond you?'

This unfortunate statement bought a nervous smile to my face, had I half this man's wit I could perhaps keep up, as it stood I was habitually nonplussed.

'I am heartily sorry for this, Joseph, I have rewarded the trust and confidence sited in me with the actions of a fool. In my defence I feel I was made overly confident by the drink and your words of encouragement.'

'Oh I see, it is I who am to blame for this farce! Would you prefer that I addressed you as the fool you are! Indeed the blame does not lie with me, no, Freddy, this is your deed, and you must own it. What is done is done, people shall say that they disappeared together, simple. It is not the fear of reprisal over this act, Freddy, that irritates, though I would add that 'tis you who would feel any such reprisal, not I. If I speak plain I would have had "this" different. You see, I was assured by the late Bertram that his estate held some promise for me in the event of his demise. I would have been recompensed, even though a beggar's path; however, had the Lady Angelica lived just a little longer I might have secured a more handsome bequest. So, you see, I stand at a loss, and your amusement at this is rather short-sighted. Should you be congratulated upon this grand performance? I do not wonder for long, if I was not the man you see before you, Freddy, I would say you looked to ridicule me! But do not concern yourself as I know you well to be an overly dramatic twit and incapable of such a sophisticated assault.'

Even the most ill-treated dog will look to his owner for the smallest crumb of affection, and to onlookers' amazement, will fetch the stick with which he is to be beaten, and I was no different. I was becoming used to finding security in the oddest of places and the strangest of addresses.

I had been too repulsed to look at what Mary was about, she was tearing at Angelica's clothes and shouted,

'Quick Badger, give me some help before the rigor sets in!'

The young lad sprung to her assistance, this was horrific! More so than the original sin – mine had been brought about by fear, but this was savage.

'Oh Lord, she breathes!' Mary screamed.

'And before you faint, Freddy, you can finish this.'

Joseph handed me a blade.

'You expect me to kill her!'

'Exactly, do I not have a right? Go on then, man, 'tis you who have hashed it. It's easier the second time, so I am told, though for myself I have never had the need or felt any trepidation. No?'

He snatched the knife from my trembling hand, kneeled beside Angelica and whispered something to her, slitting her throat. Blood filled her mouth then gushed from within, I could stand no more. The last thing I witnessed was Mary dismembering Angelica's finger to retrieve a ring. Mercifully at this point I passed out.

Chapter 10

Bleary eyed I began to wake, the sun streaming in my window. The sheer horror of the night's events was as fresh, though I think I had been put to bed. This surely was a little comfort almost heartening. I had never felt a stranger affection and had little time to despair of my situation before Joseph appeared.

'Well that was quite some night ay, Frederick? One might say enlightening for both you and I. I would ask how you feel though I may be in better position and state to tell you of this; however, I find it too early to apply philosophy, Freddy. We shall have to make do with pragmatism, and as I see it your future is set, shall we say you are resigned to this course? I feel a distinct lack of options but correct me if I am wrong? Still these things can be dull to talk of with the wrong person, and that person being you this morning, Freddy, we shall say no more about it.'

He threw a purse at me.

'A little sweetener, Freddy, you look like you suck on a quince, man! Pecuniary reward is always most welcome and has miraculous effect, do you not find?'

I could find no suitable or genuine response other than what my face must have told and though I tried to look regretful the feeling was tired and wasted. He continued.

'I shall say only one thing more about last night and it shall see the end of it, that being because you are already used to this business. There is no adjustment necessary, and no cause for redress. You shall always now turn to such remedies, their effectiveness is unexcelled, and is both practical and sensible. Embrace these changes, Freddy, before they turn you sour, or I. Now then I suppose you have not the appetite for breakfast, but some air? The morning is very fine!'

'Yes, Joseph, I do believe you are right, I cannot put this behind me but I can adapt, and, as I see, you have been most generous in your recompense!'

I eyed the contents of the purse with unchecked greed.

'I believe you have been adapting, as you say, for this moment longer than you allow. Certainly for longer than you have known I. That is my observation. There are fighting dogs in the courtyard, perhaps if you felt inclined you might allow me to win back some of that booty?'

'Oh for sure, Joseph, I cannot think of a finer remedy for the doldrums. I am assured by this most generous purse and the promise of some excellent sport that this state is temporary, as temporary as it takes us to repair to the courtyard!'

'Excellent! Excellent! Oh and, Freddy, do not think to constantly reassure me of your fealty, I understand you are with me and I would not want to grow suspicious. A man who constantly looks to reaffirm his loyalty is a man who is indeed questioning it himself.'

As expected the sport of fighting dogs was rivalled by none and most diverting as was financial solvency. It would seem that these country types could teach a thing or two to those who claimed wildly of breeding from Satan's very own bitch. As the sport was so diverting, and ruminating could do nothing other than bad, I am ashamed to say that my recovery was expedited. In retrospect, I wondered if I had deliberately sought such company as Joseph's in life. Though his was indeed the most extreme example, people often alluded to such men as entrepreneurs or fortune hunters. Who sought who was of little consequence, the ends were always the same, usually some rebuke, or mild punitive action. Alas these sanctions were no longer pertinent and if I could not acquire such infamy as that of Joseph's, perhaps by association, I may achieve anonymity.

Chapter 11

'Oh, don't you dare look at me like that, Freddy! You are no better than I!' Mary scolded me as she had guessed my thoughts.

'I wouldn't mind, but your type strip their dead of possessions too, and aren't these people sometimes kin? Is that not cold, Freddy? It is a worse sin than I or any of us could commit. No indeed, we are just not bound by your pretty laws.'

'Pardon me, Mary, what you say is both relevant and logical, though perhaps a little biased, however, I still remain shocked at your actions. The removal of the lady's finger was surely extreme? If I look judgemental it is by accident. I only wish to explain my look of bewilderment. Can you not see this as a compliment that I would not have believed it of you.'

'Well, how can I respond to such condemnation, Sir? Only that I know of many cases where bodies have been taken apart by men of medicine, even robbed from their very death beds! And there are other instances that I just can't bring to mind, you know of them, Freddy, you know of them.'

'Clever girl, Mary, you have me there.'

'You see, that which separates us is not worth your bother, it does not measure. You act as though you are beyond scorn yet I never beat a person half to death as you did. Next time you think to shame me, make good and sure that my sin outweighs yours, else I will be telling you again!' She paused little and her expression softened. 'Forgive me Freddy, I do not wish to injure you. We are still friends, and if I wanted to make you feel better I might tell you of something I saw not two hours ago?'

'Please continue, Mary, I feel duly chastised, and your philosophy always puts me at ease.'

'I am sure I am glad enough to tell you that I see the ravens come this very morn to take them onto the afterlife. Must have waited so they could go together. Some people fear them, but if they do not fetch me up when I'm passed on I shall worry. I have not a wish to stay here. I know so many tortured souls who remain.'

'I stand astonished at your psychic talent, Mary, and you are right, it has cheered me to think that they will be together. I only wonder that you cannot tell of treasure, surely this gift of yours demands development? Hah, ha.'

'Oh Mary would not tell even if she knew, would you Mary?'

Joseph often played with her like this, much to Mary's enjoyment.

'Her integrity as a reliable soothsayer would then be questionable. I have never known her use her gift for personal gain. Besides if it is buried treasure you seek then there are some very fine crypts worthy of plundering, and if Joshua has not picked them clean he might be persuaded to show you. I am thinking it might be less dangerous for the interested parties as these people do not fight back! Hah! Forgive me, Freddy, I could not help but make fun with the comparison.'

'Begging your pardon, Joseph, but I could not help but overhear and I would ask Freddy if he attends church?'

'Well I cannot say lately, Joshua, but I have, and am familiar with the scriptures.'

'Then let this Sabbath mark your return!' Joseph announced and continued with exalted dedication. 'There is gold to be had, Freddy! I, for myself, could never see any sense in filling a coffin with riches. People may say that I am missing something, I say I miss nothing and that is why there are so many coffins lighter than when first interred. It is inappropriate hypocrisy to salve a guilty conscience in such a manner. The loneliest man in life, of limited resources, may find himself rich in death in relations and fortune. And pray, what is the point in that?'

Chapter 12

For my mind this was nothing more than a bit of harmless prigging. It was not as though we were Resurrectionists. Nobody, save ourselves from the watchmen, was at risk, indeed Joseph had made this practice of burying one's dead with fortune sound idiotic and was, as ever, more than convincing. His remarks on the perpetuation of this ritual, being closer to Hell than Heaven, were made with conviction, and I believed him an authority on such matters, at least on the hellish part.

With little to do and the sun so high, I decided to dedicate this day to the Gods of Epicureanism. Some drink, some sport and good company, perhaps the more ambitious of the wishes, but more drink, most definitely more drink. Was there ever a more anticipated recreation!?

As the night drew in, we all gradually drifted to the fire, cosy I thought, and knew now why people painted such pretty pictures of the feeling. I am quite sure I had ever felt it and, honestly, was sorry for it, and I treasured it.

'Mary will tell us the story of your elders again, 'tis a chill dark night and lends itself to such a tale.'

Joshua spoke, and at this the others gathered round and pulled a chair up for Mary by the fire.

'Well if it gets me a chair nearer the blaze I have been tending all day? And if you have a mind to listen I cannot refuse. But first you must know that my gift has been passed down through my family for many generations and always 'tis the females who shine. The most ancient of these were valued and considered close to God. People of the village sought medicine and wisdom of them and were grateful for their protective powers. But my mother's grandmother, and I'd add that I bear her name, was not so lucky. She was born a natural, in a world so wholly unnatural that they would have done for her at birth had her gift not been hidden. Anyway, it was on a night such as this that a man knocked her door asking for assistance, not revealing at first that it was she who he sought. They sat him down by the fire and begged him take food and warmth and asked him unburden himself. And so he did, and was a cunning tale wrought with traps he told to undo my poor Mary. "My daughter has been missing these last three days," said he. "And I am overcome with grief and worry." He said he had been told of a meeting, clandestine in nature with a questionable individual. He told that she was blessed and at the same time cursed with great beauty and silliness where common sense should be. "I have only little information," the man said. "And if I told you that I sought a psychic to assist, how would you greet this news? Through careful channels, I have been led to this door and am already encouraged by what I see and hear." Well, Mary's husband, Edward, near threw him out the door. "Be gone, man! You will find no such person here! I do not know what led you here but I am sure it is evil! My wife has no such power." He slammed the door on him and lent by it, stricken with fear. For, as we all know, naturals were often hunted by so-called witch-hunters and had to be more than careful. Sobbing came from beyond the door and the man begged old Mary speak with him; she had to stop my Edward fetching a stick and said she found the man genuine and felt she could help. Bless him he tried to stop her but knew the gift was strong in her and so, against his better judgement, he let the stranger in. How the man weaved a spell should have seen 'him' hung for a witch, not Mary. His lies and twists, and all the while drawing her in, each word leading her closer to the gallows. She could not help him and said she saw nothing. Well how could she, I ask you? 'Twas all lies! But she asked him leave something of his daughters and that she would try again later. He left many hours later and they sat down and Edward said he felt weary and that it was a rotten night's doings, and that badness was to come of it. And though he had no real gift, we say someone was with him that night, giving warning. Sure enough, and as Edward had foretold, the witch-finders came not an hour later and took poor Mary away, though God saved Edward that night as they could have taken him and the little ones, so some mercy there. She was dead by Wednesday, and poor Edward, a broken man, never really spoke again only to forbid talk of the gift. I am with people here who may as well be kin, so don't mind them knowing of such things, but to anyone I'm not so familiar with I give this warning, "A less guarded tongue, won't just see me hung".'

'I suppose where there is no other entertainment to be had, a well-worn story will bring some relief! Praise then that there are not so many nights such as this and that we are normally occupied!'

Joseph was obviously irritated by the story, though this was my first time and apart from the pointed warning she had given, I thought she did very well. There was no need for such sabotage. Pike had fallen asleep at her feet and there was a shared silence amongst the others. The tale was fearful enough and, though I wished it different, I had to confess to a latent prejudice on such matters. In a world where everyone fancied themselves as a witch-finder, and the many purported claims of bringing these creatures to justice, historically I had revelled in their capture, though remained unconvinced of their actual power. Now I found myself wondering if the many who had gone to the gallows before were perhaps more like Mary, and surely nobody could send such a girl there? Unfortunately, they would if she were subject to scrutiny, and I was too quick to forget her actions of late. Perhaps a less familiar approach would make me see that she was indeed touched by something malevolent, as I feared was I. A thin excuse and directed at one and one only, but that was all I had. This frail irreverent ideal was what took hold, and was to see me through this most tumultuous time wrought with iniquity and sin.

Chapter 13

'You look very fine this morning, Mary.'

'Why thank you, Freddy, yes I feel it fits me well, thanks to you and that Dunwith, Angelica. It was never a dress for her, too young and too tight by the fit. It does for me where she was twice my waist.'

'Ah, now I see, "Dunwith", "done with". I must ask Mary, did you laugh at me when I enquired after the Dunwiths the other day? You see, it did not occur to me that you spoke of the dead, I believed you had wealthy benefactors! That was cruel of you, was it not?'

'No Master Freddy, I laugh at you now for I have only just learned that you were in the dark about it, I thought you jested, you see.'

'What a fool I am! Still there is no point traversing the subject as I am to church this morning, should I say a prayer for you?'

'And who do you think listens to the prayers of such as you and I, Freddy? So I shall thank you not to trouble yourself. My time for redemption has long since passed as has yours and your smart comments are not genuine, and of no surprise.'

'I only meant it in jest, Mary, forgive me, if I thought you felt injured by them it would pain me.'

'Go on! Get off with you! I must get used to you, I suppose, as you must I, I like telling people, Freddy, would you change that and ruin my day?'

'The fairer sex indeed are a mystery to me, I have never known one as well as you, Mary, and yet I remain confused!'

As I ventured from the inn I saw that Joshua along with a few others were readying for our jaunt.

'Here he is!'

'Don't hurry yourself too much, Freddy, wouldn't want to arouse suspicions being there along with the rest of the crows. We like to make a quiet entrance when everyone else is settled. And if anyone asks, 'tis old George Bramwell who's for the off today, the butcher's father. Couldn't be simpler if you are asked how you know him?'

'Thank you, Joshua, I feel prepared now, and I do believe that even I cannot blunder this!'

'Well let us hope. I would say pray but think that would be stretching our luck a little too far, considering what we are about!'

'As long as they don't bury him with sausages we are alright, ay Joshua? Not that I mind sausages, just don't want to mistake his sausage for one of them!'

Any nerves I had been feeling were banished by Joshua's and Will's humour. For sure I was very grateful to them, though kept this to myself having no wish to appear anything other than the libertine.

The church was to be found, as was always the case, at the end of a pretty lane. Not too ostentatious though definitely in receipt of some patronage from a considered individual.

Joshua and I made a polite entrance, whilst the others decided to wait outside. I believe this decision was made for their amusement at the spectacle had gone beyond reason. I myself had distanced myself from them for fear that it was contagious, whereas Joshua seemed fatigued by the humour, and showed obvious contempt for the lack of ingenuity and the same old jokes.

Thankfully the ceremony was almost through, some embarrassing wailing and a few fainting ladies was all, and the coffin was removed and carried to where it would lie. We kept safe distance, but I could not help but wonder at the genius of this whole set up! The etiquette which one applies in such circumstances definitely lent itself to nefarious activities. Grief itself can be rather off-putting in an individual and a conversation with someone stricken with it rather daunting. So naturally people kept themselves to themselves. After all, if it was an illusion they created for effect, a little less clarity of the situation was surely most welcome. And the ladies, especially, did enjoy a touch of the hysterics and some play acting.

'Mark that,' Joshua whispered to Sam.

'Joshua, why do we mark? I can only think it is to aid the discovery of this grave tonight? But surely this is unnecessary as we shall see quite adequately with torches.'

'Thank you, Freddy, for reminding me again that I must be more vigilant with you, yes, we would see more clearly with torches, if we were to use them, but for myself I do not wish to be discovered! Good God, man, have you no common sense?'

'Ah yes, most illuminating, if you will pardon the expression? Yes, I can see your reason now. You must allow that I am new to this, Joshua, and that which is obvious to you may be less so to me.'

'I don't suppose we will get rich on this one, ay lads? Still we must make good where good fortune fails us. Folk just don't seem to want the crypts anymore, and if they do it's the Devil's work to get into them, or they are snared. I'm thinking this business of ours has not much left in it. People grow wise, you see, Freddy, like to play tricks on ole Joshua. Oh they will commission a fine tomb and a damned fancy headstone alright! The like makes you feel full of promise, but more often than not they be empty promises just like the crypt and I grow weary of it.'

'Oh Joshua! Don't go on so! There will always be some fool

who will line our pockets,' a disgruntled youth pointed out, obviously harassed by Joshua's bemoaning, a trait prevalent in people of his generation.

The rest of the journey was made dull by Joshua's pessimism and the young ones, tired of it, rushed on ahead except for Pike who never seemed to mind what a person had to say. Always, whether feigned or not, and out of some sort of misguided respect, he was as attentive as his intellect would allow.

'Not so far now and we will have a good meal in our bellies, set us up for tonight. Just mind now, not too much grog, you will need your wits about you this eve.'

'I must say, Joshua, I am famished, I wonder what Mary has cooked up for us.'

My stomach growled at the thought of one of Mary's concoctions.

'Oh it will be meat and gravy for sure. She's a good girl is Mary, she'd feel shamed if she didn't feed you fit to burst. Make someone a good wife one day, ay Pike?'

'Aye, Joshua. Only I think she has eyes for another just of late, what say you, Freddy?'

'I cannot believe you think of me, Pike, good God no! No, she is just very attentive, the love Pike is between you two.'

'Yep, and well he knows it! You are a nonsense boy! There is no need to stake your claim over our Mary so often. We have eyes and ears enough, you know.'

'I suppose you are right, Joshua. I meant no harm, Freddy, I just love her so, you see.'

Although Pike took a ribbing for prostrating himself so over his Mary, he did not take umbrage. The boy was habitually good natured and the journey back to the inn was enlivened by it and made full of good humour.

Chapter 14

The night's adventures beckoned, and the dark cold night begged we leave and be on with it before the hour became too late and we were undone by the dawn. I was aware that it was a reasonable journey and so was eager to get on, thankfully Joseph spoke, and was looking to leave.

'Shall I sit Elijah in the window? So as we find our way home?'

'How so, Joseph, how might this aid us?'

The question begged to be asked, I just wished it had not fallen to me to ask it.

'Well, his complexion is positively beaconesque tonight! If there is such a word? Hah! What need have we of torches, I ask? Elijah, though uniformly sanguine, this night you have taken on a most uncommon lustre! What have you been about to achieve such vibrancy?'

Elijah remained unmoved and uncertain as to Joseph's remarks.

'You see, Freddy, it is lost on him but I see you find it amusing. I cannot help but worry of you, man. I have noted that your conversation is limited at times and that you seek me out. It is not for you and I to create a particular alliance, it would not be right. Perhaps a little more effort on your part and more time spent with these people will improve this stifling atmosphere, it is choking, Freddy, choking. And

I simply cannot bear to catch your eye one more time hoping to engage me, I find it embarrassing.'

Thankfully this scathing rebuke was beyond the present company, so my dignity was spared, and a response may have produced another so I kept my peace.

'Are you with us tonight, then Joseph?' Badger asked.

'I would not miss it, Badger. I feel a moment coming on, this being Freddy's first time. I think, yes, purely for the entertainment value and to satisfy my curiosity.'

'Shall we be off?' Joshua enquired of Joseph. 'Thankfully we are blessed with a heavy sky tonight, for 'tis a full moon and we will be spared its illuminations, ay Joseph?'

'Quite right, Joshua. If only everyone was as observant as your good self. I admire caution, though am no slave to it so it can be somewhat confining. But I will admit that mine is not a regular vulnerability, and 'tis a rarity that I should venture out with you on such a purpose. I would not have you jeopardize my safety with heroics, man, so well put.'

Elijah held the door for Joseph, such a grovelling, filthy-looking thing, and allowed it to slam on the rest of us.

Down to the graveyard we ventured, the dark chill night fuelling my imagination and what I anticipated grew wildly in my mind. What I already knew was not enough to satisfy this fear that had hold of me. A reminder from Joseph, that he was on form, bought me back to my senses.

'Why do you not join in with the japes and good humour, Freddy? I find it a little discouraging, though it is not wholly unexpected. I believe I can guess how you feel, allow me to expand. I am not given to nightmares, though their creation is not beyond me, still I digress. What I mean to say is that I know you fear this, or perhaps fear some sort of divine retribution. I have no such fears, and am not persuaded by the religious or by outlandish tales of monsters and hobgoblins. Do you see where these teachings are equally banal and ambiguous? I am not so arrogant to say that they are wholly untrue, but nothing is made beyond "me".

I pity you if you are affected, as the people who are, I consider misinformed, and in many cases quite mad. It is just a hypothesis, Freddy, but it is informed. Where the religious might have you seek forgiveness and practise self-denial for who knows how long, my way rewards almost instantly though you must embrace it. If you falter, it makes you too good to be bad, and too bad to be good! A quandary, yes Freddy, but a little courage on your part will see it gone.'

It must be said of the man, though I feared it wicked, that he could conjure from within you something so base, yet so pertinent, and suggest immorality as one does a penny panacea but with more effect.

'Oh I say there, Freddy, did one think to bring a pomander with one? I simply enquire if you aware of the smell, man, the smell! Has one has ever smelled rotting flesh before? Or ever been downwind of our Elijah? Now that's perspective for you! Hah ha! It is not pleasant if I'm to be polite. You know if that man is not already dead I'd swear he was on his way, for myself I will only entertain him outside and with a prevailing wind!'

The whoops of laughter from Sam's comical report, and Joseph's assault on my preconceptions of this situation, did for me that day and I promised myself to not venture, comment, or question again. Maybe the company I kept did lack healthy opposition, and I had no obvious alternatives, but the truth was that it was too late for such thoughts and they rankled.

I still could not see how we would rediscover the exact grave, but Joshua led confidently. His familiarity of the situation impressed, and we effortlessly arrived at the freshly turned earth.

'On with it then,' Joshua said.

I took up my spade along with the others and began to excavate, though with less zeal, which I disguised by turning over the earth that others had dug. I had no wish to be first to find the coffin, and no time passed before we found what we looked for.

'In with you then, Freddy.'

I had not developed a taste for ridicule, so with feigned gusto and enthusiasm, I levered the hinges till they gave. I covered my mouth with a handkerchief and opened the coffin. The unnerving stench had me reaching and gagging, much to the party's amusement.

'Go on then, you will soon adjust to it.'

Joshua definitely felt so and related this with confidence, though I wondered if you would ever be accustomed to such a thing.

'Joshua, do you agree that our streets are lined with excrement, yes? This said I still do not grow accustomed to the pervasive effect! So no, I do not believe I shall adjust! I might add I would want to!'

I tentatively felt for valuables. There was something, something that had slipped beneath the cadaver's shoulder. I tried to retrieve it but it was difficult and with him being so stiff. I had to push hard, then a long groan came from him. I screamed and leaped from the grave.

'God help me! He's still alive!'

'Oh he spoke to you!' Badger remarked innocently.

'What do you mean he spoke to me? He's supposed to be dead!'

'And that he is, must have had something to say to you, is all.'

'Oh that is all, is it!?'

I scrambled to my feet amongst the laughter.

'Bloody calm yourself, will you! You will have the watchman down on us! Lots of people do it when they die, their last breath gets trapped and sometimes if you push them they will speak to you.'

Joshua was justifiably irritated. My outburst was a little unchecked considering the circumstances, though Badger was insisting on continuing in the same vein. He and Tom were pressing the man's chest, and laughing uncontrollably as he wheezed and groaned, until no more sounds came.

'Come on, Freddy, 'tis only a bit of fun!'

'It is irreverent and disrespectful!'

'Irreverent? Disrespectful? Pray what do you call that which you do here tonight then, Sir, homage? I see you try again to distinguish yourself, what a waste of time!'

Joseph put an end to my despair with these few words and also put me back in my box. Though it was natural, my reaction, he would have it as fake and it fell to me to begin to question if he truly knew me better than I knew myself. Any sense of self was treated as deception, and there was no longer much to be had.

'Come on then, let's tuck him in.'

Joshua threw the spades back to the boys and offered one to me.

'Thank you, Joshua, but I think I shall sit this out, I do not wish to impede progress. I believe your boys enjoy a little too much my ignorance of such practices.'

'Aye, yes, you might be right. Go on then you shabby lot, all that jesting did was left you with another man's toil. It's him who's laughing now!'

The boys grunted a few expletives towards me, and perhaps to themselves for being so foolish and quickly set about the task of making good what we had ransacked. Not half an hour gone and we were off, and I worried a little at what state the burial was left in as it was very dark; Joseph enjoyed pointing out that I was too particular, and that it was very difficult to make a mess of a pile of earth.

An impoverished soul
On closer inspection
May still have some worth
For a Devil's delectation.

Chapter 15

Next morning I awoke in desperate need of freshening up. Save the horses trough, I had little for my toilet. A small glass and a bowl of fresh water, thankfully replenished daily by Mary. She was very attentive to me, and I thought to remember to thank her or perhaps a ribbon from town would see her smiling.

Never given to reflection, except to indulge the narcissist within, what followed as I studied my appearance was disturbing and completely out of character.

I became aware that there was no clear distinction between my reflection and myself. Both felt equally shallow, and both unforgiving. 'Look at me', I heard myself say. Look at what you have done! Yet still you cannot even own this, it has been contrived by another!'

If this was insight I did not welcome it, and was I scared enough to throw the glass which shattered against the bed and almost sighed, as if something escaped. I vowed it to be the last time I would entertain such introspection, if I now had to consider the care of my reflection then it was too much and introverted, and I would not become so. Perhaps then the company I had been keeping was a little coarse but was better than my own and, resolutely, I dressed and readied for the day. Mary would clean up the shattered glass, but I would not ask her to replace it.

I walked in on a high-spirited conversation. I felt old, and had never been as free with the more fragile sex as these boys seemed.

'If you near ole farmer Gibbons, you might think to bring home a bird or two, been such a while since we had anything but rabbit.'

A small group had gathered at the door including Tom.

'I will fetch you some birds, Mary, but I mind when you moan about rabbit! 'Tis no fun having an arse full of shot for me, or you! Don't be so ungrateful, girl! Hush now,' he whispered. 'Somebody comes!' he warned, as some paying customers entered the inn.

A rarity, I thought, they must be strange to the town either that or they were too poor to be of significance. Chance visitors of wealth and means did sometimes happen upon this place, Pike had assured me, whether they made it out alive was debatable, for sure the place did not prosper through word of mouth.

I was a little relieved to see that the visitors were local, farm hands and such like, perhaps then there was hope for me this day for I had no wish to see anybody else dead.

I ventured outside to where gathered was the usual lot. I had no wish to engage them just to take my place and feel less conspicuous; however, this was by my own fault, as Joseph had quite eloquently pointed out.

'And what do you do today, Sir?'

Joseph appeared, impeccably turned out and fit for any exertion.

'For myself I am to town, I would not object to your company if you so wished? You look puzzled, Freddy, let me be clear then, I merely think that a ride into town not so important. We are friends, Freddy, just not particular ones.'

'I would very much enjoy that, Joseph, I have errands to run and your company is always diverting. I would ask you something, Joseph, I thought to buy dear Mary a ribbon to express my gratitude for all that she does. Do you think this too much? Would it offend Pike?'

'A question you would do better asking himself, if you have the courage! If you have not then let that guide you.'

'Ah, yes, I see. Perhaps I shall take your advice if it was so?'

'Not advice, caution, though I deplore the stuff! Still let us not traverse that subject again.'

Elijah sidled up to Joseph, a repugnant sycophant, who Joseph abused regularly, and who regularly put himself forward for this.

'Not so fair today, Joseph. Still we have had no rain, so the tracks good and dry.'

'Thank you, Elijah. Observation skills better suited to the crow's nest aboard one of the King's finest, keeping watch for the rebellious French, ay!' A round of 'God Save the King' came and Joseph continued. 'But then you would be red-faced and weather-beaten, and I should not know you!'

If I laughed now I too would be trounced, I had learned this much, so feigned ignorance at the sarcasm. Others did not, and laughed openly at Joseph's smart quips, safety in numbers perhaps. Elijah laughed too, though he knew not why. He was a true dullard and I found it slightly irritating that he remained so oblivious. I would have enjoyed explaining it to him, this sly obsequious thing, but Joseph liked to leave people in some doubt as to his regard; it was this part of his arsenal that was most destructive. Not one of us survived a day without some injury, and, though I savoured the idea, I would not clarify things for Elijah, it was more than I dared.

'A great pastime of the civilized is conversation, do you not think, Freddy?' Joseph commented as we took up the journey to town.

'Though I am blown if I can think of a topic, it is quite out of character, you shall have to influence me.'

'I find "you" most intriguing Joseph, every day when I should know you better I feel I know you less, you are quite the conundrum. Perhaps then we might talk of you?'

'No, no. I do not seek self-gratification, and am very aware of my effect on people, disclosure enough. Let us examine you further? What is to be done with you, Freddy? Do you stay, or do you simply await a favourable wind to carry you home to Bath? If it is the latter, I fear you may wait forever. Some sort of parley would have to precede you, and how can this be when none will entertain you? I fear there is nothing to be done. Though I am struck by the notion that if you employed a mediator to speak on your behalf it may prove advantageous. Someone impartial, though informed, he could be under no illusion as to what has gone before. If he had influence, Freddy, if he could be persuaded. Tantalizing, is it not? But then how are you to meet such an individual when none will talk with you? It is most perplexing.'

'Yes Joseph, a fine plan but it is flawed as you say.'

'Flawed? No, I do not call it flawed, simply incomplete. Perhaps if you told me something of your previous life I might be able to offer some service. From what I have gleaned, I do not believe the situation irreparable. A good word from me, I do have connections in Bath, you see, of a more desirable affiliation, you may find yourself if not back in favour, at least not out of it. But to achieve this I must know more of your life. Your family and friends, even the smallest particular. A person's financial status, their habits. If they attended The Assembly Rooms, hah! Do you see where I may have someone who does similarly? And that an alliance could be struck, and that you in turn would naturally become a mutual acquaintance. From here one can only speculate, but surely this offers you some hope? I am no magician, Freddy, I cannot conjure good will but I can create a dynamic into which you may appear more worthy. Time has passed, has it not? Forgive me, Freddy, but you are not so remarkable. I myself have difficulty remembering who you are, and what you do here most days. Your ignominy will not have resounded, rest assured.'

'Joseph, I barely have time to laugh that you would have me cry! But I thank you for this insight, I believe I exaggerate my sins wildly and a little clarity does not go amiss. I truly find your words most encouraging, though why you would put yourself out so on my behalf is quite beyond me. I cannot help but wonder how I could ever repay such a service?'

'Oh you will adequately in the future, Freddy, rest easy. I am expectant of high reward.'

A man of many words, and I did at times find it difficult to keep up, so no wonder that these last few went unchecked. Had I not been relieved of my senses by his spin, had I not been so greedy to think that I could achieve my greatest wish – to return home sins absolved with the minimal inconvenience – I might have taken heed. For this was truly the defining pivot, in what was to become a truly horrific tale.

We arrived in town in time to catch the first flurry of ladies displaying their finery, some to shop, some to chance meetings that were never in truth chance and were purely to discuss another's misfortune or embarrassment. But however they chose to fill their days and amuse themselves the result was always as planned, to greatly affect any prospective suitor that might just be passing their way.

'Well then, Freddy, I thank you for your company, we will talk more of this resurrection of yours, yes? But as for now I must away, I have business at Gribble and Sons, the solicitors.' He took me aside confiding. 'The Toothills are missing under some mystery and are not expected to return, at least alive. Lines of enquiry have gone from relevant to ambiguous. Those who pursue are enjoying the scenic route, and finding that where the ends are frayed they shall never meet. The family are eager to divide the estate between themselves, Freddy, and the debtors. I am lead to believe by Gribble that a healthy financial settlement shall be mine within this week! I was a major creditor of theirs, of course, though the amount may have been exaggerated a little between myself and Gribble for a little sweetener. Who I do not know, Freddy, and who does not owe me, would fill a sedan chair, I am quite sure of it! So there, I am disposed to be in good humour, I might consider that you have put upon me whilst in this euphoric state?'

'Upon my word, Joseph, I did not realize you so elated or expectant.'

'I jest, Freddy! I jest. Go on then do not stand there like you would follow me, it is unnerving.'

He about turned and left me.

In circumstances such as this, where you were relatively new to a place and lacked company, if you were of the right sex you might find solace in the local inn, and there was The King's Head again! I was sure to bump into someone and had made friends therein before, even those separate from my current situation.

I did partake a healthy amount and spent a good time there. I made friends who I would never speak to again, or indeed remember. I flirted where it was not necessary, for those in my eye were available to purchase at any given time, though the exercise was good enough.

Having learned of the effects of the local brew, and in this knowledge inhibited consumption, I found my way back to the inn with little trouble and entered through the back room. The drama within was sobering enough though one more innocent may well have passed out at the sight of so much blood and a man with no face.

'Poor lamb, he will not wake now, he sleeps the sleep of giants. Still he would not have us waste time on grief, let us see what he has in his pockets.'

Mary held someone, face full of shot, and obviously dead. I assumed it to be Tom from a count of those present and I had known him to be poaching. She was basically a very hard girl but, incredulously, had retained some of her femininity and at times used this well. But not this time.

'Check the stable and I will see if he hides anything in these pockets.' She caught my look and blushed. 'Poor lamb, just a few pennies is all I can find.'

'Oh yes! What is that you hide then, Mary? I sees you! Give us it!'

Badger struggled with her as he tried to prize something from her fist.

'Come on, Mary!' Joshua joined in.

She screeched,

'No you won't have it! He promised it to me! On his death he said, so I'd never forget our love!'

'Love, Love! He thought you painful to look upon woman! Hah! Said he could not even bear to eat round you! Likened you to a warty old toad, isn't that so, Josh, 'tis what he said?'

'That's enough, Badger! I will not have you talk with my Mary like that!'

'Well she's not yours is she, Pike? Apparently she's his! Well was anyway.'

'Don't you dare go and sully my name like that, Badger! I do so belong to Pike. I'm just a little bit confused, I think it's because Tom's trying to reach me. Help me, Tom, is that you? You say you want me to have the ring on account of Badger dropping them birds you promised me? And to say to Pike, especially, that nothing ever happened between us and that the love was just on your part?'

'There! That's told you! I knew my Mary was just that, my Mary.'

'What! You believe that load of old rubbish! She's raving mad, man, and a fraud!'

Badger resumed the struggle with her, she bit him and Badger screamed,

'You witch! You ought to be hung!'

'Oh come on, Badger, let her have it, 'tis only a bit of fakery, bit of tin, let it go.'

'Very well, Joshua but only so as I can see to my hand, it bleeds look!'

'Where have the pennies gone?'

Mary screamed as Badger turned around with them on his eyes; he put them in his pocket and ran off laughing. She slumped to the floor and eyed the ring.

'No 'tis not worth the bite I gave him for it, look Pike.'

'Ah well, Mary, 'tis quite pretty though, and will look sweet on your finger.'

'I suppose.' Making it fit though was too much for this girl to stand, her knuckles had become quite manly from hard work and she screamed and threw the ring. ''Tis nothing but a bloody child's ring, I never had such trouble before! What a stupid thing to steal a child's ring!'

''Tis just a toy,' Pike said saving her blushes. 'Fit for a doll, you'd never make a penny from it.'

She seemed placated by his words and the most sincere look he gave her. Joshua tapped my arm and took me to one side.

'She ought to be bletted that one, what says you, Freddy?'

'Aye Josh, I might agree if I knew what it meant.'

'She has not ripened, Freddy, needs to be treated harsh, put out in the frost to sweeten up.'

'A fine description, Joshua, but at times I cannot help but wonder.'

'No, 'tis all as you see, she invents herself for him, I can't help but worry for young Pike, he's too soft with her. I just hope he comes to his senses before it's too late and she's carrying one of his or what she claims is so.'

'Then you do not feel her plight? Can you not pity the girl, Joshua? Once so obviously disposed to sweetness and yet to have become so sour.'

'Lucky that I am no faint heart.'

Joseph appeared and saw the gruesome crew scramble to their feet, stepping away from the body.

'I see we have a body! Did you wish to improve my day by this discovery, or are you all as stupid as you are shameless? Clear it up then, get rid! And, Mary, I shall take some wine and meats. Freddy will you join me?'

'I shall, Joseph, though I shall not partake of your supper if that is agreeable? This business has quite destroyed my appetite.'

'Oh do not be so prissy, Freddy! You shall eat and drink or I will knock you on your arse and say you try to provoke me. Do you think I toast it? And if I did, what would you say? If your intention was to insult me you should perhaps do so when you are more equipped to defend your own actions, do not forget who I am or what history you have written yourself these past weeks.'

'Please forgive my manners, Joseph, I was never famed for them and if you would allow me to offer another excuse I would say that I have had a belly full and am a little nauseous.'

'Very well and perhaps given your state there is little point in you joining me tonight. I will have no sense from you and we did have that particular matter to discuss, so no I suggest an early night. Perhaps we shall talk in the morning.'

'Thank you, Joseph, I shall take your advice and wish you goodnight.'

He did not respond, Mary had served his food and he did not glance from the fare. I dared to think of his manners not mine but in truth these thoughts were becoming less frequent; the very real fear I felt that he could read them was not a fancy but a truth and every word he spoke bated feelings of paranoia. How was I ever to be rid of such a thing?

I carefully made my way to my room, it was comical the care and attention one paid to such a detail when imbued with spirit and I laughed to myself, my general state improved by the thought of what might be. Tom's demise, ashamedly not registering even with all its violent detail.

No nightmare or introspection found me that night, quite the opposite in fact. I dreamed of a renaissance. It was vibrant and fabulous and in truth all things that mine could never be, not even the good King George could, himself, live down such infamy as mine. Perhaps five or more years' repentance and equally notable deeds, if not of heroism of at least great attentiveness, would perhaps soften people's perception. Though what I hoped for in reality was indeed very little. Would some daring soul invite me to dine to defy their neighbours or satisfy curiosity? Or some wild eccentric ask me to a ball? I knew not, though one thing was sure, I would become entertainment for some, and in time they would bore of me as others followed. Only then might I start the arduous process of re-establishing myself in society, though this time with no preordained distinctions; no indeed, it would be hard work. The more I struggled and the more it became apparent, the more gleeful spectators would be, calling it my atonement, and perhaps it would change me. It would seem then that I was to endure yet another metamorphosis, though, in nature, it would be far less arduous than those that had gone before but mostly more gratifying. I did not know it would be temporary at that point, and perhaps would not have bothered had I been aware. Still I remained unaware that in actual fact I had no choice.

Chapter 16

'There he is! Good morning, Frederick, you appear in good health this morning, you must have learned the art of depravation where the town's refreshment is concerned. The trick is to never have the last one, only take longer breaks in-between that way one may still be indulging even when one is not.'

'I wonder at this philosophy, Joseph? Do you not think to write down any of these eureka moments?'

'No, I do not, they are too abundant, and I would spend all my time doing so! But today is about you, Freddy, will you breakfast with me? We might then plot your pending reappearance in Bath town. What say you, Freddy? Shall we become conspirators?'

'I say amen to all of it, Joseph!'

'Bravo! Then we shall begin. All I ask is for clarity in the detail and lots of it, the more I know of you, Freddy, the more likely we are to succeed. I must say I have never taken on such a task, it is quite out of character but amusing enough. So whenever you are ready, Freddy, begin any time dear friend.'

'I do not understand, Joseph? Where or how should I begin, I thought you might lead me with questions?'

'Gah! I thought myself coherent in instruction, though you obviously require prodding, just tell all, Freddy! What and who filled your days and nights? Where they resided? And were they reputable? Could I be more plain, man? Lord, this may prove exhausting!'

'No, no, Joseph now I see though I am a little concerned for people's privacy?'

'Why? Do you think they're concerned with yours, Freddy? Good Lord, you are fussy on their behalf, are you not? Do you think they not regale your tale with much delight and savour every detail! Yes this is a delicate operation, though this is a fine time to discover that you have integrity! It is a pity for you that you did not apply this more regularly before. And can you afford such a luxury? Ay? But I cannot accept half the story, I will not make a fool of myself and am resigned to not spend another minute on it. However, an idea strikes me, Frederick, as a man more in need of direction never sat before me, I would ask you to consider the army? You have little funds to acquire a commission so the ranks would have to suit, though, forgive me, I have heard they feed on rats and are two to a bunk! No, no, I am certain this is just talk, such horror stories can surely have no provenance.'

A lesser incentive might have had me keep my counsel, but it was true, I either told all or ended my days dining on vermin or worse still on the ill-gotten gains of this current repose; so I gave in and after a time it became easy, and I found pleasure in divulging secrets of those once considered friends. I had not thought myself so full of spite, but there it was, and in truth it was unnecessary, all Joseph required was detail but I felt it helped in the telling.

'Enough!' he said, interrupting my vitriol. 'I do not despair of you Freddy, I may yet be able to assist you. You have been most forthcoming and honest even of your feelings, though that part was unnecessary and somewhat embarrassing. Still allow me to stand you a drink if only for your candidness. I am away to town and perhaps on my return will have some favourable news for you, we shall see.'

'Thank you, Joseph, I have faith in you as none before, I have never known such a capable fellow.'

'Capable, capable, oh no Freddy, you're confusing your

tributes surely, to call me capable might imply that I am in some way limited with no imagination. A capable man will do for you and never for himself with no ambition other than to achieve what is required. In complete contrast to this fellow, there I am, inspired, formidable, and I am not confined by humility and other such failings. Do try to refrain from such idiotic sentences, Freddy, we get along just fine with our restrained dialogue. No need, as I have said before, to try to conjure a parallel between us, there is none but the one that inhabits your imagination.'

At this he left, thoughts of vengeance poisoned those more wholesome ones of reparation and new beginnings; it could not be helped, old wounds had been opened. And though I wished the worst on these people who had shunned me, I also knew that I was lashing out, and once again placed my faith in this man called Joseph Black. A man, who in reality, was more devil-like than the picture I had, or perhaps I was just closer now and so could see Lucifer better.

'Bloody offal, don't you think?'

'What's that, Pike?'

'This work, bloody offal! I am meant to help Elijah out today but just can't spare him the time, don't suppose you can help, Freddy, can you?'

'Well he's not my favourite person, but I have little if nothing to do with myself, so yes, Pike, I shall step in for you. What does the work entail?'

'Bit of butchery you might call it, Freddy, hah, I'd pay to see you tackle it, though I think I might get a wallop from you!'

'Butchery, Pike, ah yes, I see the joke now, offal, very clever. Well I cannot say I have tried it, but am not squeamish, and what sort of man would I be if I could not rise to such a challenge? Where might I find Elijah?'

'Oh he's already waiting, in the cart outside, you might want to saddle up old Pie Crust though the smell can be a little off-putting.'

'Very well, I shall heed your advice, where are we off to?'

'To the forest yonder, half a day's ride with the cart in tow, but you will make good speed on the way back. You need not wait for Elijah, and Pie Crust is well fed and watered.'

'I must ask before I go, Pike, why do we travel to butcher meat? Surely we have adequate room here and it would remain fresh?'

'You will see all, Hah! Best not ask questions, Freddy. See if you hold your tongue, you will get more used to the way things happen round here.'

Elijah was sat at his cart looking pleased with himself until he saw me readying to join him.

'What do you want?'

'I am to join you, and be your assistant today Elijah, ask of me what you will and I shall obey.'

I tried to lighten the mood. It was pointless we were predestined to hate each other and I would have to make do with the company of Pie Crust. He set off, muttering filth under his breath and I turned to Pie Crust.

'O well old girl, I hope I am not fated to yet more infamy and that this is as innocent as it sounds. What can go wrong with a bit of butchery, I ask? And Elijah is not and I'd guess has never been up to making mischief with someone, he has the humour of a sentenced man!'

We reached the forest after a dull couple of hours; Elijah threw a flask at me.

'Drink, it will be hot work even on a day like today.'

'No thank you, I am quite refreshed. After all I have not spent the hours in deep conversation, but I thank you anyway.'

'Suit yourself.'

With this he alighted from the cart, though I say this with sarcasm as I do not believe the man could easily alight from anything. He was crippled, and puffed and wheezed constantly. As he pulled back the covers from the cart a swarm of flies rose so quickly that I breathed some in and choked.

'For Heaven's sake what type of meat do we bring here?'

Then as the flies settled I saw that indeed it was the Toothills that we brought here to butcher, or, in fact, to hide. Taken aback as I was, I had promised myself to not reveal any fragility in these reoccurring nightmares and could clearly see that Elijah was waiting for a reaction, so resolutely I stated,

'Come on then, man, let us have this work quickly done! I do not relish it.'

'Aye, you not faint then? Only I expected something else from you.'

'Faint, Good God, no, though I see you blush, perhaps it is too ripe for you?'

'No, would not call it too ripe, just about right.'

'Very well then, Elijah, let us find some secrecy and lay these people down. I would ask only that you humour me in this, allow them to lay together. I am not sentimental just superstitious.'

'Oh no, cannot promise you that, man! We have to chop them up like, don't want to draw attention to who they are if they found. Best scattered about the place, wolves won't take a whole human see, it is too big for them but they will take a leg or a head and this way all the creatures get a look in.'

He was baiting me and I was proud to note that I did not rise. I slung Angelica across my shoulder almost fainting with the smell and my legs giving as her whole body seemed to cave in as I did so, and walked on ahead further into the wood.

'Oh don't you worry about me then, I will just bring the axes, shall I!?'

Elijah shouted in vain as I could not turn back now, if I stopped I would run from this place and I would not allow myself to be entertainment again.

At a small clearing he threw down the body of Bertram; I did likewise with Angelica.

'This is it. Right there is no method or wrong or right way, just chop them up and spread around. Quite a handsome woman, wasn't she?' he remarked as I separated head from body with a sickening swipe.

"What? I will say this, Elijah, you are more repellent than the smell of rotting flesh and a mouthful of the flies that feed on it."

'Just remarking is all, seems a shame though, doesn't it?'

'What seems a shame man?'

'I just say that where there is a shortage of good meat, seems a shame. I myself have eaten it and will be taking some home to the wife to make me something nice with.'

Sickened at what I heard I could not help but be compelled to listen further.

'Suet crust, and the gravy is the best you have tasted. She got some proper recipes for it too, you know, proper old ones, got to go back a hundred years or more. Go on, take some, we have not been the best of friends, but I'm not greedy, and Mary will cook you a treat with it, so long as she don't know what it is.'

'I'm sorry, Elijah, but are we clear that you regularly eat human flesh? This is not figgy pudding we talk of, man! Do you lie to shock me or provoke a reaction?'

'Well what of it, ay? I don't know why I bothered with you, I had you right the first time I saw you! Big breeches no bollocks, always the way with your type.'

'I am sorry but I do not feel it is "your" sensibilities that are offended, in fact I do not believe you have any, no 'tis mine! Please let us make haste and have this done I do not wish to speak with you anymore.'

'Can't say I will grieve your company, you are a useless sort of a man! Never saw the reason in keeping you alive.'

'Thank you for that, for if you did I would worry about myself. Now please!'

The job could not have been more gruesome, and when at

last we were finished I mounted my ride and flew back to the inn as fast as I could. The stench hounded me and in my room I found some perfumed oils and scrubbed with what I had. It was not sufficient, so I ventured outside, and to the trough where I naturally provided much entertainment for those who had obviously been awaiting my return.

'I wonder that you have time to spare to revel in my obvious state, Pike? You did say that you were busy! Perhaps you did not have the stomach for such an exercise, ay? I think more likely a ploy though I am right, am I not?'

'A bit of fun, Freddy, 'tis all, do you deny me it? After all was not I who did for the woman.'

'And neither was it I, Pike.'

'Aye, but you came closest, maybe you should take this up with Joseph, was his swift blade that stole what life she had left in her.'

'Accepted, though perhaps a little warning of what was to come? No? It was mischief you were about, wasn't it? Very well, revenge, Pike, shall be mine to apply when chance arises!'

As ever, with Pike, this was all in good humour and though I would seek revenge, it would not be sinister in nature. How could it be with such an artless individual, and also a distinct lack of fellow conspirators!?

'Well now we have had our fun I would ask you something Pike, something that worries us all this day, did you take the shilling?'

'That I did.'

Pike twirled the coin in his hand then balanced it on his forehead and danced the dance of the condemned.

'You are a fool, Pike.'

'No Badger, I do not answer to that name any more, I am proud to say that you are now looking at Seaman Sharp. Ready to board the His Majesty's Ship, The Compass, and not three days from now either!'

'You are dead right when you say there is no Pike anymore.

You are lost boy! Did you sign for more than the seven?' Joshua scolded him, though it was out of concern and obvious to all except Pike.

'Pray, tell me why I should sign for a pittance when there is an endless bounty to be had? No Josh, I'm all theirs, and right proud I am to say it.'

'Been witnessed?'

Badger's vain attempt to retract his friend from a fate too many young men had become familiar with was all too late.

'Witnessed, signed, given me the shilling! As I say, I'm all in!'

Badger looked at the ground and kicked something which unfortunately resembled a finger; he picked it up and threw it at his dog.

'I suppose it falls to me to wish you your fortune, Pike, I feel I ought if only to divert attention from the finger that the dog gnaws on!'

My observation lightened the mood, and as we laughed Pike spoke of all that he had been promised and the countries he would see and the money he could stow for him and his Mary. Of course, what he omitted was the one enticement that turned the heads of most young ones like Pike, the free and easy women, this was all too often that which clinched the deal.

'And Mary, Pike? How has she taken the news?'

'She is all tears, Freddy, I cannot seem to comfort her with talk of gifts and such that I will bring her. She gave me this.

He produced a lock of Mary's bright red curly hair.

'Won't let you take that on board.' Badger said doing little to hide his intent at mischief.

'How do you mean, Badger?'

He was not the sharpest, but for sure the nicest of boys.

'Lice … They got to be careful of lice at sea, haven't they Josh? Nowhere for them to go but your head, and they can't get rid of them! Can eat away at a man's head so much, I have heard, he can near on bleed to death!'

'You are right there, Badger, and the bite marks so small that no ship's surgeon has needle or thread fine enough to see to the lesions. In fact, I heard, that they use whales' teeth for needles and cat gut for thread for the enlisted!'

'Now you two be quiet! Tell them, Freddy, my Mary's hair is so thick and curly lice could never get in!'

'Nice and cosy I'd say! Badger carried on.

'Hush now you!'

'We only having a bit of fun with you, boy'

Joshua patted him on the back.

'Yes, Pike, you shall be sorely missed, I have grown quite fond of you myself,' I added, and I meant it, for if it wasn't for his naivety at times and his infectious take on things I would have sworn that the free spirit, nay soul, did not exist in this godforsaken place. Though he readied himself for any chore, he did not belong amongst these people and I sometimes aspired to think just as Pike did when I despaired. You might even say that even the most hellish situation has to have something which offsets the evil, otherwise how else do you realize it.

'Be sure and watch for my Mary, Freddy, whilst I'm away. Your manners are more suited than any here I think.'

'Surely a request better suited for Mary to watch over me, Pike? She manages very well.'

'You say that Freddy but you can't believe it in your heart. I would not want her to be captured by this place, she's not gone too far yet and never killed a soul, just filched some off some.'

'I shall endeavour, Pike, though perhaps you might ask Joshua. A change in my fortune is imminent I believe, and I shall soon be returning to Bath. Of course, with the assistance of Joseph.'

'Well I wish you luck with that, Freddy, and hope it's all as your mind sees it.'

'What you up to, boy!?' Joseph halloed him and Pike laughed and walked inside.

'Evening Joe!'

Badger and Joshua followed suit, and I envied their informal casual address a little, and it was always so. I could never feel so confident around Joseph, and always began almost apologetically and as though grateful that he deigned look upon me.

'Freddy, do you care to dine with me tonight? I smell a pie that makes my stomach race me to the table!'

'I thank you, Joseph, and that I shall; it does smell rather good. I take it from this invite that you have some good news for me or do I presume too much?'

He turned without responding and entered the inn. A huge blaze had been lit and after taking a drink he took a seat by the fire and kicked a chair towards me.

'I am tired, so tired in fact that I do believe anything I have to say can be just as well relayed on the morrow. I have never enjoyed talking and eating at the same time, they each detract from the pleasure of the other.'

'Of course, Joseph, and I concur that the two coupled with exhaustion are most unattractive. I completely understand, though the merest morsel? A crumb of what has happened today would improve my appetite endlessly.'

'Yes, but I do not consider your appetite do I, man? I consider mine! No, in retrospect we shall talk in the morning.'

Mary bought two plates of pie, Joseph took his greedily and said of the other,

'Over there girl, I dine on my own tonight.'

Needing no other instruction I removed myself and took place by Pike and Badger.

'How's your pie, Freddy? I made it special for you, that meat been stewing all day.'

'It is incredibly delicious, Mary, you are a genius! I would not know it was rabbit again, the seasoning is most pleasant.'

'Rabbit, no that never rabbit. Elijah, what's that meat you gave me this morning?'

'Elijah! Elijah gave you this, girl? Do not play innocent, you know what that man is about! I cannot believe this of you of all, Mary! That you would stoop to feed me human flesh! God help me, how am I to recover from this of all, but I am innocent of intent at least I might say that!'

Mary giggled, giving the game away.

'God save me!'

Somebody shouted,

'I have eaten Bertie's buttocks! I should have known the meat too generous, though I did think the hairs a little long and in my defence an aged rabbit will grow whiskers in the strangest of places but never a tattoo!'

Shocked as I was, it was quickly usurped by relief and then laughter and I joined in, much to their amusement by asking for seconds and announcing that I would turn the other cheek! Elijah sat red-faced in the corner, though if it was not for his grunts of disapproval he would have looked nothing unusual. A man such as he was would always be avoided, and if I had not seen for myself that which had happened this day I would have believed it by proxy however fantastical it sounded. He was diseased, probably as a result of his eating human flesh, and if this shortened his years then amen to that. What hell would his be? I could not imagine further than my own, though his actions seemed to make mine more acceptable.

After this, the night was full of good humour. Joseph regained his appetite for speaking when his appetite for food was addressed, though he did little to appease my curiosity. Alas the morning seemed an age away, even though I retired late, and sleep did not find me till gone was the moon and a bloody horizon heralded a bad day's weather for all, except the inn keepers who would make their money on the back of it. It must have been noon when I awoke, and I rushed down the dark creaky musty stairs with far too much enthusiasm and found myself on my arse at the bottom.

'Lord, what was that?'

Mary rushed to my assistance.

'Are you hurt, Master Freddy?'

'Yes thank you, Mary, but a dent to my vanity, not my head.'

'Ah well, I shall not laugh at you, 'tis many a time that I have come down as you, type of stairs that see you into your grave so they are.'

'Yes Mary, though I am a little distracted, have you seen Joseph?'

'Here, man.'

His voice from the fire held all the promise of a complete drubbing and for my pride I grieved, though a few words of encouragement from him would make me forget.

'I shall join you then, Joseph?'

'Of course we have business, do we not?'

Unsure whether he was in good humour or bad, I took a drink then made that two. Joseph's form of assassination was too pure to take without some dilution.

'I have met yesterday with a fellow, who though resides in Cleveton is more often in Bath. He is more than familiar with you, if not before, certainly since your debacle. We talked for many hours, and I shall be honest did not hide our disdain for the process this shall take! It will require much prostrating on your part, and in truth neither one of us wishes to confess to knowing you. Do I sound too harsh?'

'I am a little embarrassed, Joseph, but no never too harsh. I am still being punished for my actions, it must be taken, and I am humbled by any effort on your part.'

'Well then, that said perhaps you are right for this. You shall journey with myself to town today and meet with the fellow I have mentioned to see what is to be done. I cannot do with running here and there with titbits, I would tire quickly of it, in fact I would not do it at all, and you would find yourself out of favour.'

'Of course Joseph, for it is for me to labour at this, a little of your wisdom is all I ask and have but fine words to repay this with but once re-established will produce a more pleasing recompense.'

'Forget the fine words, Freddy, you show no aptitude for them, but as for other rewards for certain, man, they shall be mine. Oh, and dress appropriately for perhaps a sortie into Bath. I do not expect us to return for a few days so a light change may be bought. For appearances sake your attire should be noted but not the topic of conversation.'

A more happy man there never was, I thought, I could not dress quickly enough. I dared but hope that this may be the first of many such ventures, and that soon I would be established and living a life more common to me than the one I had of late.

Chapter 17

As we mounted our rides for the journey to Cleveton, my initial enthusiasm turned to trepidation. I feared the elegance by which this had been contrived, was this justified caution? Surely justified. I had told so much in exchange for what appeared, to me, a simple task. Could this not all have been achieved with less detail? Surely questions more suited to a day ago, when I readily, and spitefully told all, to a man who did nothing to hide his malevolence. Nay, he wielded it with breathtaking honesty. So not for me to regret now. I either took from this what I could and rally, or step away, damage done. Might I then just as well take a pistol to my head? For there would be no going back, this was certain. So I committed myself, though it offered little respite from this malignant despair that was becoming me so often.

We rode through the rain, determined on Joseph's part, I thought, and he said little for the whole journey, nothing to reassure me. I was grateful to arrive in town, giving relief from my thoughts. Such places did not stop for bad weather, and though I missed the ladies there were many other worthy distractions. We halted at The King's Head, where Joseph remarked, 'Privacy is paramount, Freddy, and you will find no better than a whorehouse, such as it is. Yes, some do come purely for the refreshment, but for myself I enjoy a gentleman's club when in town, though still have struck many a deal within these walls.'

I laughed a little at the comment.

'I see you have your humour with you, Frederick, there is the shame, for you will find little that amuses you today, unless your own shame tickles you? Surely even this would challenge the most gifted of comics.'

'Forgive me, Joseph, I had not meant offence, just to lighten the mood, I am a little apprehensive.'

'I do not easily offend, Freddy, and saw little, if any of this, in your comment as I found no humour either. Shall we?'

He gestured to the door. Eileen was there, though busy, as were others, and fortunately they did not approach. Joseph led us to a corner, where sat Will Haverley posed with pipe in one hand and handkerchief in the other, beckoning us. A little contrived in appearance at first glance, though I would come to know this man much better and learn that simple falseness was what had him take many turns at The Assembly Rooms and grace many a fine dining table. These fellows did exist, and sometimes on pennies, though you would never guess to behold one. It was their curious nature, famously, that had people vying for their company and masterminding 'a look' from them, whatever it may take or, in most cases, how much it would take.

'You must be Frederick! Well very nice to meet you, man, will you both take some wine? Joseph, some wine?'

His hand shook as he poured him some.

'This is Will Haverley, Freddy. An acquaintance of mine, as you can see he is a tad too fond of the opium! Medicinal though, is it not, Will? For your nerves? You might think, Freddy, that a man with such front would not suffer such a condition, though I think differently. When one contrives to deceive in such quantity something must give. Am I right, Will?'

'I must disagree, Joseph, begging your pardon. I am fond of the stuff, but can equally do without it. Deception for me is sport, and I know you would not have me tire of the races, Joseph.'

They laughed together, and I nodded politely as if I knew of the stuff; in all honesty I had never tried it though it was readily available, and now was glad that I hadn't. The man was handsome and without doubt would thrill the ladies, but he had no peace from the shakes until he took some in the form of an elixir, Doctor Chadwick's poppy elixir to be exact. What I gleaned, as a spectator of this, was that he became confused and agitated initially and then euphoria took hold and he calmed. Eileen appeared, and draped herself about him, he became entangled and fought a little then shoved her back from him where she landed in a heap on the floor.

'Fuck off, you ugly old hag! Good God, man, what an awful looking thing!'

Joseph seemed amused by his exaggerated state, and Will indulged him more by shouting,

'No more! None of you please! I have business!'

A few shrieks and insults from these creatures followed before they moved to be comforted by men of no money who perhaps tried their luck!

'Shall we get on? I am quite sure we shan't be bothered again,' Joseph said phlegmatically.

'Of course,' replied Will. 'They are like weevils, are they not!?'

'Yes, though with none of the charm! Still do not feel harried, Will. It is just I already begin to tire of the dramatics.'

'Forgive me, Joseph, I forget the purpose. Frederick, our plan is to travel to Bath this day where I shall appraise you of the situation and test the water so to speak.'

'With something simple, Freddy, something not beyond you,' Joseph added.

'Might I suggest tea at Fort Simmons, Joseph?'

'Yes, but do "you" foot the bill, William? Your resources surely will stretch this far and beyond, I am convinced of it. I have great faith that my purse shall remain unmolested, in as much as we might acquire a free one?'

'Of course, Joseph, a mere trifle to please you. What say you, Freddy, are you game? Of course you are, I require no response. I am held up at a rather fine hotel, name of Banbridges, a word from me and the two of you shall have room and board for as long as you wish.'

'I cannot help but ask William, how do you manage so well? I fear you must be in need of fortune, otherwise what do you do here? I cannot accept that you do me this favour out of some philanthropic ideal! But you appear to look so well on the generosity of others, I wonder that more do not follow your lead.'

'This you shall learn of, Freddy, not being so hard to look at yourself, it is our hope, if Joseph will allow me to speak for him?' He nodded. 'It is our hope that you too shall be enjoying such liberties very soon.'

'But how am I to manage this? I say I am most excited, but know not why!'

'Freddy, do not bother yourself with such enquiries or indeed myself or Will. We have but little time, and to explain all to you might take weeks. I think, as you must own, that you do not readily absorb information that is not so concise, and your conceit may lead you to believe that this is a simple affair. No, best I think to experience first-hand, let us see if you have the stomach before we test your aptitude. I hesitate for although you are presentable, I might add that it would not do for you to be challenging there, there is a naivety about you which remains a concern of mine. Ay man, what say you? I cannot be more precise without appearing crude, do you grasp the concept, Freddy?'

'Thank you Joseph, and I am most eager, it all feels somewhat nostalgic. If my stories have led you to believe me a capable apprentice to William then let me not correct you, I am no romantic.'

'Well then, one thing I can guarantee, the sport shall be fine, ay William! And I am all in for it! Let us not delay then, if we leave now we should arrive in Bath this evening.'

I needed no prompting to ready myself and before I could draw breath we were settled on the ride to Bath.

Chapter 18

'The impregnable I think you will find, Freddy.'

Joseph halted as my heart leaped and we crested the hill that led down to Bath, my home of always. I had never left, not in my heart.

'Remember, you are not to participate, just to observe.'

'I thank you, Joseph, sound advice, and I have much to observe. I am sure the attractions, so sorely missed, shall occupy my thoughts so completely I shall barely remember to breathe.'

'Fanciful words, still I have come to expect this of you, take heed though, Frederick, you are not quite a tourist, and must not forget this is business. I do not bring you here to reinforce our friendship.'

Will reared his horse and galloped down the hill hailing the city in all its splendour.

'An enthusiast, yes, Frederick. You may find it difficult in his wake. Though I shall say this, 'tis I who makes him shine, a little bit of pressure ... as I use now on this lazy old nag!'

He kicked on his horse and cantered away.

'What keeps you?' he shouted. 'Is it too fabulous, or too fearful?'

I quickly caught him up where he remarked,

'Not the fastest ponies ,ay man? Hardly like the wind! More a couple of old farts!'

The man was too funny at times and I almost lost my seat. This was not only a perilous descent, the company was equally challenging. He manipulated my every thought and emotion with such stealth that I no longer knew how to originate any idea. I felt less than natural.

Will waited for us at the bottom, his exhilaration apparent as was his lust for such things. I felt quite inadequate, as I was only pleased to arrive in one piece. Joseph's words had yet again soured that which I looked to enjoy and I felt a little despair where there should have been joy. Neither of them, however, was to allow such reflections and though obviously fake they engaged me and listened to tales I had to tell of the place as we ventured further in.

'There is no night in Bath, Freddy, would you agree?' Will asked. 'The lanterns or recreations do not allow it. I fear you may struggle to sleep coming from the country where all that twinkles is the stars, how dull for you.'

I was careful in response, I knew Joseph would jump on me if I dismissed his hospitality as dull, so with care and as much indifference as I could manage I remarked,

'No, not dull Will, as you say the stars do twinkle and 'tis a different existence though not one I am sorry to have known. I have found the country manners most refreshing and though, with luck, I return to Bath, I do not say it shall be my last venture to greener fields and clearer skies.'

I was pleased with it, but the pleasure did not last very long.

'Honestly speaking, Freddy? You have enjoyed it? Then why do we bother with this trip! Let us about face and return to "greener fields and refreshing manners" as you so well put, man.'

Joseph's parry had me off guard and Will found it all very amusing. Funny that I should find comfort where people mocked me, but his laughter bought me back to reason and

I realized there was no intent in Joseph's words, just simple sarcasm.

Soon we came upon the very smart hotel Will had mentioned, Banbridges, and entered to a chorus of hallos from the patrons all seemingly very familiar with Will and all eager to see to his thirst and luckily ours. I was running very short on funds and Joseph had made clear that he would not supply.

'Allow me to introduce a couple of very dear friends of mine, Pip Chorliwhip and Piggy Watkins,' Will said ushering us to seats where the two sat. No real challenge in guessing who was who, as Piggy Watkins owned the name; porcine features and if that was not enough he had surely eaten his way to such infamy. So I started there,

'Piggy, how do you do, man.'

'Why hello, Sir, but have we met? I am struck by the familiarity of your address! No, I am sure we have never met, pray how do you know me?'

'Yes for surely I could be Piggy and Piggy, well Pip, myself, a lucky guess?'

'This must be the truth of it gentleman, but the real question is can he apply this luck to cards? Shall we gentlemen, to see in the new day?'

Joseph thankfully seemed to have put an end to my embarrassment, and I was quick to respond saying I often found myself in luck and to which they responded by laughing and said I was far too serious and that they merely jested. More drinks were sent to the table and Joseph eyed my reaction.

'Impressive, is he not? To live the bourgeois existence though with no real substance. I note that you stare a lot?'

'If I do, Joseph, it is only out of amazement and admiration.'

'Do you confess to admiration when really it is envy, Freddy? I do not scold, man, I judge your enthusiasm for just such an existence.'

I had no chance to affirm this enthusiasm, and affirm it I would have before Joseph began again.

'Will, would you like to deal?'

Will laughed.

'A question rarely asked of me, Joseph, but yes. Though first let me assure you that I mind 'tis you who asks, and may be a test of my honesty, nay fealty, for I cannot own the other.'

'Fealty, no I do not test it! I take that which is owed be it financial or otherwise. If you feel that I extract from you then I have become too clumsy, I would not have you so aware. Save your blushes, Will!'

As he reddened,

'This is no courtship and you no debutant. Damn cards do not favour me!'

He threw them in and gestured for Piggy to pour him wine, who obliged, and though you could not get a more distinct appearance as his, he possessed the same look as Will and Pip. It was vacant, as though their very souls had been chased from them; did I not look this way too, I wondered? I had not glanced at my reflection since I broke the glass in my room, and now I feared catching it.

'You must excuse me, gentlemen,' I said glancing at the contents of my purse.

'I find myself a little light.'

'Very well, Frederick,' Joseph said impatiently. 'Though let it be temporary. I rarely practise coercion, I have no need, but let this be one of the few times. I merely point out that the remedy is at hand, so to speak, for your current financial embarrassment.'

I was too proud perhaps to say I did not understand so nodded and decided on a turn about the place. My eyes began to fix on many an unguarded purse and the place simply bursting with every type of libertine. Joseph's words no longer confused me. Seeing the bounty at hand was too tempting and I decided on a rather spectacular looking fellow, purse attached with ribbons. My pen knife quickly disposed of the contrivance and I found myself two guineas richer; I had done this before, though for dares, and it never felt so dangerous. I rejoined the game with approving glances and the acceptance, and in the company of blaggards, was comfort itself.

The raucous atmosphere of the inn and conversations therein felt as though it had become a little personal to myself, every now and then I would catch a look or a mention.

'There is a man who sits at another's feet!'

The rowdiest of them all enlivened by the spirit seemed intent on getting a rise out of me.

'Peasant!' I retorted, but following painfully in Joseph's wake was becoming an obvious trait and the stinging comment made my position of creature even more apparent.

'Tell me, Frederick, do you sit at my feet as this fellow seems to suggest? Or do you just enjoy the unsavoury atmosphere at my shirt tails? Surely it is the former!'

Joseph needed no invitation to enjoy himself at my expense, standing up, and taking a bow from an adoring audience. The humiliation was too much.

'Ha! But I do not, Sir! I simply creep upon you unawares.'

The laughter at this comment became deafening, Joseph too amused to punish me.

'I dare any of you to comment as this cur has done!'

I grabbed his drink from his hand and pushed him to the ground.

'Come, Frederick.'

Joseph pulled me back still shaking with laughter.

'Is a wise man who does not defend himself in such cases and you are not, but you Sir?'

He addressed the fool who sought to make reparation for what he called, 'Disturbing a fine game of cards.'

'As you say, was a fine game of cards and now in retrospect

believe some of my amusement may have been shock at a presumption to increase my pleasure with your attempt at humour.'

The man looked confused and laughed nervously, which I began to thoroughly enjoy.

'Excuse me, Master, but I meant nowt.'

He turned muttering something under his breath and went to walk away.

'Tell me, did you ever see a man choke on his words?' Joseph called after him.

He had sat down looking pale and shaken, a look of terror on his face as he fell to his knees as though in agony, each vein protruding as though full of a poison. A deathly quiet descended on the inn as the man struggled for breath.

'I believe you have lost your appetite for our game, Sir?'

Joseph called to the wretch, his every muscle was contorted and was fitting violently as others stood by and watched too terrified to assist.

'I say you will think twice next time!'

That there would be a next time for him seemed to bring him round a little, sitting up coughing, and a nervous smile slithered across my face,

'I hope this hasn't ruined your appetite for cards, Sir?'

'Freddy? My appetite? Was you who drew attention to him. Perhaps you might think to hide that lack of substance in future? Perhaps then we might enjoy ourselves unmolested.'

Later in my room, luxurious, welcoming, and most of all free, I felt fortunate. Something that had escaped me for many weeks now and though was only the soft warm bed that reflected this feeling I devoured it and slept so readily that no thought found me until breakfast. The handsome arrangements set out for our morning's repast were very tempting even after so much liquor the night before. I found only Will and as I went to ask of Joseph, he stated,

'You must visit my barber, Giuseppe Armonde, Frederick. I can read your thoughts, I too feel the name a fabrication but I am no judge on accents from the continent and he is a wizard at his trade, so I do not question his legitimacy. I must say you look less dashing than you ought for this business, more like the rear end of an old ewe! Do I speak out of turn?'

'I am sorry to say you do not, Will. I have neglected my toilet of late and if you will guide me I shall happily visit with this Giuseppe, forthwith.'

'Then let us repair, man.'

Will's enthusiasm for just about everything was comical, though less so for Joseph's company. I enquired if we should wait for him.

'Oh he is gone, not half an hour ago, we shall meet him at Fortsimmons. Shall we?'

We left and Will chatted endlessly of Bath and the people I should meet, and that he did wonder that I had not met some of them before? But as we both knew, popularity and fame in Bath was as fickle as infamy could be. Will enjoyed pointing out that acquaintances of old along with their tittle-tattle would soon appear positively antiquarian. This was most welcome news and groomed and feeling more like myself we arrived at Fortsimmons. I knew of the place but had never attended. Taking tea was more an introduction into society here, and historically I had needed no such thing, but as Will pointed out there was great need now. He asked me to wait two doors back that he would get settled and then after fifteen minutes or so I was to enter and announce myself as his guest. Eagerly I took instruction and waited for what seemed an age.

As I entered I had no time to look about me as Will shouted,

'Freddy! How the hell are you? I have not seen you since your heroics some weeks back, am I not right?'

'How do you mean, Will?' I said trying to look less conspicuous.

'Come, come, man, there is no need for modesty. I speak of the lady you saved from such a nasty fall? As she stepped from her carriage, man? A lazy minded footman no less was at fault, but what need is there of such people when you are to hand, ay man? Such present mindedness is rare and does not come cheap, but what am I saying, you offer this service free of charge.'

By the time he had finished eulogizing I was at his table and quickly sat down. A lady fanned herself and giggled, I suspected from the unfortunate footman analogy. He leaned forward and confided,

'Well done! You played that down perfectly.'

'I assure you it was honest, I have not a clue what you refer to.'

'And the Lady Sophia, so taken with you, this is champion, Freddy, champion!'

He did not think to explain, and I was not so innocent and quickly realized what he was about. Perhaps if he had warned me I may not have pulled it off so well, and, though no lady spoke directly to me, approving looks were directed my way and as Will pointed out,

'If you have the ladies, then the battle is all but won!'

We wondered what took the ladies' admiration so quickly from us until we noticed Joseph, surely together if we took off our clothes and stood on our heads we could not command such attention. Lady Sophia Binchy's admiration was quite outrageous and Will quickly pointed out that she was famed for her flirtations and simply the most popular girl in town.

'If she attached herself to you,' he remarked. 'You were made.'

And fortunately she seemed very interested.

Though we had been enjoying the attentions of some very fine looking ladies, most of all Sophia, still we could have guessed Joseph's arrival had we been blind; giggles and gasps of admiration from the young and desirable, and from the more mature, disapproval. He bowed before Sophia. A very attractive proposition, with wavy brown hair, and dark brown eyes that held moons captive, her complexion flawless as she blushed at Joseph's gallantry and fanned herself dramatically.

'Gentlemen, I see you have started without me. Did you not think to acquire some manners whilst you acquired new hair?'

I, used to such verbal assaults uncommonly found myself indignant, did I dare this? Was I mad? I could not hide it and Joseph seemed thoroughly amused by it.

'Yes, well, Freddy, a pretty pair of eyes upon you, at times of ridicule will make the even most complacent of men feel other than their disinterest! Your face is quite the picture. Really Freddy, you should grow less serious man, can you not tell I jest?'

Joseph was being unusually lenient, and it was obvious that he was privy to Will's plan. Such as it was, he had done me no disservice as Sophia seemed well pleased with the whole lot of us and made no attempt to hide it.

We sat for a while supping our tea, and enthusing over our surroundings but were far more interested in capturing the attention of Sophia and her companions. Admirably done, to even as much as be passed a card to call upon the lady herself.

'This is excellent!' Will remarked, and as we went to leave he hesitated at her table, already being acquainted.

All attention was on Joseph and myself, or in truth Joseph. He kissed her hand and said nothing.

Oh do not mistake that gaze for a flirtation Sophia, I thought, 'tis an inventory of all that you are and possess.

Then it was my turn, and it was barely noted, though Will reassured me on leaving,

'Do not despair, man, though it is obvious that the lady's preference leans towards Joseph, it does not follow that she shall be lax in assisting you.'

'No, I would imagine the opposite,' Joseph added.

'After all, a lady will not put herself out for a favourite, it would bring shame upon her, as though she was desperate to win him; however, she may bestow charity upon a friend of one she regards, it is acceptable, and would win her the favour she desires indirectly. I say Sophia shall adhere to the latter if she is as wise as she is pretty. I must say I rather look forward to her attempts.'

Wiser words had never been said, and a more succinct appraisal you would not find in even the most successful of romantic novels.

On our return to Banbridges I turned to Joseph.

'Am I to understand then, that we do not attempt a reconciliation? I was counting on it.'

'Yes, for there is little of nothing to be retrieved. I have made several covert enquiries, and think this alteration sensible. Initial thoughts of reparation will not hold your weight, Freddy, there is still much bad feeling towards you. The worst perpetrator of this, being your father, does this shock you?'

'No, not at all, Joseph, if there can be less between yourself and your father than nothing, then that may answer your question.'

'Very good, though this was not my only inducement. The work would have been doubly as hard and not half as much fun. I do like a game of sport, Freddy, if I had the choice of a bag of gold or a life to toy with it would be the latter, but then you must be aware of this?'

'I would not feel comfortable in making such assumptions of you, Joseph, though if you press me I shall say that you seem to feed off the very thing, it is just unusual to me.'

'Amen to that!' Will said. 'And I shall add to it if it pleases. You may wish to call it toying, Joseph, I shall not correct you, but I would not be the man I am today if it was not for it.'

Brave words I thought as he finished off the bottle of Doctor Chadwick's elixir, but not an encouraging sight; in the shadow of such malevolence the man's very existence was as diminished as mine though it did not hurt to see it as Joseph noted,

'A little company for you, Freddy.'

If on some cold, dark night I came upon the Devil himself, I thought it would not strike me if it was Joseph; I wondered did I think this or did I know he knew my every thought, and merely asked him to clarify?

I did not remember reading for sleep that night in my chambers, it was almost hypnotic, and I was awoken by the most enveloping fear. So cold that my breath traced finger like shapes in the darkened room not lit by moonlight or hope. Pinned to my bed, only able to crane my neck, where a dark figure faceless with ebony wings seemed to wrench my heart from my chest, closer it came till it not inches from my face; death invaded every inch of my being as the wisps of my breath became its. Twisting and writhing, shaking me violently, the pain excruciating – which it delighted in, was exalted by – until there was no life left in me to give, no fight, and was gone. I fell unconscious, weak with lifeless limbs, and sickened by the assault, no other dream did I dream that night, no other quandary did I face nor was I ever torn again by the pricking of a conscious or a questioning mind.

Chapter 19

Next morning, at ten, we were to call upon the Lady Sophia. I readied myself as I would for a rendezvous with any desirable creature and joined Will and Joseph for breakfast. There was a splendid display of eggs and ham and toast. Joseph had eaten already, and Will refused it all saying he had no appetite for such things at what he called an unearthly time. Nine O Clock! I thought this was hardly early, but he appeared ragged and I guessed that he had spent the night in one of many opium dens that littered the streets of Bath.

'Shall we gentlemen?' Joseph said as I ate my last mouthful.

'I am sure Sophia would be most put out if we were less than punctual. Also you might think to wipe your chin, man!'

I quickly attended to it, and we left for 10, The Crescent. The house was her parents, according to Will, and she resided there with her brother who was quite the man about town and definitely worth our attention.

'A damned fine house, do you not think!?' Will remarked. 'Tis the best on The Crescent. I have heard quite laden with riches from the continent. It is said that her brother Phillip, has fifteen thousand a year and shall not only inherit this, there is the country estate also.'

'A man to fall in with, Freddy,' Joseph advised. 'Please continue Will, this is all sounding very promising.'

Will continued.

'He is an amiable fellow. I have had much sport with him, and on every occasion have found him to be most generous.'

'A virtuous man then, Will?' Joseph joked. 'But let us see for ourselves. I am sure Sophia has propriety enough to employ a chaperone, even if she wishes for none! I dare say she shall sit there the whole time, quite vexed. An absolute minx, do you not think?'

He rang the doorbell, and we were ushered in to the lavishly decorated drawing room, with well-appointed art, indulgent upholstery and a judicious amount of ormolu, everything pointing to the family's very deep coffers.

Sophia appeared a picture of loveliness.

'Gentlemen, you must forgive me if I look less than perfect, I almost forgot. My brother shall join us if this pleases you?'

'Of course, but I would say that it was a rare occasion that you appeared less than perfect, and this is not one such time,' Joseph said, assuming correctly that she only really addressed him.

A little flustered at his boldness she called,

'Phillip! The guests, they are here!'

'Hello there!'

Phillip appeared, tall and fair, with an open expression reserved for the very rich who can afford to not think too deeply.

'Let me guess who is who? Now I shall not cheat for I already know this scallywag Will, but I would suppose that you are Freddy and you, Sir, quite obviously Joseph. My sister's descriptive powers are mostly exact, and I have not imagined you different, Sir.'

Joseph acknowledged with a nod and a little smile to Sophia, whose pretence at polite indifference was as transparent as she was beautiful.

'Sit gentlemen sit, and perhaps, Sophia, you could ring for refreshment.'

Phillip gave his sister a little smile; it was obvious that he thought well of her and she of him as she tentatively rang for tea, but as careful as she was it was plain she was nervous.

I found myself conspiring a little as I looked on at this most desirable creature; yes, her preferences were quite obviously towards Joseph but never was there anything more impossible. I knew enough of the man to know that he would never settle for just one, how could he with such a glut of souls so ready for harvest, such as these times of liberal thinking offered up?

'Tell me about yourselves, gentlemen?' Phillip continued. 'Though I doubt there is much more to relate than Sophia has foraged for, she has quite discovered the whole lot of you!'

She blushed and said keeping eyes upon Joseph,

'Yes, I must confess to a little detective work. You must forgive my inquisitive nature gentlemen, I have many resources at my fingertips.'

'Of this I am sure, though perhaps you might take a little advice? Such tales do not always have pretty endings. Fairy tales are far more sinister than one might first imagine, in deeper understanding they often produce nightmares, but please forgive me, Lady Sophia, I am too much the philosopher.'

Joseph and Sophia's private conversation was perhaps, to the unknowing, a little strange when all I felt was that I might have taken her girlish detective work a little less seriously.

'Resources, why Sophia how can you apply such elegant terms too such silly old maids, and full of equally silly tales!?' Phillip teased his sister.

'They are invaluable to me Phillip, you know this.'

She blushed.

'Perhaps I have too much time to idle away?'

'Allow me to make your recreation less tiresome, Lady Sophia.'

Joseph took her hand in what some would consider a rather bold act, though his assaults were so delicate none thought ill of them.

'I must away today, but will return soon I hope, and would very much like to call on you?'

She blushed as response, and Phillip said,

'I think that is a famous idea! It is a shame you travel back today, I would very much have liked to enjoy all your company further, and though I know Will's company is more readily accessible to me, I find this mix most pleasing.'

'Well I need not take everybody with me. I would be mortified if I thought I suspended your pleasure, so I suggest that you keep Freddy a little longer?'

'What a splendid idea, Joseph, what say you, man?'

Phillip looked to me, whilst I feigned contemplation, but for a few seconds. Both Joseph and Will knew my answer and they shared a look.

'I would love to! It has been a while since I enjoyed such pleasant company and felt so comfortable.'

'Really, I know not whether to be confused or offended? Have I not made you welcome then, Frederick?'

Joseph paused allowing my discomfort to surface then laughed.

'It is far too easy to jest with you Frederick! It is a term that people freely use, man, I could not resist!'

'Pish, Mr Black, you do very well making a mockery of your own hospitality! You were too ready to believe he meant you!'

'Touché, Lady Sophia! I vow to give that tongue of yours more respect when next we meet.'

If Joseph had spoken to either I, or Will, in such a manner we may have run for fear of deathly reprisal; unfortunately for Sophia she was yet to conceive the abject evil that sat before her, and know that his words were as black as his name and what inspired the man was born of evil.

'Yes, well!'

Phillip sensing more went on between these two than he initially thought, continued.

'Sophia has informed, forgive me if I appear too candid, that you are estranged from your parents, Frederick? I feel she should not go to such lengths at times! You know Sophia, you may well end your days at needle point with Emmeline Sopersworth if you do not quit this prying! But Frederick, this is too awful, I tell you, man, that many tales follow you though I am inclined to believe none! Correct me please? For I know they must be falsehoods ... and now Sophia, are you pleased with yourself, he looks positively conspicuous! Forgive my rotten sister, Frederick, she is too easily impressed but it is innocent, she is not malicious.'

I felt a little discomfort, though was not through embarrassment as they thought, I merely tried to hide my design and a sympathetic ear was not what I had expected to find – indeed at their welcome I had thought them less informed, but then I had not bargained on Sophia.

'I am as you say, estranged from my family, and have been staying with my good friend Joseph, whilst waiting for this situation to repair.'

My improvisation skills I found quite remarkable, though dared not look from the siblings to Joseph.

'I shall not venture into why this has happened as it pains me but do truly hope that one day I shall be able to call upon my father again.'

"'Tis a sad business,' Joseph began. 'He has been quite distraught, and is most eager to return to Bath. We have an arrangement that if he should regain ground he must not forget this, a forfeit would be most disagreeable.'

He spoke with a degree of wit, aimed at pleasing his audience but also reminding me that his business here was not charity.

'But is this contract binding, Sir?' Sophia toyed.

'Tis written in blood, Lady, are not all the best contracts?'

He fenced with extraordinary precision, and the man was at his best under such circumstances. The conquest of Sophia, a mere trifle.

'I suppose you stay with Will at Banbridges? I cannot help but think that you might be more comfortable here? The rooms are unequalled in luxury, quieter, and if that is not inducement enough, surely the company is more refined? Sophia, do you not think it would be refreshing to have a guest?'

'For you maybe, Phillip, I am sure you shall be up for hours at pool or cards! But dear Freddy, do come and stay with us, I cannot keep beating my brother at backgammon it begins to bore!'

Laughter was less polite than propriety might have it, the two were obviously experienced socialites, but then I never found shy maidens to my liking, at least not at a game of backgammon!

'Alas, I really must away,' Joseph announced. 'It has been both encouraging and revealing, such company is too rare.' He took Sophia's hand. 'I shall send word on my return.'

Surely, secret rendezvous were in nature just that, but what these two planned was there for all to know as they really only spoke to each other. Whether he lacked wit or simply information, this was all lost on Phillip who said he looked forward to Joseph's return whilst Sophia said she longed for it with one look.

'However, I would beg a private audience with Frederick before I leave, I shall not keep him more than a moment.'

He gestured for me to join him.

'Of course,' I replied and hastened to the adjacent door.

'I shall be gone one, maybe two days at most, Freddy. If I could tear out your tongue I swear I would but in these civilized times it would never do! I shall have to make do with your promise that you shall keep your wits about you and offer up no more than the mere modicum of information that is required, your companions are light in nature. The Lady Sophia may be quite determined to discover you, and perhaps I as a result, so do not enter into deep conversation with her, you must not be persuaded. Tell me, Frederick, do you think I find her attractive? You could not be more deluded if you did. Though her charms are quite obvious, to me she appears quite ugly! And yet you do not look shocked at this statement? Am I to understand by this that you feel as I do?'

'Yes, no, I mean she is pretty enough to satisfy half the populous but I would not be so speculative to speak for the other.'

'I would tell her this, if I thought she would not believe I jested, I find her vanity quite unassailable.'

'Verging on irritating.'

I thought to placate him, and though I knew him too clever for this, I was sure he would appreciate the effort.

'Yes, really, I too am amazed to find her personally quite ill-favoured.'

He took my arm and stared intently at me with as much sincerity as he could muster.

'Did you not note the deep hollows about her eyes, I am sure that she gazes at herself so much that her very eyes retreat for some respite!'

'In retrospect, Joseph, I must agree with you though some may see it as lunacy, they really are quite sunken.'

'I suppose I shall have to meet with her, though it shall not be for the purpose she imagines. She is far too inquisitive, and thick-headed enough to think she makes fun with me. Her vanity begs a private interview with me – and I would be less of a gentleman if I thought this too bold – and shall give me opportunity to silence her. But what am I saying!? This is not your concern, unless you thought to make her your own? Perhaps in my absence? If not for her looks, as we both agree she is quite hideous, but for her fortune?'

'I can assure you, Joseph, that this has not entered my mind, I simply await instruction from your good self. This is good business though, is it not?'

'It would seem so, yes, and you have gladdened me that you do not think of Sophia in that particular way. It would not do for you to be lovelorn at such a critical stage.'

'I do wonder though, Joseph, that you shall be able to quieten the lady, she is quite boisterous. How will you manage this?'

'A sillier question I have yet to hear, Frederick! If there is nothing else then I really must go, and smile, man, you look quite crestfallen all at once.'

And with that he was gone, and I left in the company of the condemned. Sophia did not have the luxury of being so aware as perhaps those who marched to the gallows, and in their last hours did they not think things they had dared not before and did they not seek forgiveness? Poor Sophia, no such generosity was to be hers.

I took a few breaths before I rejoined the party. Will was leaving as I entered.

'Oh do you not stay, Will?'

I must have sounded like I begged, I had no wish to be Joseph's sole envoy, it would all feel too personal to me and I would rather Will complicit.

'Yes, I must be off too I'm afraid. Do not look so worried, Freddy, they are quite tame really!'

With that he left, and my company was begged.

"Tis a shame Will had to go, he is so amusing.'

'Sophia!' Phillip warned. 'You always make fun of him though he has done nothing to you.'

'Dear brother, you know he irritates me, he is always so nervous and to be frank the shaking is bordering upon lunacy! You would think he would take something for it, some sort of elixir, a poppy compound, or something?'

'Sophia! I am your brother and as so must guide you in the absence of our parents, I warn you now you go too far, girl! It is most unbecoming. What say you, Freddy?'

'Oh Freddy, I know how you shall answer, you will please your host and speak as he would have you. The mere idea of having an idea of his own is quite beyond Freddy.'

A polite pause for response or a moment's grace to recover from such damning words would appear too charitable for Sophia as she continued.

'Will is acceptable, Frederick, but he has no breeding. He therefore is left to consume as much wine and poppy derivative as he wishes. None shall guide him as none really know him, am I not right, Phillip? Can you tell me one historical fact about Will? Perhaps his schooling or lineage? Surely there is something you can impart dear brother?'

She waited as Phillip strode to the window exasperated.

'You see, we know nothing of him that he does not invent himself. It has been not a year since he surfaced, and I cannot help but wonder how he gets away with all of it? Perhaps the busy nature of Bath itself lends itself to such entities.'

'Sister, I will have you stop there, enough!'

She blushed and went to her brother.

'I just enjoy riling you, dear brother, even after nineteen years of my company you remain so innocent!'

His face softened.

'You do very well at it sister, now off with you, Freddy and I have things to discuss. Gadzooks this room is stuffy today! Do you find it so, Freddy?'

I, trying to have an original thought and still bitter from Sophia's comments, said,

'Such heated displays often have the effect. Perhaps a ride out might suit us both?'

It was lost on Sophia, who begged her leave, and skipped from the room obviously pleased with herself. Bitterly I thought after her, yes Sophia, breeding is always obvious though what lies beneath is not so – murderers, thieves, and for you, dear Sophia, demons no less.

'You must excuse my sister, Freddy.'

Phillip interrupted my thoughts laced with poison and I too used to Joseph realizing them, coloured scared that they showed.

'She has been far too spoiled, I myself am one of the guilty. Thank heavens that she is blessed with looks where she is wanting in sensibility.'

'Yes, yes,' I replied. 'As is often the case with such ladies and thank heavens for them!'

Easy words though I meant none; as for her looks I was more inclined to think as Joseph did now.

Phillip, thankfully, agreed that the idea of a ride would benefit us both and had his gig readied. We headed for the park where conversation was light, Phillip often remarking on ladies and their finery and I made the discovery that sometimes a little too much lace highlighted a lack of profile where it was supposed to have the opposite effect. He commented that this in itself was quite charming.

'The effort is astonishing in some cases, do you see, Freddy? And all done for a brief moment in time where they might catch your eye! Not to mention all else that hinges. I would feel ungenerous if I denied them.'

'And I too, Phillip. Let them fill their afternoons exchanging tales of fantasy and chance, society would stand still if we did not pretend and besides all it preens one's vanity.'

Admittance to a very salubrious gentleman's club was a treat I had not guessed upon, and as we entered Phillip said,

'A man should not be judged by one wrong action alone, Freddy.'

I knew what he hinted at, and praise that Sophia had not enquired further, happy to find that whilst I enjoyed infamy I was not so wanting in company.

Perhaps it was his modest introduction of myself, with more than a little circumspection, as a distant cousin.

'To find him settled in Bath all these years! Yet we have not crossed paths?'

That gained me only peripheral acceptance here. Though for myself this was enough, and I was soon regaling tales fit for such a gathering of gentlemen though we were none of us in spirit such. No indeed, it was only the mix that required us to perform and if a lady were ever to spy on such illuminating events she would almost certainly find herself distinguished by her form only and not by her class as she might imagine. And that in all probability find herself usurped, though affectionately, by as little as a serving wench.

Phillip joined me with equally revealing tales, and his relief at my assimilation was obvious and quite touching.

'I am sorry, gentlemen, but I must drag my cousin from you, we have an invitation to dine with my sister. She has plans for dear Freddy, I believe, and I think they take the form of a drip of a girl named Emmeline Sopersworth! Though do not despair, she has a fortune and I am assured that what she lacks in spirit she makes up for handsomely in her dowry!'

'Here, here!'

This from my following and with rousing cheers as we departed.

'Poor old Freddy,' Phillip remarked patting my shoulder. 'A night of the gentille flirtations of Miss Sopersworth is about as sedated as it comes, but I did not exaggerate her promise, she is a fine financial gain to any man.'

'Then let us not waste any more of her time, I would feel less generous if I kept her waiting longer than she already has for such an encounter!'

'No indeed, for surely it has been her whole twenty one years!'

The fun we had with Miss Sopersworth's reputation was perhaps a little mean spirited, though if she was as Phillip explained, she would have heard, and expected far worse.

Bath quickly turned about the fortunes of many and at breathtaking pace and mine was no non-starter. Though I could not relish it as one, in similar circumstances might. I had incurred debts upon my way, and not merely financial, I feared they would not readily leave me.

Chapter 20

'Dear, dear Freddy!'

Sophia greeted me with fake sentiment.

'Sophia.'

'You arrive just in time. I would have set out some of Phillip's clothes though you do not measure I'm afraid, still what you wear is suitable. Green shall show you to your room, as I am sure you would wish to prepare? We have a fine few coming tonight and I will not have you disappoint.'

'Matronly! How attractive, Sophia,' Phillip broke her onslaught thankfully.

'Hah! Phillip, you laugh at me, though I am sure you do not, Frederick?'

'I do not, Sophia, I thought you naturally so, therefore dared not laugh!'

'I see we have two comedians! Well it suits you, Freddy. I can be tyrannical at times but will assure you that I am the nicest kind of ogre.'

'I am sure of it,'

I softened a little and after all she did become the fluster incredibly well.

'Seven o'clock, then gentlemen, and away with you,'

As she wrinkled her nose, she said,

'You smell of port and that smelly old club!'

I mounted the stairs, and was shown to my quarters by Green. A little nap I thought, no need to gaze at the luxurious arrangement I found myself in. I had been used to comparable and not so far from memory that this did render itself unique.

That will do, I thought, hair still holding from my visit to the barbers. Enough, I would imagine, to catch a silly simpering girl.

I met Phillip on the stairs.

'Good, good!' he said as we descended the stairs and were met by the unmistakeable hum of a good party. Several people were already there and were quick to introduce themselves.

'Obviously primed by Sophia,' Phillip remarked, 'I can almost guess, can you?'

I laughed, and acknowledged that more was afoot here than simple curiosity. Sophia commandeered me with obvious shameless reason and took me to a chair where sat an elderly gentleman with a most attentive daughter.

'Mr Sopersworth, Emmeline. May I introduce our distant cousin Frederick Abbotsby Feltsham.'

For that was my surname, and it was good to hear. For so long now I had only been known by my forename. Emmeline looked up and blushed, not wholly unattractive, nondescript blonde hair, though it was blonde and dainty features. No, I thought, not too bad at all. Mr Sopersworth struggled to his feet and I took the chance to invest in my future.

'Please Sir, we do very well with you comfortable in your chair, I would join you if you would allow?'

And I gestured to the opposite chair.

'Please,' he said.

'That is indeed most thoughtful of you.'

'Well this is cosy, is it not Emmeline?' Sophia enquired as Emmeline took a seat by her father.

'The fire is most welcome, Miss Sopersworth? Such a cold night,'

I remarked,

'For sure it is, Sir, though I do not reprimand Sophia for asking us on such a night as it is, I thank her, she is most generous.'

'Of course, and neither do I. Though I have had a minimal journey in relative comfort, all the way from the room above!'

She laughed, and Sophia flashed approving glances at her. Old Mr Sopersworth too found the comment amusing and went on,

'Abbotsby Feltsham, I know the name, but you must forgive me my memory is not as keen as it once was.'

'And in this case 'tis right that it shouldn't be,' Sophia interrupted. 'You may have heard some nonsense, Mr Sopersworth, about our dear Freddy but you are habitually wise, as I am, and have obviously chosen to forget it!'

He raised his glass to her and she rolled her eyes and sat back in her chair.

'Emmeline, dear girl, Phillip and I are taking Frederick for a ride tomorrow, I wondered if you might accompany us? If that is acceptable, Sir?' she enquired of the father.

'Why do you ask me?' he replied playfully. 'I am sure Emmeline would be most put out if I did not allow her. The two are inseparable Frederick, as you may discover for yourself if she so wishes. Quite the double act, but take care not to pity my poor daughter, ay my dear? She adds a touch of naivety and sincerity to every prank Sophia decides to play her innocence, which I hope is not contrived.' He nudged his daughter. 'Makes these pranks all the more successful whatever be Sophia's design!'

'Father,' Emmeline began, 'I merely chose to believe the best of Sophia, I am sure none of it intentional, all pure coincidence.'

'Well said!'

Sophia rejoiced.

'I am not a joker, I am most serious, and devote at least half an hour every day to the reading of all the great philosophers!'

'Yes, dear Sophia, but can you name them?' Emmeline added much too all our amusement.

Well, Well, I thought, not such a bad girl after all, she shows a degree of wit and has something to say. The evening was passing most pleasantly, even more so when Emmeline agreed to join us on our excursion on the morn, and unaccustomed of late to the feeling, quite forgot myself.

I did witness Sophia, later that evening, receive a billet doux; this in itself not so extraordinary for such a popular girl and I continued my address to Emmeline and her father. And I did meet with her mother, at least fifteen years her father's junior, she was of no interest to me, Emmeline, or indeed her father. She showed little affection and none was returned, and soon left us to our conspiring. Phillip waved me over and I excused myself.

'How find you it all, Freddy? Do I rescue you in time?'

'It is not half as bad as you would have me believe, Phillip, I wonder that you did not have an inclination towards Miss Sopersworth yourself?'

'Ha ha, no, man, but you are right she is not too bad, though would you have found her so for less than her ten thousand a year?'

'Certainly it made it all the more sweet!'

'You are not home free yet, Freddy, she is incredibly fussy, there have been suitors before yourself and all sent away but now that she is beyond your looks and still shows interest it unfortunately falls to your charm to persuade her!'

'Hah! Such a comment is beneath you Phillip, come, man, do I detect a little jealousy? I shall wager you this, I will secure Miss Sopersworth by the summer and you shall eat your words.'

'Well then I will have to keep a close eye on you, dear

friend. I am suddenly struck by an idea that surely you will see as inspired as I do. You must stay on with us, Freddy, Sophia has warmed to you and I myself find your company most refreshing. What say you, man? Surely you are persuaded? I would feel insulted if you preferred the comforts of a country inn to the luxury you have here, though take care not to inform Mr Black of my opinion.'

'Fear not on that account, Phillip, I would prefer not to eat my own tongue for supper! I dare to jest so, as Joseph is not present, but I cannot help but wonder that it not such an extreme idea where the man is concerned.'

'Is that what it is then that made me so uncomfortable around him, Freddy? Fear? Yes I think it is and a most unusual feeling.'

'Aye, but a most unusual man. However, let me address a happier subject and say that I would be delighted to stay on with you in these most comfortable surroundings. I have never met with such delightful circumstances and did not think that I would readily find friends, or indeed be ever able return to my beloved Bath.'

'Splendid! Splendid! Now where is my errant sister? We must share the news with her, it will please her endlessly.'

We looked, but there was no sign of Sophia. Her maid, Minny, later informed us that she had retired early complaining of a headache but that it was not serious and had even sent Minny away.

Phillip was unconcerned so we rejoined the party, and even though I was having a most enjoyable time, I harboured a secret wish to retire to my room and relive this fortune that had happened upon me.

Later that night, initial thoughts kept me from sleep by their nature of excitement and optimism, but gradually paranoia and bitterness took control, and I was further deprived sleep only it now made me uncomfortable. I could never form real attachments to any of these characters; Joseph did not rejoice in people's fortune, he rather enjoyed their downfall and extracted payment through many means and to satisfy his many appetites.

The damned always choke on their evil deeds
When they tire the Devil
And is them that bleeds.

Chapter 21

'Surely the favourite meal of the day?' I said to Phillip across the expanse of breakfast delights.

'I could not agree more, it is a pleasure to share another man's philosophy at the table! Sophia for all her liberal thinking will sit at such a table laden with such inducements and I swear not a morsel passes those lips. In fact, I do believe I have not seen her eat since she turned sixteen and turned her first head! But where is she this morning? This is a shoddy display and unlike her. Minny, would you run along, and hurry up my lazy sister? I must say 'tis surprising to find you not attending her and even more so for you to be waiting on me, do you have something to say, girl?'

'Begging your pardon, Sir, but she's not in her room.'

'What, Good God 'tis early for Sophia to be taking the air! Perhaps the headache lingers, yes this is surely her reason, my sister, Freddy, is no enthusiast for the outdoor pursuits even the garden can be challenging. Very well Minny, that will be all.'

'Begging your pardon, Sir, but there is something else.'

'Go on girl, why do you look so fretful?'

'It is just the lady's bed has not been disturbed.'

'What, how is this so? She retired there last night with a headache, I have your word upon it, Minny!'

'I am sorry, Sir. I did see her to her chamber but she asked me to leave before I could attend her. I am sorry, Sir, but I would beg my leave, 'tis not my place to be present at such times.'

'Minny!'

But it was too late and the girl quickly alighted from the room.

'Phillip, I am sure there is an obvious explanation.'

'I am sorry, Freddy, but I cannot see it, I must check for myself.'

He flew from the room and mounted the stairs. I felt I ought to excuse myself at the first opportunity. This would be a scandal, there was no doubt, what nagged me I knew not but all was not as simple as a secret liaison. Joseph! Of course! Why did this dull recognition of the obvious dog me so, hadn't he said that he would have to meet with Sophia and that his intention be to silence her? I grabbed my water and drank to quench the thirst that comes with fear, fear that a guilty man feels when the door sounds in the middle of the night. Quickly I walked to the door but was stopped by Phillip.

'It is true, as Minny said, Freddy, Sophia has gone! But where do you go, man? Do you flee with fear of being embroiled in something indelicate? Let me be the first to defend my sister in her absence, she is—'

'Phillip—' I interrupted. 'Let me assure you that I do not flee, as you say, and thoughts of being compromised could not be further from my mind. I simply wish to give you room and privacy to deal with the situation, I fear my absence is quite overdue. So you can think, man, I would not wish to prejudice these thoughts with any that I might inadvertently moot.'

'No, Freddy, please you must stay, your words will silence this deafening void where I find myself lost for them. Please man, if my sanity is your only excuse for leaving then do not go.'

What could I say? I had to agree even though at every second I could be discovered, if indeed this be by Joseph's hand.

'I shall have to visit with her friends, if you would join me? I must ask that you assure me of confidentiality in this matter, Freddy? What do I say!? Of course you are a good man, forgive me. We must not delay, come our horses are being readied.'

His face was fear itself, so much so that it took my breath away; I could not name one thing I had not felt in this last six months. Fear, despair, joy and though my emotions stemmed from the selfish wish to find her safe and rid myself of this inexplicable horror, his state was still contagious and I was caught up in his trepidation. I had to have time to think.

'Phillip, I only ask that I may first collect what little belongings I have at Banbridges, I feel unsuitably attired for such serious business.'

'I shall send for them, Freddy, and to the inn for what else you have, of course you must have your things but please do not leave me now.'

'I only wish that it was all possible, Phillip, but some of my effects are in nature private, you must understand, and grant me not more than two hours.'

'Very well man, but what remains at the inn, I shall send for this, yes?'

I did not respond and pretended to fish for something from my purse.

'Very well then that is settled, though please, Freddy, hasten your return; I feel as I go mad.'

I left Phillip, no longer understanding the good in people; I felt too close to evil as it drew me in and cradled me in darkness whenever fear took me. I quickened my step to almost a run, was it from the noose that I did so, or more from Joseph? I knew not. What he would make of my improvisations preoccupied my thoughts as I rushed to the hotel, and offered me strange comfort.

Finding Pip at Banbridges was some consolation, and enticed me from my cowering and flinching that I might share the news, though not what I believed to be the truth of it. I had not yet discovered if they be owned by Black or just bells and whistles.

'Pip! It is good to see you.'

'Hello Freddy, you find me wanting company! Will and Piggy ought to be here by now.'

Unsure if I should mention the morning's events, though maliciously, I thought, that Phillip had assumed my confidentiality, and I had not actually assured him of anything, so I ventured,

'What have you been up to this fine morning?'

He looked at me as though I was quite mad and said,

'"Tis only ten thirty man! I have had little to do like the rest of the civilized world! Strange too that you find the morning fine. Winds and heavy rain suit you, do they?'

I longed to be put back in my box by Joseph, was the only place I felt comfort now, I could not maintain sensible thought or indeed sensible conversation.

'Ah! Here they are, gentlemen you are late though I see you rush and look suitably harassed so I shall forget the slight! And Joseph! A most welcome surprise!'

Piggy spoke first.

'Friends, I bring a tale so tragic and catastrophic, Sophia is taken from us!'

'What! How so, man, what has happened?'

Pip looked genuinely shocked.

'A violent departure by all accounts.'

Will began with reserve,

'Some brute has quite strangled the life out of her! Her body has been discovered not an hour ago , and the tragedy is that we should know before her dear brother! But such is the nature of Bath, nothing is sacred. I am mortified, who has done this to us, gentlemen? How shall we ever replace her?'

'We cannot,' said Piggy solemnly.

'We will not,' added Pip. 'But tell us the circumstances if they are known?'

'That is just it,' replied Piggy. 'There are none to be had, no trace of who has done this, I cannot think of a motive? It must have been an accident!'

'Yes, one would not purposefully kill such a beautiful creature. She was goodness itself!'

Will looked close to tears, though all three looked at each other as though they waited for a cue. Will looked to Joseph and blushed, his thoughts were obvious.

'Yes, though for one heralded to be so good was indeed a violent death. Do you not think, gentlemen?' Joseph began. 'After all, strangulation is a provoked method of disposal and not one that readily springs to mind be the case misadventure. And surely a pistol or something less personal, the act of choking somebody to death is in no way brief, and leaves no room for mistaken identity, I am personally aware that it takes at least ten seconds to carry out the task successfully. Surely no accident then. As for motive if pressed I would say that she made herself too busy with other people's affairs, where her own might have been better scrutinized.'

'How do you mean?' Pip asked, trying to keep up but rapidly realizing all that the rest of us did and admirably attempted to hide his moment of clarity.

Not that Joseph intended for it to be secret; he could not have been more obvious.

'Well I can see no harm now in revealing, without appearing indelicate, that for sure she had had a period of confinement.'

'How so?' asked Piggy,

'Do you mean that she has been with child? Where did you obtain this information?'

Sophia's death was of little importance anymore, more did they want of her history and as much detail as was possible.

'How can you doubt it? By your own admission she was an incorrigible flirt. I have yet to meet an innocent one! She was far too wise, gentlemen, for one who has not experienced a child even if only for nine months and a day ... do you see now? 'Tis obvious to you all I can see it.'

'Yes I see, we must visit with Phillip, to see if he copes.'

'Oh no need Will, Freddy here is set up with him and shall be all the sympathy he shall require, am I wrong, Frederick?'

'Absolutely not, Joseph, are you ever? Though how you came so expediently by the news confounds me.'

'Freddy, an informed guess, I knew as much before I left as even duller wits than you would.'

'I do wonder though, Joseph, if the arrangement shall hold in light of this tragic news.'

'Oh it shall hold. Even more so, he will not wish his own company, man, it would drive him insane! Had it not been so violent, he may have rallied quicker, such a shame. I feel for him, I most honestly do, do you see how he decays before our eyes even in his absence? It shall eat at him till there is nothing left. Please be sure to convey my heartfelt condolences, Frederick. Mind that I shall check that you have. Your new arrangement does not signify an end to our relationship.'

'I shall, Joseph, and I did not think that it ended. I am always indebted to you and must now think to repay, you have but to name it and I shall endeavour.'

Piggy's cough did little to hide his amusement and the chill he had caught spread wildly throughout the group.

'What amuses you sirs that I may too laugh and share the humour? I am confused.' I requested honestly.

'Do I look like a bit whore to you, gentlemen?' Joseph announced. 'No, there I answer for you! Payment, Freddy? I would not put it so crudely. I dare you to cheapen that which I have done for you with such words again! 'Tis my privilege to extract "payment" in whichever way I deem fit, I am in no rush. And now you may say you are confused! You have already provided plentiful opportunity, fret not, I already enjoy the proceeds.'

'As do we all, Freddy, and here, here to that!'

Will slapped my back to almost make me choke, and I remained confused.

'As for your obvious confused state, Frederick, though it obviously is irritating you, I prefer you that way!'

Though what was meant by it all would become apparent later, and whether I had known it then or later would have made no difference however I fooled myself; the urge to question became less and less and only made me uncomfortable, why dig deeper for more clarity when, here, it was dire enough?

'Very well then, you may go.'

It was too much to think that he released me so readily, had I heard him correctly?

'Go then, man. Gracious, you look as though you already miss me! Ha, ha, tell me this is not true? It would be too precious! But if it be so then let me reassure you, 'tis not forever, but for now live your life though it be full of misery! Phillip will expect you to mourn with him, a little depressing, yes, and a far cry from what you imagined, but I am sure, positive in fact that it shall not last more than a year, there. One cannot maintain such a debilitating emotion for very long, and please, Freddy, I wish for you to take comfort from my words after all they are free. Now we really must get on.'

'Yes we must,' Piggy said and took my hand and snorted, 'So long old thing!'

'Bon chance, Freddy, I am sure it shall not be too long, positive I speak for Pip too. Farewells can be dashed long and tiresome things!'

'Thank you, Will, and the same to you all. Especially your good self, Joseph.'

Joseph turned his back on me and I almost tripped rushing to the door where I had left my small bag of chattel. Just an extension was all I managed to cheer myself with as I left. But to enjoy it, surely the liberty of another less tortured soul, Joseph had left me in no doubt that I had no such option.

Sophia, it transpired had been laid dead in the road and was as a man and carriage horrifically drove over this poor wretch's body that she was discovered. He really had taken a severe disliking to the girl, I would have thought the deed enough and pertinent, no need for such artistry, he would have known that placing her so would produce effect. About her neck, crudely, a tourniquet made of her ribbons, but I guessed that this was more dramatics and he had disposed of her more naturally; after all the neck was broken apparently quite violently, and though I did not believe myself the most clever of individuals, I enjoyed relaying as much when Phillip was absent. There was much supposition resulting, and I enjoyed the reputation of instigating this, unfortunately the poor Sophia's dreadful demise proved most entertaining to even the most polite, still great care was taken that Phillip not hear of it, none more so than by myself.

Six months passed as did the weather, and as the latter improved so did Phillip's humour. Admittedly at first he did nothing to rid himself of the grief, but with care I plied him with talk of the town and tales that gently tickled and that were never so obvious to appear distasteful to one in mourning. I had also managed to forge new friendships, still I showed restraint in the hour that I returned and the amount of spirit I consumed. It became less and less that I thought of Will when someone's generosity bought my pleasure or company, and with friends such as Phillip the scathing comments that I sometimes heard of him were never to be mine. Each day that passed without word from Joseph, I blessed, though the blessing of which made sure that I never forgot all that had gone before and made more apparent that which I stood to lose. Sometimes I would wish for my success to be less, so as the loss of it be not so painful.

My Emmeline, as I now had come to call her, soon to become Mrs Abbotsby Feltsham, was proving to me more lovely than convenient as she happily nursed Phillip's malady and said she found comfort in the very deed. She laughed sweetly at my financial ruin saying,

'Freddy, you are such a joy that you must sometimes allow people to seek your company even if it be by acquisition! For if you have no funds to play for them where they wish then you leave them no choice. Do not be so bull-headed!'

I would often pretend to have too much pride, though maybe with introspection it was not such a falsehood just that I had forgotten to think of myself as anything other than a fraud.

This very day I was to dine with her, accompanied by the erratically moribund Phillip. I did so wish that this be one of his brighter days though in fairness he became less and less the grieving brother. With much care I dressed in clothes discretely made mine by who I knew not, but guessed that it be Phillip. One last look in the glass, I had always, even in dark times, maintained an immaculate toilet, well as much as circumstance allowed. I set about the door to be stopped by laughter, yes, laughter I was sure of it. Such a sound always has the same effect and so went to inspect, cheered by it, expecting to perhaps find lovers or children; nothing, though two doves were in quite romantic form and so blamed this. I now was in such a rush so as not to keep my Emmeline waiting that I almost forgot to look like a man in love as I met Phillip at the door and I felt the fire that warmed me was, in truth, not amour. However, it would do for now and I would never injure Emmeline by making this apparent, it was of no consequence.

Though handsomely dressed, Phillip always looked apologetic for it since the death of his sister and I could not help thinking, and rather ungraciously, that grief was entirely boring! So as we left I lightened the mood with a tale from the Gazette of a man suffering chronic wind, and that how he had been excluded from many places for people's fear of catching the condition.

'What a beautiful red hair, titian, do you see Freddy?' Phillip remarked as we drew up outside the Sopersworths.

'Let me see?'

And I leaned over to see from his window just a glimpse of a girl as she disappeared about the corner; I leaned back then sat quickly forward again but she was gone.

'Wasn't it glorious? A girl like that in the right situation might do very well for herself, perhaps even marry beyond her means. Do you not think? I cannot fathom if she is poor or is just an oddity, for she is handsomely dressed though wild and unkempt in appearance.'

'Hah, how foolish I am, for a brief second there I was reminded of just such a girl, how silly I barely caught a glimpse!'

'Frederick, what do you laugh at, you must tell me of this girl? You look positively whimsical! Come I shall have you tell me.'

"Tis nothing Phillip, not worthy of your attention. I only laugh at my suspicious mind. I tell you, 'tis good to be here with you and I am constantly reminded of it.'

He turned to me earnestly.

'Very well then, if you refuse to tell me. I would say that I too am very grateful of your company, dear Freddy, how would I have coped without you? But sentiment has no place at such a joyous gathering, I truly expect an announcement from yourself regarding a union tonight? As I am sure the well-informed Emmeline is, I am quite sure she knew before you had even decided upon it!'

'We shall have to wait and see, Phillip, hah! But still let us not delay I find myself in dire need of refreshment!'

We mounted the steps of the magnificent and impressive house and Phillip confided,

'One day, Frederick, just such a house shall be yours.'

'Aye if not this one, truly magnificent. My dear girl, Em, has much to recommend her.'

We entered, greeted by an eager, and slightly inappropriate Emmeline.

'Emmeline, my dear sweet girl, there are not enough superlatives to describe your loveliness tonight.'

I took her hand.

'Oh Freddy, you have succeeded in making me blush where my own thoughts did not! And I am quite sure it does not compliment this colour!'

She swished her bright blue gown, and we settled on a spot near her father.

'Frederick,' he whispered. 'I would make an announcement for you both tonight if you would allow? I am old, and confidences slip out more readily and would rather it announced than have it discovered, what say you?'

'Ha, ha, Sir, it is mine and Emmeline's wish that you do so, and it would bring great pleasure to us both if you were to honour us with your words.'

Emmeline all the while sat chatting with another and her pretence at disinterest made her all the more beguiling.

'Here! You lot clear off!' came a voice from beyond the windows.

'Oh dear,' began Mr Sopersworth. 'I fear our enjoyment has been compromised by some unfortunate types, though why they would pick tonight of all nights to set up outside is beyond me! We do not entertain such things normally. I must find Fibbs.'

He walked to the door and was greeted by the man he spoke of.

'Is there a problem, Fibbs?'

'I have seen to it, Sir. A rabble of gypsy types, thought to be fed by the cook's maid, she is a silly girl and I think took a fancy to one of them, but if you so wish she shall be gone by the morning?'

'No, no, Fibbs, I trust your judgement, and I am sure she

has learned her lesson, poor thing I expect you scared her quite out of her wits!'

'Thank you, Sir, and I do believe she will show more than a little care in future.'

Mr Sopersworth returned to us, eager to continue conspiring and before long the announcement came that, 'Dinner is served.'

And we were summoned to the dining room.

'Famished, Freddy?' said Emmeline clutching at my arm,

'Who me dear? No not too bad,'

'No I, Freddy! I am famished, ha, ha!'

We sat at the table just as Mr Sopersworth could contain the news no longer.

'Dear Friends, and I assure you all that you are as this dinner has cost me a fortune! I begin tonight with such heartening news, that of a union between my dear darling sweet Emmeline and the very deserving Frederick Abbotsby Feltsham! This, I am sure, will come as no surprise to any of you and I would have you join in a toast with me to the very handsome couple that is to be!'

The room toasted us, and cheered their approval, and Mr Sopersworth continued.

'This is fine news is it not! And for poor Emmeline who, I am told, is famished, a feast!'

'Oh Freddy, you told!'

Though she laughed and was all in good humour.

The feast, it must be said, did not disappoint, and the suckling pig and exotic fruits that accompanied did well to feed even the half-starved. The party spirit was the best I had known and a thought struck me that if it had took all it had for me to be here in such good company with such promise, I would not change it. I told so much to Phillip, though omitting obvious historical fact. I was not drunk enough on gin, or foolish enough to ever allow those villainous chapters of my life to be scrutinized, even amongst people who confessed to indiscretions themselves.

'Some air, Phillip?' I said, suddenly wishing for something sobering, and in the absence of the solitude of my room a cool ebonized night would do.

'A fine idea,' he replied, and we stepped from the party and were soon followed by others wishing for the same effect, though perhaps more so a secret desire to be rid of their ageing spouses.

'Hush now!' I begged.

From the darkness a whisper, no a message spirited upon the breeze as though a gift purely for me.

'No escape, Freddy, hah! not all your riches now can buy you that, 'tis your time.'

Then laughter that mocked. I felt myself stiffen and looked about me in vain into the shadows, there I saw movement! A pat on the back from Phillip brought me back.

'I thought I heard something, did you?'

'Ha, ha, you are as jumpy as jacks, Freddy, tonight! Too many tales of dark times, my friend, a night such as this and a tot or two too many can bring on all sorts of hallucinations!'

'Amen to that! I thought my wife almost passable not ten minutes ago! But am assured 'tis but the spirit!' somebody joked and it delighted all but me, I still needed convincing that all was right.

Phillip pointed out that if indeed I had heard voices they were probably those of the footmen and coach-hands and if not this, nought but the cold night breeze tinkering with rotting window panes and carriage lanterns. A perfectly logical explanation, yes, but perhaps if they knew little of what I did they might not be so quick to dismiss my suspicions. All the sense this group could muster did nothing to prevent my despair; I was back to counting minutes where it had become days. So toxic were the thoughts that I dared not think his name that he might appear.

'I must find Emmeline, please excuse me, gentlemen.'

I am sure I must have looked like Hell itself, he was back I was positive, and he did not come alone; I knew it would come, but faint hope had me think it would not be so traumatic. What was worse, that I had faced down Harry Godwin upon that field where a battle for honour was lost by me and denied of the other? Perhaps I would have died by his shot, perhaps not? Whatever the conclusion it would have been expedient. This hell that was visited upon me twisted my gut and owned me. I rushed through the door into Emmeline's arms; she had come to look for me.

'Freddy, you look awful! What has happened, are you sick?'

'No, dear sweet girl, no I just miss you at every moment. I was about to reaffirm my love for you and to feel the sweetness once again upon my lips of my intention to wed you. Emmeline I most truly love you.'

'Fah la la Frederick, you have had a scare! Romanticisms are not your strength, though I am, and shall be when we are wed. Tell me what worries you? Speak honestly, Freddy, I cannot think what has done this to you.'

She paused for a while waiting for response, how could I? The words were there but became confused each time I went to utter them.

'Oh how could I be so blind, 'tis that awful Joseph Black, isn't it? You have heard of him? Or he has visited you? Well, the man is a demon, and though I have never met him I have always been suspicious. He cannot touch you anymore, Freddy, you must believe this. He did not help you, he helped himself, and I shall tell you something now, I have heard that a great many of your past acquaintances here in Bath have had worries enough themselves since he surfaced. Thefts, murdered animals strung up in sickening ritualistic fashion. Freddy, I believe 'tis him, and that he enlists the help of others. How else would he have such particular detail about these people? I may sound extreme for 'tis only little what you have told me of him but I feel my assumptions are right, Freddy, do you feel I go too far or am I just about right?'

Though it was hollow, I now felt not so alone in my despair; she had surmised correctly and I took strange comfort in her words. No, she was not the prettiest or most vivacious but she was strong and what needed I of beauty? More a hindrance, even at the best of times.

'I see by your silence that it now occurs to you, forgive me for not telling you before, dear Freddy, I felt it of no import. We are not vulnerable or out of luck, we are rich and handsomely so, and my father is so well-appointed and informed that we could not be more secure. Joseph Black! Wherever you are, I swear to you that you are not long for the noose! Now what say you we forget this business, Freddy, and put Joseph Black firmly where he belongs, back in that smelly old inn that dwells in the past?'

'How can I deny you this, Emmeline, you are too lovely, give me a reason to deserve you, ask me anything?'

'Very well, 'tis a simple one, I will not take you to task, but please, Freddy, let us rejoin our party? Fun, frivolity, sweet treats, do I ask too much?'

I took her arm, if not out of chivalry out of the need to steady myself; it bore heavy on me and I would no more unburden myself than give myself over to the hangman. With enough gin I worried no more that I would collapse out of fear in front of these people, if I did, the amount of spirit I gladly consumed would be blamed.

All that night strange cat calls from beyond the window stirred me from my drunken slumber but as imbued with spirit as one man can be I found no sense in them; yet something, I was sure I heard Mary, I was sure she shouted,

'I have something for you, Freddy! Why did you want to go and make something with Mary, ay?'

Not understanding, though feeling the doom with which such words fill men, I sobbed; I remembered that much, and was not through morbidity brought on by the spirit. Either it abated, or I passed out for I awoke the next morning. The first few moments of waking are something to treasure, I thought, not yet awake but not in deep sleep, if I could bottle a feeling it would be this one and I'm sure I would see a healthy profit.

Unsolicited, my memory of the night passed began to poison my thoughts and the few moments' pleasure I felt on waking belied the harrowing nature of the night before. It was almost mischief akin to something Joseph might enjoy. I shuddered to think his name; shocked to my feet I rushed to the window, nothing. I dressed myself as quickly as I could. I had to check that all was well with Phillip and then to Emmeline's. Rushing down the stairs I did not think to glance at the very grand clock that graced the hallway, only when I entered the drawing room I noted my prompt appearance this morn.

'Good God, what time is it?' I asked the maid who tended the fire place, sweeping away the night's embers.

'Got to be six, Sir. I am sorry, I did not know you wished me ready so early.'

'Don't be silly, girl, I did not. Did the Master make it home safely last night?'

'Why yes, Sir, he saw you to bed and did laugh so he did. Said you would have a bear of a head this morning. Begging your pardon, Sir, 'tis not my place to say, but we did not expect to see you this side of midday.'

She looked to the fire and smiled.

'Shall I get cook to rustle you something up?'

'No, no, do not bother cook or indeed yourself unless you can sweep away my troubles along with the remnants of last eve's blaze?'

'I only wish I could, Sir, though all will seem better when you rid yourself of that liquor in your belly. A good breakfast, Sir, if you don't mind a little bit of advice, is remedy enough for you.'

'Of course you are right, girl, hah, yes, what worries have I? Ay? All of a sudden I feel in desperate need of some fresh air, will you give my compliments of the morning to the Master?'

'Of course, Sir, as you wish.'

I left her to her chores and bitterly thought there was nothing I would like more, this morning, than to render my worries secondary to those of the maids. She was really quite pretty, surely a lax mother had not warned her of such coyness! I made up my mind, that if I survived this day, I would visit her on the night, perhaps she would never think again of voicing such insolent opinions.

It was at least five hours too early to beg an audience with Emmeline and as I walked I became aware of every sound, every man and horse was suspicious and every corner hid something, something evil even though I had not seen him yet.

I found myself in the park and the day had begun as early autumn does, the light had more warmth about it and a low ghostly mist still clung about the trees. This was not a place to be if what you dreaded was ungodly and the scene reminded me too much of the first morn I met him on that road. I quickly turned and raced from the park.

'Take a breath.'

An elderly woman touched my arm.

'You are hounded, aren't you, touched by evil? 'Tis that what makes you mad and will do for you if you care not.'

She spoke with urgency and foreboding, dressed in coloured rags, and wore many talismans about her person.

'Bloody fortune teller! Leave me be, you stupid, stupid old woman! Ever look at yourself, do you? I think not, you are a farce, a deluded simpleton!'

I went to walk off.

'I'm just a reflection, Sir, I meant no harm. When I awoke this morning I dressed in clothes that were not mine, that would not seem to fit however much I struggled. And where yesterday my path to this very park was straight, today it became crooked. Made me wonder who I was to meet today? Then I saw you and if you see that I am deluded then look about yourself for 'tis you who is so. Oh and you need not worry about seeing me right for my wisdom this day, it was free, if you cannot think sensible then you must find a place that you can, that's all, Sir.'

'Ridiculous woman, how dare you speak to me in such a pernicious manner, off with you, or I shall find a stick to beat you with!'

'Beating will do you no good, Sir,' she said as she waddled away. 'What's done is done, and if you have a mind for beating then better put it to use elsewhere. Flush him out, for he hides within you.'

'Infuriating woman!' I shouted after her and went in search of company that found me less transparent.

I mounted the Sopersworth's steps not knowing whether horror lay beyond the door or hope and it was answered, nothing out of the ordinary. Though I gave searching looks and was ready for the worst I was shown to the drawing room and all remained well.

'Emmeline, my darling girl, it is good to see you.'

I embraced her perhaps a little too keenly as she pulled away, she was not afflicted by an exaggerated sensitivity.

'Freddy, you are here a might early? Sit, my love, I shall send for tea.'

She starred boldly into my eyes.

'I thought you were settled last eve? My dear, you really cannot have this man Joseph Black whip you so, he is evil, and the very type to worship it. I had so hoped I had allayed your fears. Dear oh dear, I shall have to try harder! He has no power here or ever will, and if all you have to bring on such nightmares is a suspicion, then I shall not fuel it by humouring your state. Let the man enjoy the torment he rains by hurting those you once loved, for you do not now, do you dearest? As they turned from you, you must respond likewise. Freddy we have had nothing from him here have we, hmmm?'

'This is true, Em, but I am sure something was amiss last night. The voices outside here I swear I heard them and the gypsies at the kitchen and, Em, I saw a girl with red hair disappear around the corner not five minutes before we entered.'

'Well what significance has a silly girl with red hair? I despair I really do, hush now Freddy, the man has made you sick but with time you shall repair, you will see I am never wrong.'

She placed her hand on my arm with such tenderness that it made me feel I had been starved of it all my life.

'I want to believe you, Em, I really do, perhaps I am sick, and you are right I have had no clear sign from him. Oh Em, if only I was as brave as you, I might believe I deserve all this fortune, but fear, Em, fear, it makes a coward of me.'

'Hah! What nonsense you speak, did you not seek to protect me this very morning? Pray what time did you leave? I shall venture that you have not slept much for fear of my safety. That is true bravery, Freddy, and as you see it makes me blush. I have never felt such a princess I tell you honestly, but I would not have you do it again. No danger awaits me, Freddy, as it does not you.'

The maid brought in the tea and was sent away without serving.

'Enough chivalry then, dearest Freddy, I do not require it for my vanity. What you have done this morning is rich enough for me to feast on for many years. Perhaps when we are old and grey you might save me from humiliation if I take to wearing powdered wigs and patches! Come take some tea, Papa shall be reading for breakfast and I am sure your appetite needs no encouragement.'

I thought, as we headed to join her father, not every poison has a cure though some concoctions lessen the pain and make the demise more bearable. This was just such a potion; the relative safety of this house, Joseph would not wish to acquire the notoriety that would be his if he were to petition this house aggressively and these were not the Toothills. They were connected even as far as King George's court and this coupled with the abject trust and belief that my Emmeline had in me made this false security seem almost sensible.

As to my demise, which for sure would be grisly and would not allow me to catch breath, I thought perhaps it was always to be so; even before I met Joseph Black, even before the duel, but then maybe the man had just been waiting, for this was how it felt, like he had always known of me and forever owned me.

Sitting at the breakfast table, lavishly adorned with smoked meats and fruits left over from the night of feasting, I felt a little comforted though this had an uncommon effect. Where did I go from here? I could not remain within these soft walls, it was not real, and I felt trapped. Before, I had faced the horror of what was happening to me, I grasped it, and in retrospect it began to almost feel good; now I felt unprepared, unaware, and could no longer stand it.

'Excuse me, I must go. I am sorry to you, Emmeline, and to you Sir, but I find this too confining. I must act for myself and all instincts are insisting upon it. I am not a prize poodle, I thank you.'

I went to leave hastening to the door.

'Frederick, dashed rude, man, and quite unlike you, do you sicken for something?'

The figure of Mr Sopersworth accosted me at the door and he grew other wrinkles which I had not seen before, those of concern.

'No Sir, if Em has not relayed my new circumstance to you then I am sorry for it but I have not the time to explain.'

'Well, no, she has not. What have you kept from me, girl?'

Emmeline looked as though she would cry though remained silent.

'Wait Freddy, this is not permanent is it, your design to quit us?'

'No Sir, 'tis temporary. I am sure Em shall explain all, but for now you must excuse me.'

'Oh father,' Emmeline began. ''Tis nothing but a suspicion he has! I curse Joseph Black I really do. I told Freddy, Papa, that you would see to him if he ever dared—'

'Stop right there, girl!'

Mr Sopersworth looked to scold her.

''Tis not your place to speak up for the men in your life! I am afraid you will have to postpone that luxury till we are without sense! And if your betrothed wished for assistance he would ask himself, I see now why he rushes and finds the company confining. Dear girl, you do us both an injury. Forgive me, Frederick, if you must away, then you do so with my blessing.'

'Sir I thank you, though I would ask you not to be too hard upon our Emmeline, she is too young and innocent to apply wisdom and I would not change this in her.'

I hurried my escape, eager; but for what I asked myself?. What had I planned to do? Indeed, was there anything that could be done but wait? Bear another of Joseph's excruciating tortures. Would he be merciful and put me down quickly? Would he hell, I knew it too well and charged to I knew not where, perhaps to the ends of the earth where I would gratefully fall from it if I thought it would rid me of this demon. And that was how he captured you – the hypocritical word that had this place an earthly paradise in truth hid what was indeed a favoured hunting ground of the malevolent and that it was only by default or monastic solitude that one might achieve the promised paradise. Most I knew of were touched by evil, though I had never recognized it before. Perhaps that his was pure, and that I could see where others would admire it and desire a similar effect that it now became apparent, and strangely in the dissecting found myself in awe.

Occupied by these thoughts I blindly went home, and wondered at the door if I should share my worries with Phillip, but then wasn't that what he wished? To do nothing and for me to do the unravelling? Then I might crawl back to him, where he would revel in turning me away, after all where was the game in it? So I decided to hold my counsel and wait, at least this way I might remain some worth to someone.

Chapter 22

'Freddy! Where have you been man? I thought you quite mad to take the air so early but I see by your pallor that it has chased away the night's devilment! Come, I have news for you.'

Phillip ushered me to the drawing room, and I thought was it paranoia or did people make reference to the devil habitually? It seemed frequent and hindered me where I would choose to forget my alliance with if not the Devil himself, at the very least one of his generals.

'I have had a visit this morning, Freddy, the man Joseph Black. The little you have told of him was too ambiguous for me to either keep him at the door or greet him as an acquaintance, so I had him come in and I listened to what he had to say. This is delicate, dear friend, and I only ask that you remain calm until I have told all.'

To listen keenly and maintain a look of vague disinterest is incredibly difficult I discovered, I could not have been more horrified and yet I knew I could not show it. Phillip continued.

'He came with news of a child, Freddy, that I am sorry to say has apparently been born to you. Let me finish.' He held his hand up to stop me jumping to my feet. 'Mary, tell me what does the name mean to you? He seems to think it will mean more than owt. Frederick will you please stop hastening to your feet I have not finished! He has implied that a man of means, which you soon are to be with your pending nuptials, should be able to furnish this Mary with a comfortable life for both her and baby. This will also insure silence on the matter. I have known of many such concords Freddy, and you are not alone in this indiscretion.'

'Thank you, Phillip, and if you will allow I shall now speak. Mary! Mary, Lord, man, if you ever did which, honestly, I confess I have, then you would know that you were not alone. And she is promised to one, though this is no barrier to nefarious dealings, and gives her not a moment's concern. No man, if she has a child then good luck to her and the fool she snares to look after it. Good God, I cannot believe her to have the gall!'

'Yes Freddy, but 'tis Joseph who speaks for her, I believe you forget this and seem to have an odd allegiance, or perhaps are indebted to the man? Else surely he would not have bothered.'

'Yes Phillip, you are right I am indebted to the man, and it fills me with dread that he is intent on reaffirming this. Do you not see where this is mischief? What am I to do? All is lost I am sure, and though was not much to boast of, I liked it Phillip, I liked it all.'

'But surely you over dramatize Frederick, or is there much, much more to this than you have said?'

I reddened quickly lost for words, any excuse now would seem dishonest and he got up and walked to the window.

'I would not mind Phillip if she had but the ingenuity to line her pockets from her efforts but the girl is a simpleton. Hah! Imagine, I a father to such a girl's child, ridiculous, I say again ridiculous!'

'Of this I am sure, Frederick, but mark, nature does not select more compatible partners if you choose not to. No my friend, you must see to this business and quickly as others have done before you. I shall tell you now, as you seem suitably calm, I have asked your Mr Black to call on us this eve, after dinner as privacy is paramount and the servants will be busy in the kitchen. I took the liberty in your absence,

Freddy, and I am convinced you shall make me right.'

A lengthy pause was now required, for me that is, I had much to swallow and Phillip granted me this by directing a lengthy stare out of the window.

'I cannot escape this can I, Phillip? It seems such a vicious assault, though I know not what or if I expected different, and if God were to grant me an extension to become accustomed he would have to multiply all the moons and all the dawns to come up with a figure yet this still would not suffice, not to how I feel at this moment.'

'Frederick, you do not think straight, can you not see this as a fortune in disguise? Yes, you are compromised, but will all soon be done with along with our Mr Black, can you not see this?'

'Perhaps, Phillip, yes perhaps you have a point and that all this business will be done with and be less painful than I expect. I will allow myself to hope this for it comforts me.'

'As every man must, dear friend, if he did not then he wouldn't arise from slumber if he had no hope of a sunrise, and he would not eat cook's cake if he did not believe it as fabulous as her last! Hah! You see, you laugh, all is not so bad, ay man?'

'No indeed it is not, Phillip, I have come to know of the happy circumstance of a clever escape, this with luck shall be my second. I might add that I prefer the accommodation and company to its predecessor, for it was never so full of promise and opportunity and there is why I cannot tell you more of it.'

'Of course, I would have it no different. Enjoy it, savour it, Freddy, I do not share everything either.'

It was easy to feel persuaded and encouraged by Phillip's words, and briefly I felt almost fortunate but I did not delude myself that Joseph was purely out for monetary satisfaction. No, he wanted me to suffer, to feel tortured, and forever be unsure, but how surprised was I to realize that I could endure it, for as long as he stayed ignorant to that fact. Best then let him think me done in and no longer sport.

Something else occurred to me and was equally astonishing, not a few months back I would not have dreamed of hiding something from the man but the lengthy separation had had me grow in confidence and, I hoped, common sense. Yes, I dreaded the man, and thought him evil but now began to doubt him supernatural. These waves of euphoria and despair occupied the afternoon, but to my rancour the latter proved more compelling and I retired to my room, hoping that the solitude let me ready for the night's pending drama.

I looked at myself in the glass with some perverse vanity that he deemed me worthy of such pertinent attentions; I felt as those did with a noose about their neck, or at least how I imagined they did, and every second I checked that it was still there. Here was strange security, as if I would succumb to far worse if he slackened his hold. I was a fool to think that I had enjoyed my liberty these last months' gone, I had felt his grip throughout the whole term, and unfortunately had grown used to it. I could not see a future without him, and yet I had none with him, purgatory then was a solitary state. I had once imagined it full of tortured souls and I was sure it was, but I was not to know them and was sure now we passed each other regularly sharing nothing but a sentence to be alone. And why would this be different? For it would not be a hell if you had company, and even the worst man is a better companion than the demon who resides in your conscience.

As I descended the stairs for dinner with negligible appetite, the little maid who attended the fire on the morn, bustled past with a bundle of fresh linen, she was pretty though I would not have cared.

'It is Beth, isn't it?'

She looked down and blushed.

'Why yes, Sir, if you will pardon me I have to ready for the change tomorrow.'

'Oh do not rush from me, pretty Beth, I have thought of your kind words this morning all day.'

I touched her cheek knowing she dare not flinch. The politics of a well-run house have unspoken bylaws, that if a master takes to you then for fear of losing your occupation and home you dare not turn from him, or indeed speak of it.

'Thank you, Sir.'

She went to go again.

'Such a pretty blush, Beth, it becomes you well. Beth, tell me if I am too bold for what I am about to ask? Would you visit with me later, when my business this night is done? Of course in the privacy of my very own quarters, I know too well of the jealousy that exists in such grand dwellings between servants and such like, and forgive me again Beth but one as handsome as you would for sure court such feelings. Such soft precious words you gave me, and I long for more, do I ask too much, sweet Beth? If you felt you would be compromised then please feel at liberty to state this.'

'If it pleases you, Sir, though I am sure I am not what is best for you. Begging your pardon, Sir, 'tis not my place to speak out so.'

'No, no, Beth, not at all, you may speak as you feel, however, I must correct you on one instance, that is that you are exactly what I need, dear sweet girl. Go on then, you may go girl, until tonight.'

I finished just in time, as Phillip emerged from the dining room.

'Come, come Freddy! I am starved!'

'Hah! Yet I am not one minute late, Phillip.'

'Ay but 'tis long enough when the smell of good beef fills the house!'

I joined him not knowing if I would manage a mere morsel beyond my lips, even a mouthful seemed an exhausting process as Joseph's grip tightened, his hands might as well have been about my throat.

'The hour draws near, Frederick, and I cannot help but notice your anxious state.'

Phillip acknowledged this, obviously noting the lack of good beef passing my lips, the smell had sickened, and only added to the nausea I suffered. He continued.

'Let us retire to the drawing room, it is much more comfortable and I would have you more so.'

'I am a little anxious as you say, Phillip, but believe it is the not knowing. I was cheered by your wisdom earlier, mine being temporarily excluded as is often the case when thinking of Joseph Black! But still I hope he is not long, it seems like lunacy I know to wish his company, but I want this business done with. I must know his agenda as I have suffered such nightmares this live long day and would have them done with.'

We sat by the fire where the clock passed time with such deafening encores, and then he was there.

'A Mr Joseph Black for you, Sir,'

Green showed him in.

'Gentlemen, Freddy, it has been too long! Tell me have you missed me? Hah I think not, I hear such tales of your new life and this being a very admirable set up.'

'Joseph, it feels an age, please Sir, sit.'

'Oh I shall, I really am done in with all this business, I am sure Phillip has informed you somewhat.'

'Why yes I have, Sir, but if Freddy wishes me gone I shall.'

'Whose house is this? First ushering me to sit and now excluding people from conversations in their very own drawing room! Hah, you are not changed Freddy.'

'I simply believe that Frederick has a right to privacy and is also a common courtesy, it was a gesture, Mr Black, he has already intimated that he wish me near. Have you not, Freddy?'

'I have Phillip, and Joseph you are, on this rare occasion, wrong. I do not believe I take liberties, this my home and family now, we share everything including histories.'

'Damned convenient, ay man, but are you sure you wish for complete transparency?'

'Oh, I am sure I do not, Joseph, perhaps some things are best kept between us. Forgive my impolite boldness, it is a result of much worry, I believe you are here on behalf of the girl Mary?'

'I shall leave then, Frederick?'

Phillip got up and readied to exit.

'No, no man, stay, I shall not embarrass your friend here.'

'If that is a solemn promise, Mr Black, then 'tis good, and I thank you, you seem to enjoy this moment a little too much. We all have delicate affairs we would not wish public.'

Phillip sat down again and Joseph began.

'Our Mary, surely Frederick, not the girl Mary! I am sure she would not wish such a cold informal address from one she obliged so many times! Which brings me to my purpose. Yes, I do have news for you of her, and you are right I do assume advocacy for the child. I fear her wits too dull to speak out for herself or indeed to be taken seriously. Do you not agree gentlemen? For sure she would have been turned from your door had she arrived with her claim.'

Neither I nor Phillip spoke, I through previous schooling that Joseph rarely required an answer speaking for both himself and the person he was addressing; as for Phillip, I knew not why he failed to defend himself but seemed placated by Joseph's attitude and was more intent on listening than I had hoped.

'Frederick, I am sorry man but she has had a child by you, it was only when pressed to give up the liberty taker that she yielded your name. Not Pike's, Freddy, yours. Are you not ashamed? Do you think nothing of taking another man's betrothed?'

He held his hand up as I went to speak.

'No I shall hear no excuses, I know them all and you too well. It did not occur to you that Pike would think it his and Mary would not correct him? Or was it just about right that Pike awayed when he did, and you left the poor girl with a secret that bore heavily on her? So much so, in fact, that she would have nothing to do with the child at first and was this that made us suspicious. A good, honest and loving girl and you have abused her. Still that is your fashion.'

He rolled his eyes to Phillip, who I was sure looked to believe Joseph; it was evident in the return of gaze.

'Joseph, do you expect me to believe, nay take care of this girl and child, on the extreme off-chance it be mine? One night, man, one night,' I almost pleaded to Phillip. 'She is hardly virtuous, Joseph, even you must agree? I have even known you, man—'

'Yes well, we have all had a poke, Frederick, she is not half-bad when you are close to oblivion, which I am regularly, aided by spirit!' He and Phillip shared another look. 'And you are aided by your own conscience! But Phillip, I ask you, 'tis the dates, and the girl is sure of it. I would not be here if in doubt.'

'Quite so man.'

Phillip stared at me with earnestness.

'Frederick, did you not agree this day that it be your indiscretion or lead me to believe it so? I am sure I am not mistaken, and there really is no need to defend yourself so rigorously, you further injure the girl with tales fit for bar rooms. Please state your purpose if you will, Mr Black? I am sure there must be some requirements.'

'Thank you, Sir, you have made sense of the situation. I must say it was all getting rather heated and, in my defence, I do but care for the girl and past experience has taught me of this man you feel fit to call family, but then that is your affair and I did promise to speak not a word of it. As for the girl Mary, to speak plain she shall require a regular gift of money substantial enough to care for her and the baby. Of course she shall stay on with us at the inn, but I feel she deserves a handsome annuity.'

'And Pike, Joseph?'

I began with foolish bravado, again forgetting momentarily who I addressed and checked myself.

'Forgive me, but shall he return to a loving family, woman and child? Or empty promises of faithfulness? Surely, Joseph, if you care like you say the former would be more preferable.'

'I am sure, Frederick, but none expect him to return. I would hope none foolish enough to believe that he enjoys good health aboard The Compass, and believe that if he is not already dead then he is close. I am fortunately reminded of your limits, I must make a note not to hurry and seek your company in future.

To answer your question Phillip, I plan to secure the girl's fortune. I would add that it must be contractual, legally binding, not that I doubt our Freddy here, there is no question in my mind.'

'But, Sir, you take this as verbatim, and yet I have heard you call this man tonight nothing short of Machiavellian, how can this trust be so vindicated?'

'Phillip, your attention to detail is astounding, I am surprised you have not considered a legal profession, not for monetary gain of course but as an exercise there is nothing more invigorating, I myself enjoy similar exertions! But to answer your most pertinent question, Frederick and I have an understanding, I do not feel the need to expand as you have requested to be spared embarrassing detail. I am amazed you do not note a lapse in his jocular attitude when in my company! I will say he is not the man you think you know and leave it there.'

'Frederick, do you not wish to defend yourself? I cannot believe you are accustomed to such libel, yet you are not fazed by these accusations. I must then believe them, for you do not correct me.'

'Phillip, my relationship with Joseph is particular, and I care not to argue with him simply because he is impossible! Hah, you must allow for differences in personality, Phillip, he applies wit like you do cologne! Will you gainsay me, Joseph?'

I thought it admirable recovery in such dire circumstances to make light of what Joseph said and hope Phillip not sophisticated enough to understand his assault.

'Hah, I see more is afoot here than I have knowledge of. Poor Freddy, I had not wished to make you squirm but unfortunately for you the environments you create have less clarity than they should and squirming is a product of it. Do you not agree, Phillip? Though I mind that you have said that he is not scrutinized.'

'I believe you still enjoy yourself, Mr Black, but 'tis not unsettling, Frederick seems almost comforted by it so please continue.'

'To continue then, of course we must consider the future Mrs Frederick. Hah, I laugh for I only this morn discovered his real name and now it eludes me! Perhaps for there have been so many and I take none of them seriously! But yes we must consider her, and also her family, people of considerable means keep keen accounts and a sizable amount disappearing from the family coffers regularly would no doubt be questioned. I am sure we all agree that this should remain between us three? Therefore my idea, if agreeable, is to have the account set in my name and Frederick can carefully infer that he is financially indebted to me, nothing more needs be said, simple, yes? Many families accrue foreign debt as a result of marriage, do you not find it clever?'

'I for one, Frederick, find it most workable, how do you find it?'

'I too, Phillip, I cannot fault it, and for myself shall not lose out.'

'Mark that, Phillip, 'tis his avarice! I pity you I really do.'

'Oh no gentlemen, Joseph you know that especially in such formidable company I sometimes struggle to express myself as I would wish, I am not so greedy. I simply meant that I shall have to confess nowt. My thoughts were not of any financial state I might find myself in.'

'Ha ha! So easy, is he not, Phillip? Maybe you do not find him so?'

'Hah! Yes man, the happy fortune of acquiring a wife must be coupled with a happy fortune, I am sure you are not so green, Freddy. Our Emmeline though a beauty inside is not so much to look upon, ay man?'

'I see that you two make fun of me in my state and am assured that you wish to cheer me, so, yes, I think I can laugh at it all!'

'Almost enjoy it, ay Freddy, so long as you don't feel duped.'

Phillip did not understand the last comment and Joseph secured a private audience with me with those few words.

'All this said, we must now finalize these arrangements and I would venture Freddy that this be done with a solicitor friend of mine, I do believe you know of him, Gribble, yes? It would mean you would have to journey back to Cleveton with me, but I do find an honest man of the legal profession scarce to say the least and I have had many favourable dealings with the man. Would tomorrow suit? I can call on you at, say, ten, and have you home in time for evensong! Business finished.'

He paused as if to go on but really he savoured every minute of my excruciating situation. I had never wished to journey that way again and did not relish the thought of the company either.

'I am sure that a ride into Cleveton with your good self, Joseph, as companion would be most welcome.'

'Champion, perhaps we shall chance by the Toothills, Freddy? I know you are particularly fond of them and I have heard Angelica is looking extremely well just lately. We shall have much to talk of, perhaps more so myself as I can guess or have gleaned that which has occupied you, all quite predictable, and I have no wish to hear it again.'

'Very well gentlemen, I do believe our business is concluded for the night, I would offer you more refreshment, Sir, I know not where you lodge but surely something warming is advisable on such a night?'

Phillip quickly dispensed with the cringing scene and my embarrassment was averted.

'I thank you of course, but I must refuse. My palate, being

as it is, is used to more sophisticated potions and is confused by yours. I know not whether to like it or detest it. And surely a good spirit should not set such conundrums. I would rather my senses dulled than enlivened.'

'Very well, perhaps, Sir, our differences are more pertinent than mere spirit,' Phillip responded with more intellect than I had credited him with.

'As you wish, though was just a comment upon your beverage of choice, hah! I do believe Frederick that your condition is contagious. And now gentlemen I shall take your leave. Until the morrow.'

And he was gone again, but with no relief for me, I had not this for many months since first encountering him.

'He is strange, Frederick, I cannot help but wonder if he has another side? I knew not if he made light with you or tormented, you shall have to enlighten me for I say I cannot fathom it. But then he seemed genuine about the girl, so that is something to be had.'

'Philanthropic, he likes the term.'

'Yes, well I have no argument there, perhaps a little too attentive? I tell you I was almost embarrassed at one point but then I am a coward for not laughing! Am I not? I now see where you might find him intimidating, I swear that he could walk around naked and people would still say he was dandy! Hah! But instinctively I would not cross him.'

'You do not surprise me, Phillip, I do not even in thought and I cannot laugh at it.'

'No indeed, old friend, I believe this day has been tiring for you, I myself have some paperwork to attend to and I would suggest you retire early, you look almost grey.'

'Thank you, Phillip, I believe I shall.'

And with that he left me to find his spirit not so poorly equipped, and had several tots before returning to my bed chamber.

A rap at the door and the promise of relief in the form of Beth.

'Dear darling Beth, come in, come in goodness you look warn out, girl! Sit, sit.'

She curtseyed averting her eyes though I saw them skip fleetingly to the bed.

'I would rather not, Sir, I would dirty your chair and 'tis not my place.'

'If I say so girl, it is, I seem to remember this morn you saying it was not your place to question my reason, yes? Come Beth.'

I took her hand.

'I have something for you.'

I picked up a dress of Sophia's that I had acquisitioned earlier and had laid out on my bed.

'Here, this is much prettier, and will become you well. Come let me help you.'

'Oh no, Sir, I couldn't, was my lady's dress, Sir.'

'Beth, Beth.' I held her too me. 'So attentive even to your dead mistress, it is quite moving.'

She pushed me away.

'I would like to go now, Sir, please.'

She made for the door but I barred her escape with my hand.

'Beth, dear girl, tell me for I am sure I am losing my reason, have I dismissed you? I am quite sure I have not, so no, Beth, you shall not go. You will stay and wear the dress, for it pleases me.'

I went to unfasten her gown and she gasped and pushed me again.

'Twice girl, twice you defy me, no, Beth, I cannot have it!'

I lashed out and knocked her to the floor, she sobbed, and held her face as I kneeled beside her.

'What have you made me do Beth?' I laughed then held her too me. 'If you did not wish for this then why did you come here tonight?'

'You told me to, Sir. And for fear of losing my position, I would be homeless, and my family would starve, Sir! I have three sisters, you see, and one of them crippled, as for my father he is a good for nothing save looking at himself in the bottom of a tankard! Please, Sir, have pity, I will do anything but that. I did so hope to marry, and none would have me if I did not have my virtue. I am not so fair to be forgiven the loss of it.'

'I have not spoken of it, have I? Again you put words into my mouth! But a warning, young Beth, keep your flirtations in check! I talk of this morning girl, then on the stairs your eyes betrayed you. Yes, I am sorry Beth to discover you, but it was you who wanted this and are now you are too feared that you might lose everything. I am a man after all, girl.'

'I am so very sorry, Sir, and I thank you for your wise words. I shall be mindful for what you have spied in me this day, and would beg my leave, Sir, if it pleases you.'

'Oh no need to beg Beth, you are not half-bad in the twilight but quite odd to look at really, be gone then.'

She slipped away uttering apologies and gratitude under her breath. I leaned against the door finding the whole affair rather amusing, not at all fearful of repercussion.

'Oh I could not, Sir, was my lady's dress!'

Hah! Good God had I lost my mind! Girls such as Beth had proven to me, historically, to be the perfect antidote for a dismal day though I had never felt murderous intent before now. I would have killed her, what had stopped me? Faint hope, but then that was Joseph's genius; a prison can only be so if the exit is beyond you and you have but hope. And what of Phillip's words? Did he collude with him? No, no it was all too rich! Eulogizing on the merit of it!

Paranoia was incredibly preoccupying, almost addictive, for me anyway; I missed it perversely when it was absent. I never knew that the human mind could think so diversely. There were so many facets and more discovered daily. As for the girl, Beth, she would not fuel my state and I felt a little of Joseph's power, it was magical, knowing that she would sooner take a dozen beatings than ever breathe a word about what had transpired.

Aided by the drink I had absorbed, and gratification knowing that poor Beth would have no rest, I slept a deep dark sleep only waking with the sun, though it rose later at this time of year and it had to be seven. I would have to rush to be ready for Joseph, composure itself for such an event took all of two hours fifty nine minutes and even then I would be late and ill-prepared. At nine I ventured to breakfast, appetite eluded me, and the thought of small talk made me aggressive. I eyed Phillip as he began to speak of the papers and it quietened him, saying that they were full of nonsense and that a man could do better by consulting a psychic, their predictions and assumptions, he said, were about as credible! This unfortunately irritated me more, considering that I had met with one the day before, and perhaps it was my, too loud, announcement that he was an arse that had him rush his breakfast and leave me to my nightmares.

Chapter 23

All too soon came the announcement that he had arrived and I rushed to the door almost falling into him, ill-prepared as I had thought, even the man's shadow impinged.

'Hah, damned greedy of you to monopolize that view of my boots, Frederick! Up with you then unless you wish to shine them?'

'Joseph, hello there, rather clumsy of me yes, I do apologize.'

'Oh no need. It would be tiresome if you apologized every time you admired my boots! I have with me horses though I see Phillip has generously furnished you with a rather handsome one, honestly Frederick, I believe you would be more comfortable on my bay. He is less conspicuous and after all we are to Cleveton and even beyond perhaps? Just for the night. It is a possibility. We may get waylaid.'

'Waylaid? Joseph, at the inn?'

'Why yes, unless you have a solid objection.'

'No, no, of course not, I only think of Mary and that she might object, or worse think more of my visit than intended. I would sooner sleep in a barn than cause her to hope.'

Ha, ha. Good God man, I see you have become careless as well as pompous! Your haughty attitude and vanity will do nothing for your safety where we journey to. I do not talk of myself, for 'tis my boots that you aspire to and are guided by, I talk of others, Frederick, men that consider themselves your equal, indeed some would be presumed superior if wit and talent were to be judged. I declare if they knew how you thought! And as for Mary, she does not long for you, man. Did she ever? No she anticipates my return with favourable news of a fortune that is to be hers. Poor girl would be more than happy with a few guineas, but I shall not keep her short. You look puzzled at this, Frederick? No let me guess, you thought that I would hand over considerable monies without a care. Mary could not manage a fortune, no, it would take her places she was not welcome and would for sure end in tragedy.'

'Yes I see, I am sorry if I looked as though I would question your motive, original thoughts do not favour me so well these days. I would rather that I had none. You shall be her trustee in this then, Joseph?'

'Yes, for a moderate sum, 'tis why the arrangement shall be perhaps a little more ambitious than one would think for such an affair, I have to consider myself. You do get there, Freddy, but with just a little encouragement.'

'Thank you, Joseph, but it has just occurred to me that Emmeline, my betrothed, should be alerted by my absence if I do not call upon her at least once today. I would request a slight detour, so as I might give her some explanation.'

'And what would you say in the company of the infamous Joseph Black? I am sure she would be quite taken back at the sight of the two of us on a morning's excursion and so predisposed to chit-chat. No, Frederick, after all there really is no need, I have sent word this very morning that you have been taken from town suddenly on business and that she should expect your return imminently, or as soon as is permitted.'

'Joseph!' I almost shouted. 'Oh God, man, save me. Who has delivered this message? Please stop, Sir, I cannot ride further.'

'A messenger has delivered it, you fool! I would sooner speculate a penny on one than jeopardize a very healthy commission with something les considered. It is all in hand, she suspects nothing.'

'Oh, thank you! Thank you for that, Joseph, I might have guessed, nay should have known that you think too elegantly to allow for mishap.'

'Why bother thanking me, was it not for your peace of mind?'

Even still I was enormously relieved, and was strangely thrilled by the violent shaking it was almost enjoyable I thought, enlivening. I began to wonder, do I seek this? Am I deliberately naive? No, I was not mad yet, but then my companion may have a different perspective and, painfully to me perhaps, more insight.

'I see by your demeanour that you thought never to travel this way again. Rather dour, as though never to return to Bath. Did you think you might not want to?' he said as we exited and picked up the road to Cleveton.

'What? No Joseph, I already grieve the place, I have a life there and I believe I can be happy but I am also aware that I am indebted to you. This I truly have never forgotten.'

'I do not doubt it, but to return to what I was saying, sometimes circumstance can take you from places, from the familiar. All the while you are gone you long for what was and care not for the present, in fact it can pass you by. In some cases, I have heard that people have lost fifty years of their lives to just such an evil, the human psyche, I have heard it described as such. I have often pondered it but never been able to deduce anything from these thoughts and conclude that it is unnecessary and a form of mental discomfort.

I wondered, perhaps I am a little vain, but that you might have thought of the inn at all? And all that went with it. Perhaps in times of stress? When a man looks to be free of the shackles of an honest existence, if only for a second? All I require is a wish no matter how fleeting, after all a man can be forced to rely upon something, manipulation is perverse but will suffice, but to have him long for it, now there is the genius and nothing can be more pure. I mean to draw a parody for you, Frederick, in that previously Bath was as much of an anachronism to you as was the inn but still you managed as much devilment in either. You are sure it is not you rather than geography?'

'But Joseph, I never meant to stay at the inn.'

'No, but neither did you think to ever return to Bath! And now here we are, Frederick, on a journey that was in no way imperative, if you believed you had no option but to return then you are a greater simpleton than I already credited you. We both know 'tis not all as it should be, and I would have been receptive to offers. You talk of a debt to me, whilst this is true 'tis not purely financial. Dear friend, how I choose to extract what is mine is as pleasurable in any form, and the more you hide in dark places, Frederick, the brighter you shine! You might wonder why a jeweller will often display his finery on a black back drop.'

I could not help but enjoy the analogy, and as we journeyed I played his words over and over again often missing what he was saying; if this annoyed him he did not show it, in fact he seemed almost amused by it.

Being allowed to indulge my mental state was something that I had missed, and it grew wildly within me. The rare times, of late, that I had managed private thought noted that this state kept me warm in the harshest northerly and had me miss the rain though it beat on my head and soaked me through. You would think that those who purported to care for me would allow me my own mind! A rage came over me and I saw that Joseph studied it.

'As I say, Frederick, you do get there but with a little coercion.'

And I was grateful, relieved, for where I knew not my own mind there was somebody who did utterly. And though, at times, it caused me pain I still felt less weary, and was not aware that I was so afflicted with exhaustion until I began to travel this road again.

Chapter 24

After a journey that was in a small way epic, there was Cleveton. I had never seen it from this angle, and remarked on this to Joseph who replied succinctly,

'We were on the Bath road, and as such Cleveton shows her best side. Flashes her eyes, and hoists her skirts as any self-respecting whore does.'

And he continued, that the road I had frequented, though it came from the sea was in no way a significant port to either travellers or smugglers.

'A drink first, I think, Freddy! Yes, the hour is late but Gribble will wait on my thirst.'

'Well said man, I am quite parched!'

'Perhaps, though not through inane chit-chat as I, ay? I noted sincerity about you for most part of the journey, more than you thought, I venture, to digest?'

We stopped outside The Kings Head and whether from the thought of relief from such a thirst and a hard saddle, or something seated deeper, I was heartened to see the place and said as much.

'But surely!' he remarked. 'You have not missed our Eileen? Hah!'

'Perhaps a little, perhaps her comedy?'

'Yes, but oh if she knew it! I say she would scrape a healthier living from it than she does with her more biblical choice.'

Sharing laughter, or if I so dared, good times with Joseph were rare.

'And all the more enjoyed for it!'

He interrupted my thoughts.

'A lucky guess Fred, you marvel at us enjoying a time together, perhaps you would not find it so astonishing, and more frequent, if you did not struggle so much. A tired man is more honest by default than one who has had a good six hours!'

'And I might add to this, Joseph, I feel somewhat liberated.'

'There man, that was not grovelling, was it? No, was truth. I know enough of you to know you would kill a man, or woman if needs. You would steal a purse to feed yourself and you would rather bed a pox-riddled maid than pay for a well-oiled whore – the word, economic, springs to mind. You are perhaps more independent of me than you may have thought, and I think you manage well if somewhat lacking in finesse. Still, 'tis not such an accolade and purely on the surface, and is there but to be admired, vanity, ay Freddy!'

I was too tired and thirsty to comment and as his words were always scholarly no fit response became me, but I felt I must have looked grateful if not for the seat for the refreshment; although not a word did we share till the time came to leave and the night fell about us, as did a ferocious chill.

Ushered into the dark foreboding establishment that looked like it shamed the street and cowered from scrutiny – Gribbles. I knew not who greeted me, as both father and son both wore cobwebs and dust enough and their attire blended perfectly with the dark rotting beams and prevalent mould.

'Gribble,' Joseph began. 'This is our Mr Frederick Abbotsby Feltsham.'

'Honoured I am sure, Sir, please to both take seats.'

'He is like a toad,' I whispered to Joseph.

'Yes, but he is more secure in this than you are as a rich man at this moment.'

I am sure he had masterminded my elevation to companion purely to enjoy such a moment. Still perhaps I was too sensitive and though it shook me I smiled.

'Mr Black, as you requested of Gribble, the contract is as you designed and I shall not take up more of your time. All that is required is for the gentleman to mark.'

'It is done!?'

'Why yes, Frederick, a little pre-emptive, do you object?'

'No, no, Joseph, but am I allowed to see it before I sign?'

'Of course. Gribble would you mind?'

He groaned and shuffled to the cabinet at the far side of the room, a more generous description for sure had never been given for the place was barely a foot from him! He stooped and struggled back to the table, the other Gribble penned in by the three of us and the desk disappeared into a cupboard, which Joseph saw fit to close with his foot and was duly thanked by the incarcerated.

'Good God!' I remarked as the man produced the documents. 'Why so much? Surely this is excessive?'

'How so, Sir? Are you accustomed to such matters? You seem to think this an extravagant amount.'

'No, of course not, Joseph, you know this to be untrue.'

'Poor Gribble looks quite alerted! Do not worry yourself man, as you said 'tis how I designed it. Your ink?'

He handed me the quill and waited.

'The amount, am I to know of it?'

'Of course, Freddy, though it shall vary so as not to appear suspicious. Tiring details man! All is in hand, your mark please.'

And what did I care of the amount? He would undo a handsome arrangement by appearing too greedy, but if I could have spared a month, for it would have taken all of it, I would have liked to study the contract, however, I signed with confidence and was resigned to whatever lay within its bounds; strangely enough even if it had contained my own death warrant I would not have crossed the man to refuse him it.

'Grand, grand, now let us be gone, you cast a depressing shadow over everything Gribble, what do you save for, man?'

'Thank you, Mr Black, always a pleasure, your condescension cheers me so, Sir. To think that you might take an interest in old Gribble, Sir.'

'Oh do not bother yourself!' Joseph said as Gribble showed us to the door. 'I am desperate for clean air and would rather expedite it!'

'As you wish Sir, Mr Black,' he said and slumped in a chair most appreciatively as we left.

'Now then, Freddy, I do believe the inn is the sensible option, 'tis too late to even think of a journey to Bath and I am sure you are just a little curious?'

'Of course, I would not attempt it, 'tis lunacy, and you are right both times, a little scared but curious indeed. I believe I own the right.'

'Very well, then let us hasten, I feel a good pie and a warm welcome imminent at least for myself! Hah! I enjoy myself endlessly with you, Frederick, you are like a fruit that ripens perpetually and am shocked to discover that I have missed you!'

We set off, a small distance, and if I anticipated, or dreaded what came next I could not deduce, but had not felt this much in so many months.

Chapter 25

All was as though time had not yet passed at The Hangman's Hitch, all except for a girl nursing a baby and a prettier picture I had never seen. Artless and unaware, Mary sat with child; I had no wish to call it mine and was under no spell but still I delighted in the scene.

'Freddy!' she screamed. 'Dear Freddy!' Then she blushed. 'I forget myself for surely you do not wish to see me? Considering the young one here. I had no wish to bring shame upon you, Freddy, I have not the wit to do so.'

'Mary, I am more embarrassed than angry.'

I knew not what more to say and desperately searched for fitting words.

'It is just that when Joseph took me to see your fine set up, it made me think that maybe our child could own a little of life's fortune too. Oh do not worry though, the people were kindness itself and did not wonder at me with a baby. I remember the cook's maid with particular fondness, Freddy, we all did have such a time, did we not boys!?'

She laughed with Badger and a few others, who had joined the spectacle that I felt I was becoming,

'I see. I believed as much as I thought I saw you, your hair is quite unmistakeable, Mary, I do hope it was not deliberately embarrassing.'

'Oh, don't you scold me, Freddy! I was about a bit of teasing and have done no harm!'

'I am sure Mary, but even still it made me uncomfortable and I would not have thought you so thoughtless.'

'Touching, is it not?' Joseph remarked. 'I am quite sure that there is the real romance, but with no fortune, Mary, Freddy can only see the inconvenience. Poor man, he is lost.'

'Joseph, you promised me, none of this.'

'Oh, pish, Frederick, none of what? She is under no illusion, my words hold no promise for her, ay girl? She is as sensible as she is ugly!'

Mary's smile went briefly from her face, to return falsely; I felt her pain, which was remarkable as I believed myself only capable of feeling my own.

'Go and see him then, Freddy, see if you can conjure a likeness! God knows we all have! 'Tis almost a party game, even old Joshua drifts a little when he looks upon him.'

'Not Elijah though, ay Joseph!' she shouted as Elijah entered the inn.

'Not that one, not never.'

I sat beside Mary and looked into her arms at the child.

'He is fine, Mary, strong, and with your hair!'

'I see that, yes, Master Freddy. Though the rest is you, as we all believe, and I have named him as such, I hope you do not mind?'

'I do not, but cannot see myself in him Mary. Yes, I shall furnish you with your fortune but not with a salve for your conscience. I despair at it, but there is no point traversing it, 'tis all sown up, and in hand.'

'Very well, Freddy, but I would rather be called a simpleton than a liar! And I do so hope you do me the courtesy. I only wondered, Freddy, that you may want to know him? Joseph thinks it would be burdensome to you and I would not wish that. I do so promise, Freddy, if it takes that expression from your face, that I have no plans to look to your father for anything, especially since things are so bad between you.'

Badger blushed as Mary swooned.

'I cannot see why you would visit with my father either, Mary, or indeed why you would mention him as though part of some conspiracy!'

'No, no, Master Frederick, I am just nervous on account of seeing you! I had no idea you came this way, such a treat for Mary, ay Joseph?'

'Aye, you will be spoiling her!' said Joshua. 'Go on then girl, baby needs something, doesn't he?'

She was not so stupid, and quickly made her escape keeping her gaze from me.

'Honestly gentlemen! If you think to visit with my father, then I wish you all the luck! He is a vile man, and for me has done all the damage he can do! But for Mary and the little one, he is cruel and unscrupulous, and would derive much pleasure in their pain.'

'Astonishing is it not, gentlemen? May I present the much lovelorn Freddy, I believe you will find a most unsuspecting if not disbelieving audience, Frederick, though for my part I feel you sustain my suspicions. I am a vain man, am I not! Hah! Yes I laugh but, honestly, I find I have much to adore about myself as do others. Do not hurry then to uphold this statement! I might say of the others that their literacy and understanding restricts them, but you?'

'I would say of you, Joseph, and forgive my tardiness in replying, that you command great admiration from myself. Though I am mindful you might find such insignificant, and only in your condescension acknowledge it. So I rarely speak of it, and have found before that it irritates you.'

'Yes, yes man! Frederick, you were not blessed with much, but at least where humour is absent there is bountiful misunderstanding! It really is quite funny, I feel as though I would never tire of it!'

I had to laugh, and in small part agree, though what had brought this fine mood he courted with myself, in particular, was somewhat worrying. I contemplated it as discretely as possible with such a man until after barely a minute I could stand the thought or his gaze no longer and gave it up for lost.

'Aye, aye Joseph, I have a mind to agree with you about our Freddy. You seem very keen to protect our Mary where none is needed.'

'A good observation, you must agree, Fred. If even, please excuse the term, Joshua, a dullard can spot your attentiveness then can we both be wrong?'

'Can we all, Joseph? A man would have to be both blind and deaf.'

Badger roused the small crowd, and I began to wonder if I was being lead or just being discovered, both equally terrifying, both with consequences, and all would lead to me being further embroiled in this situation; there was the oddity. I did not fear it, more anticipated it, I had no thought of Emmeline or Bath other than to see it as incumbent on whatever might be.

Badger spoke again, and the profuse amounts of whatever he drank did nothing to improve his humour.

'Greed. I sees greed in you, Frederick! I would not have thought you would have the bollocks to be so blatant, but there you are and have either gone mad with it, or spoiling for something, ay?'

'Poor Frederick. Come, man, you may sit with me. Oh and Badger, greedy? I should say so, for 'tis his money that she and the piglet will grow fat on, I believe he owns the right.'

'Thank you, Joseph, for speaking up for me, but I beg you not make me out so callous. Poor Mary must think very little of herself today.'

'Nonsense, here girl. Explain to Freddy that you are nought but a scheming minx and conspired with the Devil to fall pregnant and say it begot by our Freddy!'

She sat beside me.

'Well Joseph! Can you not hold your tongue? Did we not swear that Frederick should not know of it!?'

Only Mary could get away with such addresses to the man, it was her boldness, and that every word she said of him was always meant to flatter.

'What then, Frederick? Libertine? Well if you are then you are for sure the meekest one I ever heard of, poor lamb. Do you think then that I am not swayed by your money? When I look at that baby, young Freddy, I see a child who will not have much luck as his father did not. I wonder that a little money might make that easier to take, after all Frederick you did not want, and you owe him a fortune as you blessed him with yours.'

'Oh well put, Mary! I would call it poetic but I do believe you have overheard me talking so, yes girl? I do not mind, you know that. Only that I am recently laughing at my vanity with Frederick and do not want to render him senseless with more humour!'

'Yes, I owe you a lot Joseph and I thank you for that. Forgive me if I coveted your words, I shall not do so again.'

'Oh, I am sure you will, Mary, I am sure I should feel pride but, no, I find it irritating. It is habitual.'

Mary of all would not expect me, or even, I hoped she would understand that in such a situation a different man who felt something would make an effort to defend her. I remained silent, and cursed it for it no longer satisfied me to do so, but challenging the man was yet too terrifying to consider, though I would enjoy the thought even under his watch.

'I am sure I can guess your thoughts, Frederick, do my blushes give it away?'

'I do not follow, Sir? Have I missed something?'

'Oh, I am sure you do, and, no, you have not missed anything. I would not have thought you brave enough to talk to me as if I was a fool, Freddy! 'Tis you who is the fool, man, and you do not need to say it for me to know you wish to defend our Mary. It is written on your face and your pathetic eulogies earlier are a complete giveaway. How your own father was not fit to receive such a girl – I could go on, could I not? You shock me, I had rather hoped your motive more selfish, or born of fear of reprisal when you return to Bath, which you must, I need not remind you I am sure. That you find this all rather cosy is quite obvious, and that where I may have jested that you were indeed feeling inclined towards the girl could not have been more perfect.'

'Please forgive me, Mary. But, Joseph, you are misguided in this and I beg your forgiveness that you thought I insulted you, surely you are aware that I would not, nay could not?'

Mary, shockingly, and rather irritatingly, was finding it all quite amusing. Could she not see I was struggling? I had thought she had cared something for me, had I been so mistaken?

'Hah! I told you so, did I not, girl? Frederick, I must commend your punctuality. You see we had a wager, and I must say that I forever excel at sport! He still looks confused, girl! Ha, ha, allow me to bring relief, Freddy, please. Mary here would not have it that you would so defend her, and said that no amount of spirit or feigned camaraderie on my part would chase you out that hole. But I said that you were in such a fragile state, and that men who are despairing can do quite insane things! I must thank you for proving my theories right again! You have great aptitude there. What say you to our little prank, Frederick? Is it not the most amusing thing you have ever heard? And your reactions, so studied with impeccable delivery, hmm? What say you, man? I have quite recovered from the insult, for we together have made the fool of you! Yes?'

If I spoke now then I would have no time to dwell on the excruciating ordeal I had just been subjected to, so speak, I thought. Why I would be rendered so confused at a very normal assault from Joseph made little sense, until I looked to Mary and found her smiling, willing me to find humour in it and was plain she had meant me no injury. The revelation being that I had not thought her opinion so important to me until I believed it low.

'Excellent, such acting, such talent Mary, though I should not have doubted it!'

'And myself, Frederick, what say you to my talent? Did I not draw you in? All day I conspired to do as much, and knew that Mary would be most willing. I am sure she had longed for your laughter but I treasured the shock upon your face! I cannot, simply cannot erase it. You are most rewarding, Frederick, never disappointing, such entertainment is scarce!'

'The only thing lacking, surely, Joseph, is a full glass. Mary could I bother you to bring us some more wine, you look as though you need an occupation.'

She blushed heavily, unaware that I only meant to see her laugh again.

'Of course, Frederick, what was I thinking? I shall fetch some straight away.'

'Hah! You see 'tis not only I who can be so entertaining! Blushes suit you though, girl.'

'Aye well, I had that coming, Frederick. I will say though that you can fetch your own bloody wine tonight if you need some!'

'What sort of serving wench is this? Ay gentlemen! She flatly refuses to serve me, and will not indulge my fantasies of an obliging miss with no wit nor plot! I know not whether to enjoy it more or take her in hand!'

'Go on then, Frederick, I dare you! There's not a man here who would wager on you.'

'I know what "I" would wager on Mary!' Badger hollered. 'That pie being spoiled! Or will we have to see to it ourselves as well?'

She poked out her tongue to Badger and lifted her skirts in defiance to which Joseph began to cough.

'How lovely this is, incredibly embarrassing, but lovely. Be a dear now, Mary, and get along, I am beginning to feel nauseous and 'tis not wholly your smell. I must make a note that today I discovered that a man who is falling in love is not only blinded by it, his sense of smell is impaired! What else shall follow? I do not know, though I beg you do not feel the need to educate me.'

She curtseyed flamboyantly and left me thinking that I had not enjoyed something, such as Mary, ever before and that I had not been privileged enough, in life, until this very moment to experience such bon viveur. Yes, of course I had said I had, and convinced myself of it, but therein was the lie and she only highlighted the fact. Still I did not curse her for laying waste to memories that had oft time entertained me, it did not seem to matter, for if this was the only time I would ever truly experience such a thing then it would suffice to see me through to my grave and even beyond.

'Ten minutes! I have timed you, 'tis a long time to think of someone, Frederick? Especially one who you intend to leave, you do intend to leave, do you not?'

'But of course, Joseph, and if I did not I am sure you would take much convincing to allow me to stay.'

'Not much actually, but I have no appetite for speculation tonight, more for rabbit and wine. Do you eat, Frederick? I note the hour 'tis handsomely late and you might consider that you have much travelling to do tomorrow.'

'Oh no I would much rather eat, Joseph, I am quite starved! And would join you if you would allow me?'

'In such a small place, Frederick, the appearance is that most do join me without any encouragement! So if you do not wish to eat outside with the dogs and horses then do not bother yourself to move, it would make no difference!'

We ate together, drank together, though not a word passed between us and eventually I found company in the others who had consumed enough drink between them to forgive me for what they saw in me as greed. Mary's company was most sort after, and I barely had chance to speak with her but found gratification in the kiss she gave me as I retired. I never found sleep so readily, or indeed so heavenly, as I did that night. I remember my last thoughts being that surely not all treasure was so obvious, encrusted with jewels, or heavy with precious metals, some needed more careful detection but where equally as breathtaking.

Chapter 26

'Up with you then, Frederick, must push on! I will allow you to take the bay as far as Cleveton but then you shall have to pick up the coach. If you hurry you will catch the midday.'

'Pray, Joseph, what time is it? I had hoped to enjoy some breakfast at the very least.'

'I swear I have never known such optimism! You must allow that the fare here is not up to much, the breakfast alone can lay a man low for at least half the day! No man, come, come all is settled here and I am sure in truth you are more eager to return to Bath than you credit.'

'Pardon me, Joseph, but I am not ready. I had wished to spend a little more time with yourself without question, and Joshua, most certainly Joshua. There are things about the place that I have missed, you said as much as we journeyed here, and have revealed this to me.'

'Gracious Frederick, you sound quite desperate, and what of Mary? It is deafening what you omit to say on her account. A fancy Freddy, 'tis all that is, though I do not personally find it a captivating one I do understand that for you it is. Poor Frederick, you look quite crestfallen, I really should not allow it and you shall have many such fancies when you return home, ay man? I would wager much prettier ones also than Mary, and whose toilet is more a daily essential than a yearly celebration of all that's been relished and passed as Mary's is. Please pardon my crudeness but I am all amazement at you!'

He gestured impatiently for me to rise.

'Joseph, please, I would willingly add to my debt if you will allow me this day to indulge this state, even if it be but a whim. Surely I do no harm? And I feel I must or it shall set me alight.'

'Save your poetry for Mary, Frederick. If someone were to pass by the window they might think you made love to me! But I am not a cruel man, upon reflection some good may come of it, so yes, you may stay, and for as long as you wish or until your luck runs out. Practise your love making on the girl, man, but for Heaven's sake do not make me privy to it. Perhaps if she were handsome I would not mind, nay, I might find it entertaining, but she is not, and I feel but embarrassment in her wake.'

'Thank you, Joseph! I would contain this elation if I felt it mattered but I care not who knows it. I care not for anything but this very day I awaken too and in that, hope salvation be mine for only good can come from such purity. I have nothing to gain by it.'

'I might disagree for evil can only be but pure and offers no salvation if 'tis the divine type you seek? Salvation in itself, Frederick, is not a holy word. I would willingly save any from the righteous, as I felt I did you, though to this date receive no thanks for the deed. However, the lack of grovelling aside, I believe you think of me most days and 'tis enough. Now get to it, man, before she runs off with another handsome libertine! Mark my wit there, Freddy, I do not wish to alarm you! However, we do have a binding contractual agreement to consider and though I have no wish to impinge upon your euphoric state I feel I must! Indeed, you have described your wish to remain here an indulgence and I may be being too particular, I am habitually, so therefore conclude that my concerns are unfounded. After all, forgive me but I have made myself laugh again, surely this does not measure? Mary and a baby begotten by moonlight, are there not many such nights that have been enjoyed? Though I feel this morning that you would have it that there had been but one! And ventures into who knows what to put food on the table. Frederick, you cannot seriously compare yourself to Badger or Josh, they have known no different, or do you wish to emulate Elijah? Hah! I am still laughing that you consider it as an alternative. I really am incredibly comical today! And even though you look quite crestfallen I am sure you agree. Poor Frederick, I can see, and am quite sure I have cast shadow enough, they are simply things to think on, man, and I had thought they would have amused you.'

'Thank you, Joseph, for if I was a little confused as I woke I find I am not now.'

'And will be, or can you elaborate?'

'I cannot at this time, forgive me, Joseph, but I have much to think on.'

'Then enjoy it, Frederick, your time here with any you wish, excluding myself. I shall not be put upon by a whimpering wreck, and I find you lately most attentive to me, 'tis nauseating in truth, quite nauseating. I find it incredulous that I am about to say what I am about to say for it will only add to the revulsion I am feeling, but remember it is not so serious nor so final when the time comes to leave, I had not planned to liberate you so readily.'

'Hah! Yes, I thank you for your clarity and wisdom, Joseph, tell me do you breakfast?'

'No Frederick, do you jest? I have many a time observed you, however, partake of it and though I felt the urge to inform you of certain facts did not, as you always seemed to, relish it so. Perhaps Mary's charms were to blame and thank heavens I am not as deluded as yourself! For you see she enjoys thrift and will, without prejudice, return to the pot which has been gnawed upon or, in more likely case, spat out. So if now you do not feel as if you could enjoy her efforts this morning, there are some berry bushes and some fallen fruit that probably have been pissed on, but still they hold more attraction!'

'Oh dear. If I cannot convince her that it is Lent and I must fast, then I am lost! Ha, ha, I believe I am a few months out!'

'Yes, and she is most particular about tradition, I envy you none of it but if you have the stomach for the girl then I cannot see how you would struggle at her breakfast. No, more so think of it as a feast. People's peculiarities are most entertaining, even yours hold some fascination, but still I must away as I have business elsewhere. Do not feign disappointment at it, Frederick, you know in truth I would enjoy too much the spectacle.'

With that he left me to my speculation, which I revelled in and thought if the promise of Mary was half as fulfilling as what I had imagined I would indeed be a happy man, and blessed my misfortune for I truly felt it be fortune in disguise.

As I ventured downstairs, I noted a distinct lack of care for anything beyond this place, and as for Joseph he would answer this conundrum for me, and it was the first time I did not dread his manipulation. I had found solace in the oddest of thoughts, that my debt to him might well be extracted in a more personal manner, but did he know this too well? I knew that he did and knew, also, that what mattered to me now was right here; he would find no purchase in Bath.

Chapter 27

'Good morning, gentlemen! I hope to find the atmosphere less feudal today, I am sure you are all quite subdued after last eve's admirable efforts to relieve the place of all its liquor!'

Joshua looked up, pale with blackened eyes; he had obviously consumed enough of the poison long before he had finished.

'Aye, morning to you, Frederick, and rest easy for there is none of us that can even raise a thought let alone a fist this day. I would ask if you be off, even though we have been informed of your plans, but I have not the will nor stomach to antagonize you at present. I find if I maintain this position I can look enough alive so as I am spared the grave, and if I looked like I cared as you entered I am glad to say it is working. You will find Mary, for 'tis who you seek, outside collecting fruits, 'for a special breakfast for my Freddy', so she says. And you can thank Joseph for it, he gave her the idea, spared you the slops. Unusually charitable of him, do you not think? I would laugh, Frederick, but, as I say, am not inclined this morning.'

'Thank you, Joshua, I shan't pretend that I wish to stay but I do wish you better and take courage in that it is a temporary state, I at least can offer charity in my prognosis. Hah!'

'Take as many liberties with your fancy words as you wish, Frederick. At least what we suffer is curable and is a "temporary" poison.'

'Aye man, but I do not wish mine any different.'

I ventured into what could not have been a more perfect morning and to see Mary gathering the infamous fruits.

'Freddy, you have spoiled my surprise so you have! I wished to have these ready for you as you woke this morning, I had not dreamed you be about so bright and early.'

'Please accept my heartfelt apologies then, Mary, I would not have knowingly denied you this pleasure.'

'No, I do not feel denied for we can sit here and eat together? I expect you are not so used to such manners, they are thick I know but why would I pretend differently, ay Freddy?'

'I would not enjoy your company more, Mary, in truth I would not be here, for 'tis all that you are that wakes me so early and makes me forget that which I deemed so important.'

She blushed upon hearing my affection, and I immediately wanted to speak more to her.

'Now then, Freddy, we are both red-faced! You because perhaps you didn't mean to say that, and me because I was glad to hear it! Sit you down next to me, Freddy, and eat something. I would hush that tongue of yours a while, yet until you know what you are saying. 'Tis a might early for such treats for me and I am careful on your behalf, the day is so bewitching and you must admit these fruits are very fine to look upon, so quiet now, and eat.'

My response to this could not have been more honest or comical; I had no wish to eat fruits that smelled of the piss pot, but then I could not have been tempted with anything else. Yes, I had an enormous appetite, it had woken me this early, but it was for this girl and all the wonder she filled me with.

'Dear Mary, I would rather share a small moment with you than this bounty before us, I find your company sustains me more than any such delights.'

She threw an apple at me, which, I am sure not deliberately, hit me on my head and knocked me from my perch.

'Hah, hah, Lord I am sorry, Freddy, but you deserve it for your boldness! Have I yet given you permission to make love to me? Well no, I have not. Come then, Frederick, let us enjoy this morn I have a mind to think I never saw a prettier one.'

'I shall not complain then, dear Mary, but I ask only that we enjoy this time together and that you allow me to speak plain when the sun is higher and you can more readily receive my addresses.'

We sat for a while, and I allowed the morning sun its ascension. Every now and then she would turn and smile at me, and in return I gently held her hand. Surely this small act of tenderness spoke more than verse or rhyme could, especially for a girl such as Mary. Fine words and pretty phrases simply made her laugh, but still I found purpose in them, for was such a thing to see her laugh and I gladly would perpetrate it if she so wished.

'Who is that girl, Mary?' I enquired after a great ox of a girl, who walked by us, and seemed to curse the earth with her every gaze.

'Oh, she lives here or about, Freddy, and is a wudjie woo.'

'Wudjie woo, Mary? Another one of your words? Let me see if I can do better with this one. Wudjie woo, no I really cannot fathom, you shall have to tell.'

'What's to fathom Freddy? Wudjie woo, would ye woo.'

'Aha! Now I see, and would any woo, Mary?'

'Not likely I says, she has hard bones, and is sour as old cabbage!'

'Ha, ha, poor girl, damned for sure, but with such a pretty word! Do you know Mary you are quite the genius, I feel I could call a girl such a thing and she would believe I cherished her! Ha, ha, do you come upon these terms yourself, Mary?'

'Oh yes, Freddy, 'tis all me, I have my journal if you would ever care to look.'

'I am sure I would love to, dear girl. I mean it most sincerely.

Pike was right about you, Mary, though this place and people become more pleasing to me you do not belong here.'

'Hah! Freddy, if you are not more guarded I might have a mind to journey to Bath and tell that sweetheart of yours how you make free with me! And how would she take such news, ay Freddy?'

If it was a threat I would gladly receive more and daily. What a witch you are, I thought, and to become it so majestically.

'Mary, if I told you that all those castoffs you possess and silks and finery became you more than any lady who had decided to call herself one, would you believe me?'

'I am sorry, Freddy, but I cannot believe you mean it and I will listen to no more!'

'Mary!'

'Oh tush, Frederick, I do not scold, I tease you! And 'tis not that we grow more pleasing to you, 'tis that you do to us, we were always pleasing! And I cannot sit here with you while I have a rabbit to skin and gut and a little one to see to. Would you love me so much if you went hungry tonight, I wonder? Mark that Freddy, I said you loved me! Hah, hah, but I run to not hear your excuses.'

'Mary, I have none.'

'None, if you are sure then you will kiss me.'

I got up and walked to her where she stood by the trough.

'If you attended your toilet more diligently, I might promise much more. I laugh for I do not feel embarrassed in requesting it!'

'Toilet, Lord, Freddy that is not for me! Do you remember who you talk to? 'Tis I, Mary, I am not some fancy piece set up in Bath. You might get away with such liberties with such a one, but not with me. And so, no, if you will not kiss me as I am, then you shall have no kiss!'

'I see you leave me no option.' And I pushed her into the trough. 'Now then Mary, what smart comment have you to say to that!'

'Hah! It means nowt! Oh 'tis cold in here! I don't like washing, Freddy! But now I am started I might as well finish. Though mind that it is not for a bloody kiss! I would sooner kiss Elijah's arse at this moment!'

'Allow me to fetch him, I am sure he will be most eager. Dear Mary, you know I meant no harm in it, you are not too angry I hope?'

'Get you gone then! I cannot do this in front of you, can I? And mind none come out for a while! And no Freddy, I am not angry, you make me laugh so you do and I am glad to see this side of you. You are not so bad to look upon when you are not cowering, there is no need you must know that now? 'Tis what's inside the man wants, not your head, at least not a while. Trick is, Freddy, that you stay amusing, but if you cannot then you must run. Mind though that none truly leave here, none escape Joseph. I never dreamed that somebody would come along that would want me, even if it's just a fancy of yours, so I did not mind being set here.'

'And now, Mary, tell me in truth, will such an existence raise you in the morning and send you to sleep at night? Or have I brought about a curse on you who I know only too well, no peace Mary. I shudder to think that unwittingly I have promised you much more than I can deliver.'

'You make me question myself, Freddy. Do I like it? Well I am not sure to be honest, but will sleep, and tell you in the morning. For now though let us not speak on it further, I am not so quick witted to be able to keep it between us, and think them therein might string you up! Mind, not out of a sense of gallantry, I am not that foolish, I just believe they would enjoy it!'

'I believe you are right, unfortunately, so let us be private for now, Mary.'

As I walked towards the door I turned about to look at her again; had she beguiled me? But then that was deception and I did not feel her capable, at least not unaided, and still she would have no comprehension of what she did. I could be certain that her innocence remained, I had known of enough schemers, including myself, to know that, though guided, Mary was wholly natural, and with not the wit or genius to mastermind such drama. It was beyond belief, but then everything about this place was, and I began to wonder if I could ever leave or even, perhaps, if I wanted to, for sure I was in no hurry. For the love of a girl, who stole from the dead and kept company with devils, I was impatient. I wanted to hasten to a happier end, not furnish her with pennies to keep her from me. Surely then love is heavenly, I thought, and so offers at least some redemption for sinners, such as I.

Chapter 28

'Now what I ask you, puts such a smile upon a man's face, ay boys?'

Badger, as youth dictates, was eager for the confrontation.

'Calm yourself, boy,' said old Joshua, who had been acquisitioned to care for the infant in Mary's absence.

A most attentive host he was, and had made toys for the child, I would imagine from cat bones.

'There are many ageing cats about then, Josh? Just I seem to find you frequently in possession of their bones!'

'Not so much ageing, Freddy, but definitely in want of a purpose.'

Though he laughed, Badger was set on continuing with aggression.

'Come on then, Frederick, I asked you a question?'

'I do beg your pardon, Badger, but you made an announcement and directed it at all, so I wonder that you do not request another to quell your curiosity.'

'Sit you back down, boy!'

Joshua held his hand up as Badger rose with intention.

'She is not your kin and you have no stake in her!'

'I must question my reason, for I believed I came to sit amongst old friends but I find the atmosphere more acerbic.'

'How so, Frederick? I thought we spoke boldly and plain enough last evening.'

'Why yes you did, Badger, and perhaps to a stranger it might have seemed foreboding, but as we are more than familiar with each other, and have not yet quarrelled you will forgive me if I saw it as harmless baiting.'

'Now come on, Badger, his words have truth, and if you ask me you are in desperate need of a purpose! I have a mind to give you one, so take this baby, and be careful you keep him content! I have had a full morning of its yelling and have just managed to quieten him.'

He passed the infant, giving no room for a rebuff with nothing more than a wink. In the absence of Joseph, most looked to Joshua for approval, and any independents were lucky to be of no consequence. Rich men, be it in fortune, spirit, or soul were plundered regularly here, however, they were never so devastated so as they would not rise again and offer up more harvest.

'Badger,' I ventured. 'You look a deal awkward with the boy, might I have him?'

'Come on Badger, he has bought and paid for the rite, give him the baby.'

'Oh, you will hear no argument from me, Josh, I am no wet nurse, unlike some, ay boys?'

He looked to raise a laugh but managed little as his support began to tire of him.

'You see, Frederick, I remember being young like that, and though I am barely at thirty two, I bless the day I turned it. 'Tis my true age now and I swear it.'

'You swear it, do you, Josh?'

Badger laughed as did all.

'Yes, it is so dark in here 'tis difficult to differentiate between old and young! Why I even look upon this baby in my arms with quizzical fashion for I am sure he must be all of fifteen! And then surely it is settled that he is not mine!'

The comment was received so well that Badger fell into a seat laughing, and I was gladdened to think that in all that I had lost I had gained qualities that I would be loathed to part with; cynicism – some may question why but still I enjoyed it – recklessness, and a peculiar wit. And if I was glib about them, it was to not have them deemed less important for in secret they fascinated me, and ferried me from this plateau I found myself frequenting.

Chapter 29

'Having no wish to dissemble my thoughts or, indeed, there being a need, I take my seat at the fire for 'tis cold and no, Frederick, the scene does not sufficiently warm me.'

Joseph's shadow as he entered, seemed almost painful to those who hushed and cowered at it, that in itself is not so extraordinary, but still something was afoot.

'Joshua, please take the infant, and Freddy you might join me? I feel a debacle is imminent, and I must at least try to prevent it. As for the rest of you mutineers, I am shocked to see you so taken in by a man obviously struggling to comprehend the peculiarities his life offers up. I do not find the man difficult, and with shrewd assertion he can be most pleasing, but this is carefully, most part, guided by myself, and those who have taken instruction. I am disappointed to say the very least. Odd, that I should be, and perhaps I am not? 'Tis simply my plot gets away from me? Still it shall run, for the ends attract me, they really are uncommonly pretty.'

None looked up, and Joshua, apologetically, took the baby from me. I for one was not despairing, there was something in his tone or choice of phrase, nay inflection, that oddly cheered me. I could not imagine that I had played him, he was unassailable even to the divine, and enjoyed regular sorties into their realm. But perhaps my happiness was an oversight and something he could not, in all his plotting, escape, for as much as he twisted I seemed to do likewise and though I would not be his undoing, he might think of me as I did of him and there was some retribution in that.

I joined him eagerly, but would not speak unless required. I had learned enough of the man's vanity to know he could turn in a breath if you in any way detracted from his brilliance.

'Now, Frederick, you must allow me some conjecture for if what I assume be correct then 'tis not a rare man that would be bemused. If it were only society you sought, then a brave man might tell you to look elsewhere, though I do not call him brave more misguided. 'Tis a strange society here, but have no doubt is refined. I have personally undertook considerable efforts to make it so. A veritable banquet of bespoke attractions and, yes, of most part thieves and the like, but then I find this depends upon the digestion. To conclude, one might say 'tis the sort of society that is the richest and that all others are tempered in order to allow a lesser man appear sophisticated! What say you, Freddy? Do you find your appetite more satiated? Or are you green at the gills and desperate for more of your insipid repast? I believe I have the answer. You have a mind to remain here for at least as long as you create an impossible future for yourself and Mary, to become united, yet 'tis not so simple. Do you forget that you are for most part indebted to me? I wonder how you think to repay this? I have not finished—'

He held his hand up as I went to speak, though what I would have said was a mystery to me. I faltered a little, but the state was temporary, for I felt I had him whatever way he turned. But then if he sent me from here? No, that would not do either, for my memories would comfort me. I felt exalted, I felt it was I who became unassailable for the core of me was beyond reach.

'Obvious complacency, Freddy, can lead to the assumption that the perpetrator of such loses respect, but I personally believe that he simply suffers a serious, yet curable malady perhaps bought on by the lack of aforesaid company and judicious amounts of villainy and devilment! 'Tis obvious that you think yourself incredibly clever, and I watch, and am saddened to think that you plot as I speak. Frederick, even the dullest of souls can read your intent, allow me to demonstrate.'

He beckoned one so painfully slowly, that at first he did not respond to his name and was only when Joseph hurled at his head his goblet with incredible accuracy that he got to his feet with measured pride.

'Boy, why do you think Freddy here so distracted?'

'I think, Master Joseph, he plots to be gone from you and thinks you fooled, Sir, if that pleases you? And I would say I am proud to have been his undoing! You there, why do you hang around, ay? When you look upon us all as though beneath you!'

'Enough, enough, be so good as to sit, was a simple exercise is all. Do any of you ever speak with that boy? He gave his opinion most readily as though he often lacked company.'

The boy sat back down, guided by Joshua, and blushed, and enthused with his limited vocabulary until he was hushed by another more alerted by Joseph's rancour.

'Joseph, I swear to you this day that I have not thought of this but must be truthful and say that you are right in some part. That I find my wishes altered, and that fortune leads me here where I find more happiness and chase the peace it brings me. Of course I question that I am in reasonable mind, but say I prefer this, be it madness, to any sanity.'

'Oh quiet man! Your poetry does not disarm me! Gadzooks this is a fine pickle! You know you must leave here, Freddy, there is the small matter of an annuity, and I do not speak of Mary's. Were it not purely financial I would still enjoy the contrivance of it for my sins.'

He held his hand up again as I went to plead, though I had not a penny worth of fortune or soul with which to bargain, all was tied up rather neatly.

'I am softened a little perhaps, Freddy, and feel uncommonly lenient. Not given to sentiment or romantics as you must be aware, but still I am struck by a pretty proposition that I would put to you?'

'Please tell me of it, Joseph?'

I could not wait to speak a second longer that he might end my agonies as he got to his feet with obvious intent to amuse his adoring minions and conjured again.

'You may remember that I said that if this be pleasing to you, Mary and child, that your departure from here need not be permanent? Well 'tis there that I begin, and make apologies for such a short story, for 'tis there it ends! Hah! All men have such fancies, Frederick, and neither Mary nor your future spouse will expect less of you. The finances will remain and I would add that upon reflection, Frederick, I find you most fulfilling and had not expected such richness and gratuity, or had I? I am afraid you must endure the suspense for at least the present or until you're next eureka moment. Now then what say you to this plan, man? I would have thought you shocked to find such charity, and would have attempted to embrace me at the very least!'

'Of course Joseph, I am ashamed to appear so ungrateful, but only dreamed, nay aspired to live a simpler existence. I am afraid the divine nature of my feelings leads me astray and indeed I wonder be they truly divine if they inflict so much pain now?'

'Simpler! I ask all here, what could be more so? Yes, you will have to attend to your wife's needs and provide her with heirs, but she is not so hard to look upon, is she, man? And can be more less than often, I am assured historically that neither party in such cases feels slighted, ay man? 'Tis perfect and you simply withhold your astonishment at its genius for you feel that you ought to have thought it first! Before delving into ideals which are the preserve of the purist, be they celestial or more pleasingly as you find myself ... I have known, in fact, in majority, I am familiar with people who regularly and without check sample both hoping that one eradicates the other to order! They are uniformly entertaining but have no hope of ever being acceptable to either. I do believe Dante's purgatory be a fine example of their predicament and would explain their situation more extensively, as I for one cannot be bothered! Though you may think to read it more studiously if before it left you blank, of course assuming that you have read it? 'Tis the fashion, is it not, to read these prophetic works? I find it odd his practical knowledge of the subject and the comical light he makes of it; one might mistake it for bravado, and is in my eyes simply a foreboding to victims who fail to commit to neither one thing or the other and so is of no relevance to me. Still I digress and we are still to hear your resolve upon the matter at hand?'

'Yes, yes to all, Joseph. Here I find myself a little lost as to what I commit to? Yet I have been guided thus far and have a fortune I would not trade, so no, I do not mind the terms, Joseph.'

'Hah! Well put, man, and let us drink to it all! Where has that blasted girl got to now? Mary!'

Mary appeared to whoops of admiration. More than acceptably clean, and wearing a very pretty dress very well. This all suits me well, I thought, and fancied that any other life I lead would always be superfluous and inconvenient to this one. As for the baby, if dear Mary in all her innocence was convinced he was mine then surely he was just that and always would be for she had no slight nor scheme in her. So I would accept it in good grace and fancied fantastically that there would be more between us.

'Who has the baby then, does nobody watch him? Joshua! How many times have I asked that you not leave young Freddy with your flea ridden cur! She will be nursing him next! Lord help us, 'tis not a lot I ask?'

'Oh shush now, girl, she will do no harm. Can you not see she loves the child?'

She hesitated above the scene of baby with cringing dog and, resolutely, as only a girl in need of spoiling might, said,

'Very well then, for she does seem very pleased with him, all snuggled up like that, but mind you, Josh, if she bites him I will bite you!'

'And undoubtedly it would fester and become septic. The

mouth is most definitely unholy. Personally, I would rather a nip from the mutt.'

'Thank you, Joseph, for your wit, there was me thinking I looked quite fine and took me all of the morning with special care, but 'tis your candour that keeps me from making a fool of myself.'

'If you think to look for spoiling from me, Mary, then I would advise you not make it as tiring for yourself as it would be fruitless. Surely Freddy here is enough for you? Now go! And fetch some wines for us we are celebrating somewhat, and make good use of that pretty dress with a dance and a song if you have one.'

'Why yes, I think I shall oblige you all with that! I have a mind to get noticed today, growing used to it so I am, isn't that right, Freddy?'

'Flippant, Mary, 'tis another word for your journal,' I added trying to catch her eye for longer than the second she allowed, but she did not turn.

'Ay Freddy, 'tis a nice word, and a fine way to describe me, for I know it already. And you might wonder that I would have to care more to feign it.'

So she pleased herself and pleased the crowd and soon all were in except Joseph and myself. I was yet to acquire the artless manners, or enough drink to really enjoy such unbridled entertainment. Joseph was more intent on the bottle before him and his scathing observations, which frequently he voiced with too much honesty and accuracy.

'This could either be described as a celebration in honour of a most agreeable compromise reached, or perhaps a prelude to a most exquisite destruction.'

Joseph, now tired of passing insults to those of limited wit found me more delighting in his candid appraisals.

'I would suppose how you decipher it all will depend upon your mental and emotional state for I am sure the two collude on fantastical levels at present, and also upon how precisely you assess your inherent worth. Until now one might wildly assume that you were possessed by an eagerness to please, brought on undoubtedly by a thorough ousting. It has been quite comical and in all fairness one could stake money on your performance, but insider knowledge is in my view cheating and what is the point to good sport if it is applied? I do not subscribe to it, no, I would be doing your questionable wisdom perhaps an injustice, though if I did not mention that others have before I am sorry but feel that they not so insightful as I and so cannot be damned for it. 'Tis subliminal, yes, but truthfully could not be so bold if you were laid open by surgical means, and therein, if you cared to look, Frederick, you may find shackles. Only now I feel, and must say enjoy, this opportunity to speak so boldly with you as liberal wine swilling and the toxicity of love found has you without a care for tomorrow. I believe you conspire to be rid of these binds. How? I cannot fathom, and do truly tell you, Freddy, that it has made you brave, which does not suit you and I can forgive the temporary insanity. The ideas you are nurturing, will be fruitless, and painful in defeat. So let us agree that the spectacle shall run to its ends and hope that, for you, it has them. Still 'tis nice to be without care, as you appear to me now, Freddy, and I should allow you this liberty, but feel I must point out that 'tis now that you do "truly" care and are once again vulnerable.'

'Joseph, forgive me but am preoccupied with the happy chance of finding such fulfilment in a most uncommon place and girl, and I say you are right, that I do have something to care for now but I cannot feel fear anymore and 'tis most perplexing. I find I am thoroughly enjoying some freedom from it at present and hope you do not misconstrue my happy manners as any form of disrespect.'

'Aye, well perhaps I do not and a mad man is incapable of sensible insult, but you might think that the prison you inhabit is too complex, ambiguous say, for you to fully comprehend at this stage. I say, you did not flinch when I remarked that you were shackled, is this also bravado, or perhaps that my remarks seemed lightly put?'

'It is not bravado, Joseph, or indeed failure to comprehend

your wise words, 'tis resignation and out of respect I do not flinch for it is only by your benediction, and the very shackles you talk of that I remain in Mary's heart.'

'Well indeed, if truth be that you are in hers then that all seems very convenient and I am shocked by numerous acts of charity I have bestowed upon you! But this has become very dull, has it not, Freddy? Let us drink more and think less, for tomorrow you must journey back to Bath and I would not forgive myself if I engaged you further in this ridiculousness! Ha, ha, you see, Frederick, how easy you are still! Drink, drink and enjoy your girl for you will not see her again for a time that would respectably be next full moon. Lord help us though if we are due an eclipse! I once again amuse myself and you too I see! Good. Let us have more of it then, damnably drab business these love affairs.'

'I have but one more thing to say on the subject if you will permit, Joseph? Must I leave tomorrow? Is all set? I had hoped this business detain me at least one more day.'

'No question in it, man, tomorrow it must be. Would not wish to alert the girl too hastily of your errant heart. Still will be but three weeks and you shall return, ay man. I fear I must now withdraw from your company, Frederick, I cannot abide moping and there is company here that is improvement on yours at the best of times without the aid of this poetic prattle.'

Stunned I might be that his comments did not hurt, and that I did not notice his departure for Mary stepped admirably into the breach and was all that filled my eye.

'So you are to away then on the morn, Freddy? La! If it were that all my beaus paid the same attention to me I would be as bitter as old quinces. And I will not ask you to stay on if that is why you look to me!'

'Mary, I am sorry for it, but I have matters to attend to, and though you might think I do not truly give my heart I tell you I did not know a man could live without one, yet I leave it here tomorrow. I must, but in all eagerness shall return very soon.'

'There he goes again! Hah, hah, Freddy, I know you must go! I have ears enough and I have asked you for no promises.'

'But I do swear, Mary, most sincerely that I am yours and yours only.'

'Oh, shush, Frederick! We must live on something, ay? Come on no more of your nonsense and dance with your Mary.'

'I gladly do so, Mary, and even more so gladly look the fool for am not used to this particular way of dance.'

'Ha, ha, we shall have some fun with you then, Frederick, but there is not one of us who knows the steps and mostly make them up, I am eager to see yours as any!'

'Just a little courage,' I requested, but more of the bottle, and though it would do for me tomorrow it would also do for me right now.

I swiftly drank the contents to roars of delight, which had the lucky hap of diverting attention from my foolish attempts at the dance. Mary noted that I was more affected by the drink and selfishly took me aside so as all she had to contend with was my love making and though I was a novice there was much improvement, she said, on my dancing.

Strangely, on waking the next morn, I found myself in the company and hold of Joshua. We had obviously fell where we were slain by the final few flagons, and it being cold I excused Joshua the indiscretion and carefully released myself from his grip. I had hoped I would wake with Mary, and vainly looked around the place for her; she was probably fetching some bounty for my journey. It would be discarded, I laughed, but still would fill me enough that she had thought of me.

'Well then, Frederick, do you make ready? You have some journey to complete this day!'

'Joseph, I do of course but have only just awoken, how do you find the day?'

'I find it well, I have been enjoying some of its promise

this last hour. I did not drink as you, and limited my intake last eve. There is much to discover in a room full of drunkards and it amused me endlessly. Still we must not delay, let us have you ready, I shall see you as far as Cleveton.'

'Might I wait on Mary, Joseph? I would like to say my farewells to the girl.'

'No need, really, Frederick, you all but did so last night and I have informed her that your journey must be expedient. You will not see her this side of midday, she visits with a friend here or about, but did say to wish you courage and speed and that she will wait by the moon till she sees you again.'

'Did she really say all those things, Joseph? It so gladdens my heart to hear her speak from hers!'

'Hah, hah, no, she did not, I have only just invented them! I am constantly amazed at my endless talents and to know that I too have one for poetic verse, it is just too much!'

'Ah, hah, yes I see, Joseph, and comedy! I am to marvel at your ability there.'

'Oh do not be so sour-faced, Frederick, you must allow me to indulge. You did not truly believe that I would deliver love addresses between the two of you, did you?'

'I am foolish, and perhaps still a little inhibited by the drink.'

'Yes, and all this silly love business has turned your mind, man, but it does cheer you now, yes? Pray you can still recognize humour? I meant to put it where it belonged. 'Tis no great love story, Frederick. You shall have your Mary, and keep your wife, but 'tis not epic! You must see that.'

'Of course, but perhaps it only lacks this quality to one on the outside, I myself find it consuming, and am sure I can vouch for Mary.'

'You are sure? As am I, of course. She feels as you do, and 'tis just that she is more guarded with her feelings, yes, I am quite sure this is the answer. But what do we do here? We really must not delay for you have a coach to catch, and as you travelled light we can away presently. A horse is readied for you, shall we?'

He gestured to the door, and knowing that I would return perhaps rendered this vacation less gruelling but still I felt many things, in short his battery. I joined him at the door and stepped into the frosty morn, and as the sun had risen for sure it would fall and there would be moons enough to watch till I returned, and I knew that he would watch for them as eagerly as I.

'Pensive?' he remarked as we rode.

'Perception of a mood I sometimes think, and laugh, is somewhat liken to psychic ability! I am made more aware, upon your acquaintance, of a plethora of talents I had not yet discovered, Freddy. I say you bring out the best in me, now come, was I right? You are elsewhere at this moment?'

'I stand in awe of your insight, Joseph, but, come, surely there is enough psychic in our Mary and that you are just well-informed of my current state.'

'Ha, ha, yes, you are right! And do you note that they are always so damnably ugly these apparent psychics! Yes, odd-looking creatures that look to unworldly realms for their acceptance as perhaps this one too decorative?'

'How would you have me respond, Joseph? With such bold thrusts delivered I either call myself the lesser man for not enquiring if you included one I love in the damnation, or I enter into battle with a greater man in many respects and lose face once again, perhaps more. So I decline and am more comfortable with being the former at least in your eyes.'

'No it was you who included Mary in my assault, and 'tis you who struggles alone with it. She need not be an embarrassment, man, it is not as though you will attend a great many balls with her, and you may say of her what you will when amongst friends in Bath for they shall never know her. Come Frederick, laugh with me, 'tis comical, is it not? A little less sincerity would not hurt you at this point, for as you see we arrive at Cleveton and we must farewell. 'Tis no small journey you take to Bath, but be sure you have enough time fall back in love with the place and equal time to learn to despise this one. Contractual agreements aside, you might remember that I have invested time and thought in this little tale of yours, Freddy, and would not wish it treated with a less than careful hand.'

'Your wishes, Sir, bring me comfort, knowing that between us there is one purpose. And I thank you, Joseph, for your company and this very fine ride, until we meet again then.'

'Yes, for who knows when that shall be!' he remarked over his shoulder as he rode away, and I too used now to his surprises gave him no reward by either stopping or enquiring further to his meaning.

'All the way is it, Sir?' the coachman enquired, weather-beaten but with a strange vanity – for his attire was immaculate and he had made a knot which wasn't a bad attempt at a ponytail. Add to this a patch below his left eye and you have not a bad description of a man used to keeping company with high society, though only by default. For sure the tales he regaled would be much exaggerated but entertaining enough to elevate him in opinion amongst his friends. 'Not that there is much in-between,' he continued. 'I suppose you could say that about most things in life though, ay Sir?'

'Yes, all the way, and take a care to limit your observations to the milestones, I have had my fill of apocalyptic dispensations and would much like to enjoy the journey for what it is.'

'Aye, you have much to think on I can see that, and there is plenty of room for you to do so, being my only customer you see today. Strikes me as odd, so it does, seeing it is midday, and the good half of the week? Still, who am I to say, I just ferries the folk here and there, even those who have nowhere to go! Ha, hah, you do get them, Sir, I don't mind telling you. Boards my coach, pays me a fare and says to me, "Where do we journey?" And do you know what I says, Sir? I will make you laugh so I will, I says, "I will take you to Bath but you will have to pay your penny to St Peter for owt else these ponies won't outstrip that devil on your heels!" Ha! Yes, it always does that, Sir, just what you are doing now, given you something to think about, ay? And I do not charge extra for the entertainment, Sir, I truly believe 'tis all part of the service.'

'You are a dedicated man indeed, and thank you! Was that the last observation? Pray that it is!'

And I boarded the coach a little harassed and was never so glad to be travelling alone.

A consuming dread that I would too soon forget Mary ate away at me like disease. Why this thought should inspire such a feeling was confusing, for surely if I forgot her the act itself would be painless? And I comforted myself that I had become too accustomed to the man I had been and that time, being limited, had had little time to adjust fully to these new feelings. Still I feared the outcome. I questioned if I would ever act alone again, coupled with this the doubt that any of it was honest, or but a fantasy that Joseph amused himself with in the absence of more enthralling entertainment. That I felt like I was escaping again haunted me, and felt it not my voice I heard for it filled me with fear and dark nightmares, sad that these I would not wake from. If lucky they might become history, and I gambled a moment's peace that they might. My wild speculations became so enveloping that I felt my only escape be alighting from the coach in transit but was prevented thankfully when it came to stop.

'We are here? We are here!'

'Hah! Yes, Sir, I think you might have slept the live long way by that, or was it your troubles that occupied you? No, I shall not venture further knowing your palate for unsolicited comments does not run to those of a lowly coachman. I thank you, Sir, for your custom, and wish you luck and happier times.'

'Not a moment's rest have I had, and yet you are so bold to think that your wishes may have some effect upon my life! However I do have something to impart, if a man has the look of worry or is preoccupied leave him to be so! You may well be rewarded more for your silence at the end of the journey than with your ill-founded wisdom or smart quips!'

'I shall take it from that then, Sir, that there is nothing for my troubles? Just looking as you do, I half-expected a penny, or two? 'Tis the way, is it not, of your society to condescend us less fortunate mortals and I am shocked to find you less than generous.'

'Are you? Are you indeed, well I am heartily sorry for your disappointment and solemnly swear that I will not darken your day again by avoiding your services in the future!'

I left him, a little satisfied that as he had unwittingly added to my discomfort I had in turn deliberately added to his. Bitterness, I thought, was much undervalued, and kept good company, at present, with hatred and resentment, acting as a fortress to any softer feelings I kept sacred within me.

Chapter 30

Where to I wondered? Phillip's club? For sure he would be in residence, or onto Emmeline's? But then perhaps she would be too expectant for a believable delivery of my joy at beholding her. I just could not muster the emotion; perhaps my length of absence might aid me as it had been not two days, and surely she would expect me nothing more than glad, but as we were apparently in love I felt I needed either practise or to find confidant in Phillip or similar candidates. Things of such delicate natures were often handled by the burliest of fellows in such places and more the better for it! Though it would seem the very antipathy of such precious arrangements, and as I had no wish to hide the matter particularly, the club it would be and was thankfully not far. I had, however, no wish to be spied by one of Emmeline's many friends taking tea adventurously in the vicinity, for some still owed much to the belated Sophia and were oft time caught not two doors away daring disapproval, so I acted as though preoccupied and with quick step came upon my design.

'Phillip, I had hoped to find you here!'

A head or so taller than any others, he had the ability to form an uprising against men who mobbed darkened corners singularly.

'Ah ha, gentlemen I surrender unto you the fellow who took the liberty of preoccupying our thoughts these last days gone! Freddy! A real pleasure to see you returned. Now please, you must tell us all of your adventure, we are quite parched for anything exotic, that being anything more than a mile outside Bath! How found you fair maiden? Was she obliging? And the baby you begot? Is he very much like you? Or does he favour the general populous? I declare there is not a man here who has not, at some time, been similarly inconvenienced!'

'Aye and I am right proud of it too!' an enthusiast spoke up.

'And the enigmatic Mr Black, was he terribly frightful?'

'In answer to the latter, Phillip, I am surprised you think me so base, it was purely business I declare and have not lost my heart. And as ever Mr Black did not disappoint.'

'Come, come, man, you looked done in! Gentlemen make way, my friend here is exhausted and his levels of sophisticated brews dangerously depleted, allow me to tend to his condition.'

Finding seclusion under such scrutiny, though all in good humour, was no easy task for Phillip but a small settee by the window proved adequate, often vacated for fear of being noticed by those who might spoil the sanctuary within.

'Now tell me all, if you so wish, Freddy. I say I have missed your company.'

'Thank you, Phillip, and I your company too. I find myself lacking in friends who I feel I can trust entirely with this, so am grateful to your ear, if you will? I suspect you deduce that my business took me places I had not foreseen with regards to "fair maiden" as you so put it. That your judgement leads you to believe something has happened between us, you are right of course and with the luxury of time and relative privacy I find her a delight, and she has much improved in my esteem.'

'I am glad I am right in this assumption, you have a look about you of fulfilment and 'tis your God-given right to feel this. Of course we shall take care to not make it so apparent as to embarrass your Emmeline. But she would be an innocent, indeed, if she did not already suspect. And as the fairer sex excel at finding such matters inconsequential, let us not be too concerned. Pray though, more of this business that took you there, is all in hand?'

'I would be generous if I say it took more than five minutes! And I am as sure as one can be who is contractually embroiled with Mr Black! I find in summarising this whole affair it renders it less worrisome and am glad of your plain speech. Tell me of Emmeline, has she fretted much?'

'I do not believe so, Freddy, I think the girl is as resolute as she is stoic and have yet learned more of her this past year that she too is compassionate; these qualities alone set her far above her contemporaries and she is an exceptional catch. You are a lucky man, Frederick.'

'As I am fully aware, Phillip, it does not concern me that she may well admire me more than I do her, for 'tis natural, but I will say that I would not readily part with her. I do believe that was upon Emmeline's instruction that I began to feel once again, and to be susceptible. Life offers up such pretty circumstances to those who do not hide, and she is a dear sweet girl, who I now am eager to reunite with, no longer reticent, and I thank you for reminding me of her goodness, Phillip.'

'And now, if you have had your fill of this very fine wine, though the thought leaves me confused, we shall repair as I believe you would like to attend to your appearance before reuniting with Em.'

'Why yes, Phillip, I find I am suitably refreshed and you are right my ensemble is distressed and not fit for such as she. Let us make haste though, I do not wish to prolong any secret agonies she feels over my absence.'

So we made the short journey to The Crescent where the remarkable gallery of properties never tired, and held court to all others that did not bare the same address. Wonder then that my father, a redoubtable figure, did not think to purchase one to fortify his status further? For certainly he would have managed one of equal grandeur. He had argued that they were lacking in character and individuality, but I suspected that as he aged he grew less generous, and with that to be mine eventually I had never pressed the point; I had dreamed of an inheritance magnificent. Personally, I must say, I would never be influenced by antiquarian idealists who furthered a division where one ought not be. Oft time referring to those who resided here as the 'tag rags' and would cross the street to avoid any pleasantries that might otherwise pass between people of the similar distinction. However, my thoughts were the luxury of independent men with riches in bequest; I had seen mine off with a cowardly act and now must look to other means of inheritance. Emmeline would prove most profitable come the day. My thoughts were both wicked and vain for I at once wished that I share it all with Mary in preference to Em, but what sort of society would tolerate such a girl? I decided that things were more ideal than my romantic heart revealed. As much as I believed my feelings for her were deep, on returning to Bath I found I rather enjoyed the place and company after all and would be fool indeed if offered more to Mary by punishing myself. In truth, it was but a fantastical notion and enjoying it did little to quell its surge.

'Freddy!' Phillip called to me as I descended the stairs,

'Enjoy the liberties you take, and those that you are about to, but for Heaven's sake, and Emmeline's propriety make good that look upon your face! 'Tis only one thing that can preoccupy a man so! Can you think of owt else? If the girl and all she is be not enough for you then thoughts on her dowry surely must?'

'Hah ha, thank you, Phillip, I should have taken more care with my expression when I attended my appearance, but I am sure she is woman enough to satisfy in the confines of her drawing room!'

'Frederick, you are as transparent as the finest muslin and lucky for you that she never tires of the stuff! I shall dine at the club tonight, perhaps we might meet there later?'

'Of course, and I shall not be beyond nine. You might think to order for me I have a devilish appetite upon me.'

'Yes, of course you do, man! But I wonder what he make you hunger for? I have a notion nothing so simple, be careful of complexities, Freddy, I would not wish to lose you.'

I barely heard his parting words, but his sentiment was felt and respected with a few moments' conjecture as to what he had meant. No answer came, and so I hastened, unaffected, to Emmeline who would not set me such conundrums I was sure.

I did not wait very long for a very enthusiastic Emmeline to appear, her immaculate dress and air yielded sophistication and a definite attraction. Not so obvious to be called startling or even to turn heads, but a pleasing countenance that owed nothing to bitter nights spent plotting the downfall of others more agreeably favoured. Had she been more devastating, she may well have not been so sweet-natured and I would not trade it in her, besides recent experience had taught me that a more satisfying bounty could be reaped from imperfect fruit and was quite settled on the fact.

'Here you are my errant Freddy! How I have missed you. Do I sound overly dramatic? Oh dear, I do, don't I?'

'Emmeline, you mirror my affections perfectly, girl, I too have felt this separation.'

'It was a shock to hear you had been taken from us on business. Freddy, can you say who it was with?'

'I shall explain what I can without making you blush, Em, but still you must be brave for 'tis not how you would like it. I am irreparably indebted to Mr Joseph Black as I am sure you may have suspected even prior to this. Em, he has a design to retrieve what he can and having not the financial free flow to satisfy, he finds he has an appetite for other means. 'Tis not all as it seems, dear Em, and would rather speak of it no more, I will not have him impinge on this most joyous day!'

'Oh Freddy, I knew as much, and fully expected him to act so! What sort of a monster would he be if his essence was less than tyrannical, and as you wish tell me nothing more of it. Come, sit with me, I have much to relay to you instead. I might begin by saying you look somehow different, my love, as if you are somewhere else, but 'tis something other than Mr Black that changes you? I am sorry to say that you seem less sincere.'

'What can I say, Em, all is how I have relayed. Please girl, do not be so inquisitive, you may find things you ought not and I would not hurt you by affording you more insight.'

'Perhaps, yes, you are right, Frederick, but look to me dearest, do you see what I have here? You see this fine piece of lace, Freddy? 'Tis fine, is it not?'

'The most, Em, it becomes you well.'

'A person would take great care of such a thing, would they not?'

'It would be precious, Em, and would take pride of place.'

'Then let me be so to you, Frederick. I am not as ill-informed as you might think, and mothers before mine knew of their husbands' little fancies. I was not raised ignorant of these circumstances and was prepared should they, and in all probability they would, occur. I merely ask you not abuse me, or be rough with me. I have seen such marriages where a wife is disposed of regularly with no affection, it must be the cruellest type of agony. But I shall not believe you capable of such treatment, my Freddy, and I do not require confirmation, simply let us be together when we are together, is it such an unreasonable request?'

'Em, I am shocked by this revelation that you could believe me less than yours. Do you think there is room in my heart for another? No Em, you are all fulfilment, and have not been usurped, there is too much to love about you, I may quote Phillip in saying that you are exceptional.'

She paused for a brief moment and discarded the lace.

'I am assured by your words, Freddy, and shall never ask you to speak of it again but am happy that I can still inspire the poet in you.'

I picked up the lace.

'Would you allow me this as a keepsake, Em? To remind you of it from time to time when I see you look as you just did? I am yours and yours only, and though sport may take me places it will never take me from your side.'

My word would have to make amends for much deceit, and if I was culpable in creating of her the very thing she dreaded then I was sorry for it; however, I was sure she had not the inclination to be individual and would now have some conversation to share with other dissatisfied spouses. She would rally, even come to enjoy it; after all, how would the ladies fare at The Assembly Rooms if they could not huddle and despair! They would be singularly without purpose, surely then I only attended to her needs? This was not such a wild assumption more candid observation.

'Thank you dear, Freddy, and so prettily put. I swear I do believe it, but find I am a less than attentive host! You must wish for refreshment, poor thing, let us take some tea and I shall inform you of plans made for our pending nuptials. I find it a much happier circumstance than this condemned discourse.'

'Of course, Em, I would be delighted to hear all that you will allow, for I am aware that I cannot know it all! It shall be a most welcome and anticipated surprise.'

She rang for tea, and as her plans unfolded I found that it would be easier than I had thought to maintain her blissful state, for I was sure she did not know that I only thought of Mary, and how I might expedite my return to her side. Phillip had assured me that the bloom would fade and I would find it less urgent within me, but I could not see it, surely no one man had felt so much before?

Emmeline's laughter bought me back to my senses.

'You see, Freddy, poor Papa spends more time in his study than ever and Mama is all consumed by it, I have never known her so attentive!'

'Your poor father, Em, an overly attentive spouse might well be why he retires, do you not think, Em?'

'Hah, ha, yes, Freddy, I do believe you are right after all, poor father!'

The afternoon I spent with her lacked attendance as I dreamed of less stringent parameters with Mary, though never allowing myself to forget the importance of this arrangement. I would not have thought to have held the girl before me in contempt, but still it was how the meeting fared and even if I was selfish it was not so rare.

Later I would meet with Phillip and, less inhibited by judicious amounts of good wine, would confess as much to himself. I wondered that he took it both well and not so, as if it injured him and was personal – perhaps he had grown fond of the girl subliminally but I cared for none of it. Nothing would tempt him to rile or indeed ruin her with such a notification.

Chapter 31

The commencement of a battle; Bath in her most royal majesty offered cultural exploits, fine wine and good fare, pleasant company. In stark contrast, which became odder to me as days passed, was a different society though no less hungered for. The inn at the end of the world, where those who congregated sought neither forgiveness nor amnesty, offered a porthole to an unworldly realm full of villainous exercise and volatile assemblies, and if this were not enough to make you take flight an audience with an entity most definitely born of Hell would. Those who remained perhaps did so by default but more so by wicked trickery. One might be intrigued, curious even, but it would only happen there by chance. As happened to me, for Joseph Black was the most satanic, punishing, and vicious individual you would ever meet whilst earthly bound and yet still I was drawn. Still Mary, a daughter of his design, managed to manipulate my thoughts daily and had in result accrued a number of gifts pertaining to love surely, for they were purchased boldly and under the scrutiny of those who would busy themselves on my behalf. I had also attempted poetry, and written carefully in a journal I had purchased with intention of gifting it to Mary. Still, I wondered if she would appreciate the sentiment or even misunderstand? If she laughed, be it to my face or behind my back, I would feel it, I would know it. In the waking light when all was new and the sun first rose, 'twas easy to think in the comforting haze that all was as it should be and was as you dreamed. But as the warm haze became bolder, so must you rise from your slumber, and accept whatever clarity it afforded you. Such long days I had had of late.

'We are but half-way there.'

'Freddy, half-way where? Pray. what are you so deeply distracted by?'

'Forgive me, Phillip, I merely mark the moon and should do so in silence.'

'Not at all, man, but forgive me if I do not share your occupation or interest, I am quite done in and really must retire. Still, I am a little inquisitive as to its purpose? The study of a demi-lune? Come on, Freddy, 'tis cold and dark, and I cannot rest until you tell.'

'I simply wait, Phillip, for it to be in its entirety, I have a promise to keep.'

'Enough, man, for it involves that bloody inn and chit of a girl and the whole damned affair is of concern to me! Such a time you have spent gone from there yet you are sure of your love after only two days? I ask you Freddy, 'tis all as it seems?'

'Your worry touches me, Phillip, and I might share your concern if I were in my right mind. Do not look so worried, dear friend, I have yet finished. I am bewitched by her, yes, but know her to be affectionate and caring and would not have won the heart of the boy I told you of, Pike, if she were sinister.'

'I do not doubt the girl, of course not, you have recommended her most fervently, but I doubt her strength of will whilst captive at that place. Black I know to be an antagonist, this I concluded whilst not biased by your word, but upon meeting him here. I do not like the connection Freddy and I fear a little for Em.'

'Please then, Phillip, allow me to allay your fears, and though you have considered me the very best of friends I feel I must explain myself, though is contrary to the term. If you feel persuaded to protect my Em, I might first remind you that I am acutely conscious of my situation and upon my oath no harm shall befall the girl and say your concern unfounded. The act itself might arouse suspicions in her that she will sit with uncomfortably, being such as she is a most honest girl. I am also angered that you believe me less of a man, or is it that you harbour feelings for her yourself? I must say you seem most complimentary, and it would not be unnatural. She has been more than caring, and sympathetic this year gone and I mark that you considered her exceptional! A fool indeed would allow such treasure to slip from his grasp.'

'And yet she does not, ay man? Upon your union she shall become sister to me for I have considered you brother in all, and yet sadly of late we seem to feel less for each other. I have already made clear what I believe to be the cause of this and think that your relationship with that God-awful place might be healthier if more distant! But still I find I must check myself. Freddy, I do not wish to quarrel with you more, let us forget this, and perhaps you might forgive me a forthright opinion that was voiced out of care.'

'I do not dispute it, Phillip, and 'tis not just the hour that is too late for such discourse, so I say let us retire as brothers, but leave blood feuds to the continent as we lack that very ingredient! Hah!'

'Hah, hah, yes, we are not blood, so no such excuse to expect loyalties, but in its absence I am still happily surprised by them!'

That night in my chamber I plotted to escape the next day and take a brief vacation beyond Bath, beyond Cleveton, and beyond salvation – was the only place I was not regularly made aware of my conscience in that all those around me had not a mind to discuss their own. I needed no such excuse of course, my time was my own and if I wished to visit with my Mary, it was precisely what I would do. I was certain Em would not be so inconvenienced, an understanding of late had flourished between us and she seemed happy with our separate arrangements. Perhaps happy is too extreme a word, more so she showed great resolve and I grew to like her more than when she resembled a silly girl who fawned over me and blessed the day that a man ever took an interest in her. I wondered if, secretly, she sometimes blessed the day Sophia was taken also. For Em was doomed whilst the girl lived and courted her company, to be forever overlooked. If my opinion, this counted for owt with her, then she would continue this way for I had told her that she had greatly improved and maturity suited her, best to leave temperament to those more becoming, it always looked so awkward on the plainer girls.

Chapter 32

I planned to be gone before any awoke, and I knew with anticipation I would hardly sleep and worried little about being discovered. I drifted in and out of sweet light dreams, nay promises, and as soon as the first lark marked the morn I escaped and went to fetch up the first coach heading for Cleveton. Thankfully, it was not manned by the fellow who had brought me here, still I thought that I may have been more receptive to his charm – if indeed that was what it was – being in this happier state, I now see a little conviviality was never so missed as was when the dark surly fellow ushered me in and roused his horses with a deathly lash that made my stomach lurch.

Cosseted from the weather, and within these confines I laughed a little at my daring-do and enjoyed the thought of the chaos in my wake. Phillip would worry less and would attend Emmeline but for sure would not disclose me to her; all was set for sure, but for a simple matter that had eluded me and had done so with devilish cunning, Joseph Black. Why had I not thought!? Such boldness surely could only be by his beckoning? This I hoped for at least, but was a presumption, and one I could not validate without appearing belligerent; he would not be taken with it. Perhaps he might see it as initiative? More likely that I dared to imitate a liberated man and make choices for myself. I would run the ten miles already ventured if I thought he would not be insulted that I dared leave him standing there if in truth this was his doing and he waited on me. As absurd as it sounded I had to consider it, and decided on my course to stay and turn back at Cleveton with as little notice as possible.

On arriving I thought to maintain an anonymous state for I wished to return to Bath unscathed. Too many spies occupied the place and were forever eager to win favour with Black. So I vacated with care and in trying to look inconspicuous managed the opposite, and alerted one, or two passersby enough to enquire of my business. I had not met with them before and only hoped that they did not know me by reputation or association. I waited for the coach to about turn and head for Bath but with no reward, and when I asked of him why he waited he replied,

'I have no time for tourists, Sir, and if you will be patient I will wait an hour or so longer, I have those who rely on me, you see, Sir, and begging your pardon but another penny from you will not change that.'

So I waited on and after a while found a little courage, perhaps brought on by hunger and the smell of the confectioners, and decided it as good a place as any to hide. Such a pretty girl waited on me that I disguised myself admirably as though I had not a care but for her company and conversed with her boldly enquiring of her situation. For certain she was single, and could not have been more than sixteen, so rakishly I offered her tea at Bath that afternoon and that she would find fine lodgings with a lady acquaintance of mine if only but for the one night. These bold gestures were nectar to the morally challenged and also to any pretty girl who may be recipient, and would be chewed over later by both parties for the liberty taken! I enjoyed much her coy refusal, was as good as acceptance from such a pretty girl and as the yell came for the coach to be leaving I made my apologies most handsomely and took my leave. Through it all I had not yet forgotten how to bring about a blush and took it as verbatim that had I remained she would have, with polite coercion, of course agreed to my proposition.

'Forgive me, Sir, we appear to both have the same purpose

but not a separate path!' I went to apologize to the fellow I had stumbled across.

'Joseph! No, 'tis not you! God, man, what do you do here? Heaven, do you make fun with me?'

'No, it is I that must own to that, are you not pleased to see me, Fredrick?'

'I had a ridiculous thought, Joseph, I was taken by an urge to visit with Mary but was only inconvenienced by the fever for a few miles and was about to take the coach back to Bath, I swear this to you.'

'Of this I am sure, Frederick, your course is obvious but excuse me I must thank Millicent, my pretty pointer, for was she who sent a boy with a mouthful of bonbons to fetch me from my business. Such a lovely face do you not think so, Freddy?' he said as she ventured from the shop, and caressed it with his finger.

'I am amazed you did not see her deceit, for surely you did not believe her taken in by you? Hah, hah, yes, and so bold to think me not of great notoriety both here and as far as you have ever been! You have become careless I think. Run along now, girl, I cannot find you attractive for I know not if you are mine.'

The girl curtseyed and blushed and ran from him to the shop where a gathering of old maids at least offered some retribution as they scorned her as she passed.

'So crestfallen, Frederick, so defeatist, I will tell you that you have learned something today, and it was not such a futile exercise. If you can judge a woman's worth by her weight in grain then you will have established a rule to live your life by, for at present, man, you are simply out of control! Take this very instance, a little extreme do you not think? For the one you have dared all for? Such as she is. It goes without saying that I am not well pleased with this wild and thoughtless act, but what is astounding, is that you risk your own sanity on a girl more accomplished in evil, where others may sew and sing and paint, and are virtuous if their talents are limited. Of course, I know you shall say that she is soft and has charm, but consider what drives the girl? What she will do to achieve her ends, and that you yourself have witnessed. Would you venture your last guinea on her fealty, Freddy? Would you? If I offered you insider knowledge I would deem myself a cheat, and besides you may well thump me! Hah!' he added and mocked me with every ounce. 'Come, man, I do not say forget her, just that she is not memorable, and treat her as such.'

'Perhaps Joseph, perhaps you are right, and I elevate her thus high that the stars may make her shine where she labours. I am not sure, but sure it should be less important. But do you tell me this as a friend or as tormentor? Can I ask you this without insulting you? I pray so. I know you to be a candid man, do I mistake this for, however unwitting, a propensity to belittle, and cause injury? I am regularly confused by it, for at times you deliver as though sustenance yet other times your words can be vitriolic. Tell me, I beg you, that I am too sensitive.'

'You question too much, Freddy, and I make mischief with you if I wish, and since you seem to admire my bluffness I will tell you that in order to find someone amusing there must first be something of the fool about them! But still questions aside, what are we to do with you? It would appear you have missed your coach!'

'Lord!'

I swivelled round almost losing my balance.

'Somewhat inconvenient, for I do believe there is not another one today. A room is what you need, Freddy, and I can think of but one place, can you guess?'

'Hah, yes, I must concede that until you spoke it was looking dire, and I promise you, Joseph, that this eventuality was not contrived. That you allow me to put upon your hospitality without notice is indicative of the fair man you are in essence, I wish I could but retract my observations but perhaps you will not mind them so much if you see them born of envy? It is what I deduce on being happily surprised by you again.'

'My hospitality? No, no indeed, Frederick. I talk of The King's Head and not the inn. I cannot reward your temerity and I see you too well come about my broadside with fancy praise and a pitiful attempt to confuse! You will find yourself a whore and steal a side of her bed for the night. Dare not pick my pocket again; you will find no goodwill there.'

'My apologies, Joseph, how could I have mistaken your meaning so absolutely! Of course The King's Head is a fine establishment, at least fit for a traveller who finds himself marooned. I am become too expectant of charitable deeds, and sometimes feel I am all but penniless and share booties with beggars, though have not their credibility. How can I beg favours when I look as I do?'

'Yes, 'tis fair to say that you would starve but for the fact that you are my type of beggar, Freddy. I will not be put upon by the more legitimate less fragrant ones for I cannot throw a penny far enough as I am always such a distance from them. A valid excuse, I am sure, and that said you have convinced me that I am too hard upon you, so yes, you may stay at the inn, but no, you cannot share my ride, how you get there is your affair and forgive me if I rush from your ovations and exaltations, they have no worth to me, I might even accuse you of stealing, you fool, for I believe they dim the light about me, you must learn, Frederick, that not everybody in life wishes to be likened to celestial beings seeking flagellation.'

He turned to leave and as he disappeared into the fading light he remarked glibly,

'I shall expect you at some time tomorrow then, Frederick, that is if you set about it now, but then surely you shall have to about face. I do hope it is worthy of such an exertion and that you have good legs!'

I felt my purse and it was well enough to acquire a horse that could keep a trot for the next ten miles or so, and so ventured to the blacksmiths. Ponies were often bought and sold here and one that was destined for slaughter, and to grace a table or butcher's window would certainly fit my requirements.

'Closing up, Sir, for the night, I have a bed to go to if you have not, and I shoe horses, Sir, so have nothing that will fit you! If you want shoeing then the best I can do is chase you with my iron! Hah, hah! I bless the day that I can still laugh for 'tis hard grind with little reward.'

He swore under his breath.

'I just mean to enrich your day, good fellow, in buying an animal from you, if you have one? Is but for a short journey and your worst will do with no fear of reprisal, I ask little, do I not?'

'Ere, Doric, get and bring out the mare that rots up my good straw. I will see your money, Sir, and as you are not fussy I will take it too.'

'Of course, but, good man, how much do you ask? I am yet to see this animal.'

'Well I am sure that depends on how desperate you are, Sir, begging your pardon for I might just as well take myself home.'

'A guinea's worth of desperation, seems extravagant but I am as you see.'

Doric brought out the animal, very long in the nose and with more whiskers than an artist's brush, and I am sure it had never been likened to a thoroughbred until now, for to me she was of great value and would not part with her for any purse. However, tomorrow was another day, and I may well wish to sell her to the butcher to recoup some of the outlay.

'Did you think, Sir, that you would need a saddle and such? I would be doing well here this day if I had another one of those gold ones, as you see on the wall there, saddles and all.'

'I suppose I must, I am no heathen and cannot say I have ridden bareback since I was a child, and with such a God-awful road to navigate … so yes you may have another guinea.

Perhaps in hindsight I had laid out more than the butcher would pay, but still I was eager to be on my way and left without wishing the thief any goodwill.

Empathy was something I would not have imagined I would feel with this poor wretch of a beast, but as we both stood condemned I found myself taking it easy on her and a few words of encouragement I hoped made her task less arduous.

'Faith, faith is a marvellous thing, do you not think, old girl? I have it that you will carry me this journey and you must have it, in me, that I find a man willing to pay me your cost or 'tis the butchers you go to.'

All said with an affectionate tone and as was only God who heard me or understood me that dark night and I found I cared not, if nothing else I had managed to liberate myself from him.

A deathly stroke
The assassination of hope.

Chapter 33

'What! I stand amazed! How came you, Sir, to be so spirited here? You must have acquired an animal surely, or did some kind pilgrim offer you passage? If it be the latter then show me to them, pilgrims by nature are thrifty and have heavy purses from want of expenditure!'

'I am sure you feign your surprise, Joseph, and no I do not have rich pilgrims to offer, sadly,' I addressed all solemnly.

'Yes, but I see you say that with relief not regret, still I have no expectations of you and am sure, friends, that he would have brought us treasure if he could. Now, Frederick, before you continue, or Mary spies you, I beg that you limit shared affections until I, or the two of you, have retired. I have not a secret wish to be privy to this banal courtship.'

'Aye, and so say us! Freddy, you see how we treat them mange ridden curs of ole Joshua's when they be a chasing each other? 'Tis distasteful and is why they get a boot up their arse, well you are not so far off that yourself!'

Badger, as ever baiting conflict at every eventuality, and though it was edged with humour I never had the guts to return fire.

'I must congratulate you, Freddy, for your show of urgency has been efficacious in creating mass nausea, and you have disarmed a most hostile committee.'

'Oh shush you now, Joseph, or I will spit on your pie, and the rest of you!'

Mary joined me putting down the fractious rabble.

'I will not say I am surprised to see you, Freddy, not that I am given to vanity, truth for sure I never expected to see you again! But when Joseph told me that you ventured this way I knew a gentleman like you would not be put upon to walk a distance! So I knew if you came it would be tonight, and as you see I am for ever your Mary, if indeed it is what I am to you? Though why you would venture here for owt else is beyond me!'

Strangely I found her assumption a little embarrassing, though to call it such was not generous and though I wished a little intervention from any, her loveliness was still apparent. Her hair and her eyes were still very pretty and she was disarming even if it was disconcerting.

'Well, Freddy? Have you nothing to say?'

'Only, Mary, that the Devil is mischievous tonight and prevents me from speaking it, but my reason for being here is as obvious to me as is to you.'

'Surely this love be blessed by the Lord,

A spineless fop and a smelly old board,

For Heaven be full of just such matches,

Or is the Devil too smart to say, 'tis his eye you catches!'

'How sweet, you see, Freddy, how opinion is divided? Some are inspired to create poetry whilst for others it is mischief and some manage both, but still such a tender reunion I am yet to see.'

'Thank you, Joseph, for that, and I truly believe you mean your pretty words, but as for you Badger, just shut that mouth of yours! This here is an educated man, who does not believe in such fairy tales about devils and such like, and pretty soon I shall be so too, for sure you will teach me things, Freddy?'

'Of course, dear Mary, but I have not been schooled to disbelieve only to avoid such things.'

'Pray then that you all send your children to his tutor! For in avoiding evil he has attained great respect for it and enough to adhere it to some practices. And though none of you speak the word, for 'tis vilified, you blindly go where Frederick sees more clearly, and has learned, I think, that in the knowing other riches can be found.'

'A fine summary, Joseph, and I wonder why such volumes are written upon the subject and indeed in some cases considered precious that we are not supposed to be somewhat influenced.'

'Well said, Frederick, and mark that most here that have felt fear in their life may well believe that it was brought on by evil, and I would agree with them but also have them know that those who must be blamed for the fear are those who teach us that evil is to be avoided. It is perplexing, and you might see me as a more honest man in the knowing of it, a purist.'

He paused for adulation and received it even though it was obvious they did not comprehend.

'I say that we all, except Joseph, go to the Devil in our own way and there is not much he can do with us if we cannot understand his fine words, ay there?'

Mary lowered her eyes, and curtseyed reticently before him and if she intended to name the Devil amongst us, she did so unwittingly.

'Go on then, girl! I do not give you board and lodging for blushes and kittenish banter! We all need feeding and though it be pie again, with imagination one can generally dispose of it, but keeping it down now that requires more particular application!'

'Well you know what you can all do then! What an ungrateful lot!'

And I was thankful of a less embarrassing interlude as she disappeared, for her adoring gaze had been fixed and disconcerting.

'You seem a deal quiet, Freddy? I would have thought it difficult to contain you not three hours passed? Perhaps the cold night air offers a little too much clarity, but in her defence 'tis not Mary's best angle, looked upon askance. Clusters, simply clusters of pox marks. Have you ever surveyed the lie of something by looking at it just such a way? Of course, this said you might call her an adventure but never a beauty. Still there is much to be said for a warm-hearted girl, much I am sure.'

'Joseph, I have long since been reconciled to her appearance and try not to note it out of respect, I just feel mighty tired as if I could not harbour another thought, even better I would have them sail by.'

'Hah! I never, till his day, knew a man reconciled to a woman's looks who did not possess a handsome dowry! But there I am all for sport, and admit it, you have proved me wrong, Frederick! As for your thoughts, well, man, the day you give up hope is the day you shall stop thinking, but trust me, thoughts are imperative to this relationship of ours. I apologize if you feel I have been remiss in controlling them, and do so again if this statement startles you, but you must admit that if I did not carefully manipulate your environment, say, for I think you still find my presence in your subconscious fearful, fate would have dealt with you long time since and with severity. As for hope, for 'tis not purely divine in nature, and I find I indulge in it too, I have an example for you and shall share it with you now that you are receptive. I hope that your mewling offspring, if it is such, quits his state of hysteria for 'tis unnerving! Do you think him in want of exercise? Nothing like a bracing midnight stroll by the shore, I would take him there myself but the poor might cannot yet walk. Mary! Mary! The child! I do believe I am damned, Frederick, also, for he is the only living being I am aware of that will not capitulate for me, and I do not speak his gibberish therefore he is beyond manipulation.'

'Ha, ha, Joseph, I swear you are a genius, for now I feel that my thoughts be sweet sanctuary if I can make them deep enough to drown out that wailing!'

'Joshua!' Mary screamed. 'Will you please take the baby? You have all the magic old, man, not one of us can do as well.

Please Joshua, I cannot manage all your dinners as well as your baby!'

Joshua made plain that it was only with a male child that he could bond so and, a little embarrassed, took the baby from an irate Mary, scolding her for yelling so around the infant.

'I wonder what that man sees in you, Mary, you have nothing to offer him now.'

'Sort of said it all there, Mary, ay boys?' Badger remarked with sudden interest. 'Just I felt sure that all was set and he was Freddy's child.'

'And so he is Badger, thank you! You and Josh can just quit conspiring against me, enjoy yourselves, do you? I cannot be held responsible for what I say when that demon is yelling so. Freddy, will you allow me my mistake and not punish me for it?'

'Shush now, Mary, and Joshua give me the child. I had younger cousins in another life and am a bit of a genius at amusing them.'

'Go on then, Josh, give the baby to his father, and all I meant by the remark was that you all seem to take an interest in bringing him up to respect none, and that you are all to blame!'

'Hooray!'

'Well recovered, Mary!'

Joseph joined in the ovations.

'You are lucky to be so pretty or you may have frightened Frederick off, but incredulously he remains, so I am convinced that a confession of even worse still could not raise him to beat you.'

Such scathing comments, for a girl less than she, might be devastating but was odd to me that her contemporaries failed to impress me as she did. Perhaps it was true that physically she was not so attractive, the pox had marred a once very pretty girl, but mentally and emotionally she was heads above and would be her heart and courage that would warm me in years to come.

She was kept busy, deliberately, for the rest of that night and our relationship was the subject of much comedy, but as all retired or fell into slumber she came to sit by me and as tired as I was I had waited for her.

'Lord, Freddy, you look done in! It is true I am not a shy maid but I still know not where to put you? I am just not sure where you would like to lay. My bed is soft, Freddy, and I will not disturb you as I am tired also, but I am happy, Freddy, more happy than I have ever been.'

'I too, Mary, and am amazed. I do not insult you girl, I just did not think myself capable of such a deep emotion. I believe I was limited. There are times, Mary, when I wish I had been privy to my recent history but only for the fact that I might have known of you. This said, I would add that I am just as tired as yourself, ha, ha!'

'No, there will be no romance tonight, Frederick, and I have a mind to ask you if you snore?'

'No I do not, Mary, but you do!'

'Ha ha, well then that chair must look very inviting!'

'I am sure all will be well, dear girl, just a bottle if you please to render me senseless?'

'Oh, I will render you senseless with a bottle, Frederick, just not how you think!'

So chastised in a most affectionate and oddly romantic way, I followed her to the chamber and both too tired to offend any sensibility, and certainly hiding my sobriety, fell into deep sleep, and I remained innocent of a foreboding future that I, aided by Joseph, had meticulously created.

Next morning I awoke alone, but Mary had placed a small posy in my hand, more witchery! I thought softly to myself, a potion to lay me waste and unfit for society apart from this. I lay there and decided that I would remain for at least as long as the potion was effective, and any pending tribulations awaiting me in Bath became comical, contemptible even, and so I dressed lazily remembering the gifts I had brought which she would delight in.

I took a seat by the fire and looked about me for Mary in particular, but noted that Joseph was absent so enquired after him.

'He will be out front with those who have a stomach for a bare knuckle.'

A boy called Kane informed me, small and sickly-looking and I would venture that his physicality denoted his state of health quite precisely and that he could be found most times, even on a summer's eve, huddling with Joshua's mutts for warmth. Mary would often coax with warm broths and he would complain of his head, that it hurt always, and I must say it was a fine specimen, overly developed, and a milliner's nightmare. Was it only his physical state that kept him from Hell, indeed what mischief could the devil make with one who cared not for anything, except that he might be rid of his ailments, often concluding that he would be better off in the ground. None asked his help or opinions and perhaps he was lucky in this, but if this was the sacrifice one had to make to be rid of evil practices, no wonder the world listed with all but a few Samaritans. I, now educated, believed I knew very few if any.

An ugly thought came to mind, that Emmeline resembled just such a person, and I found the idea repellent. Poor Em, bound to do good for she possessed little else, except for a pretty fortune, became less in my esteem and how I would hide this from her would either be troublesome or too much trouble. I would not know until I met with her again for her memory was dim at present.

'I may venture a penny or two,' I said over my shoulder as I left. 'I would venture a guinea on you losing if you could make a fist, no riches to be had in that but the fresh air might improve your health!'

The boy Kane did not answer, simply curled up with the

dog, a stranger would be challenged to distinguish either; I laughed and went in search of sport.

'Let us see the colour of your money then, Freddy?'

Two of the young ones wrestled, and it was such a dirty fight that the source of so much blood was indefinable.

'I will venture a florin, Josh, but as this be a disassembled scene I know not who to bet upon? I cannot distinguish at any one time!'

'And that being the case, Joshua, surely you may win either way? I for one have not bet a penny and just enjoy the spectacle, though they are brothers I am sure they would readily kill the other to rescue pride. I wonder, Freddy, if you now see the attraction of investing in people, such sport can be had.'

'I thank you, Joseph, for seconding me, and Joshua, I do believe I shall be educated by Joseph this time.'

'Aye, you are right there, Badger,' Joshua replied to an obviously disparaging observation Badger had made.

I turned to stand by Joseph hoping to avoid another confrontation with the habitually angry youth, but Joseph had more mischief in him.

'Pray do tell us all, Badger, you have something to say?'

'All I says is, is that fool of yours is not a man's arsehole.'

'Well then, Frederick, what have you to say in reply to such condemnation? Do you attack it with passion and vehemently protest your manhood? Or do you hide about my shadow where none but angels sent to punish dare be? Both options take more courage than you possess and so best step back from me, and fear not, the moment has passed for you to defend yourself.'

I guessed by his last statement that even this devil, perhaps, had adversaries, and in a small way made him, if not human, a little vulnerable, though the idea seemed fantastical.

Shaken from my speculation by the loud clatter of well-shod shoes, a coach drawn by Spanish greys thundered upon all, confusing all except Black. I knew instantly the figure that emerged.

'Emmeline! Lord, girl, what do you do here?'

'Aye, aye!'

'How do you do, miss.'

'Are you lost?'

Just some of the heckling she was subjected to before I managed to relieve her.

'Frederick, please, I must speak with you privately.'

'Em, what is this?' I checked the coach. 'Lord, girl, you travel alone!'

I took her arm and tried to coax her back to the coach.

'No, no need. Dear Emmeline, we have yet to meet but still feel I am acquainted with you, can you guess why? Ha! So serious, I jest, girl. Frederick, you must introduce us properly even if well you know who I am.'

'Of course, how rude, Joseph, this is my betrothed, and fear not, Em, he only knows of you through my praise.'

'Mr Black, I have heard much of you and so forgive me if I forgo pleasantries.'

'Oh but this is a real treat to finally behold you, though not all treats are sweet. Some grow mould and become bitter on being left out too long. But still 'tis not the case here, I am sure, dear Emmeline. But what is this? Such impudent actions girl to travel this way alone! Do you wear breeches beneath those pretty skirts?'

Emmeline did not take her gaze from the man and became so awkward that I felt I must interject.

'Emmeline?'

'Oh hush, you must continue this inside. Please?'

He held his arm out for her, who too proud to refuse as though injured, took it, and was led inside.

'Our girl Mary shall be with us soon, and of course bring

refreshment, is that not so, Frederick? Is she not the most accommodating of girls?'

Ushering us to the fire he pressed on the point, but I was not so worried, she would not dare have me discovered, she was too cheap and too accommodating as the man said. Dear God my thoughts were harsh but then was not I always, if only in thought. My sleep afforded me my only comfort, a divine state of unaware.

'Of course, Joseph, I as you am not concerned.'

How I enjoyed my parry but it was obvious I would never think as a genius. Still I might enjoy his treats.

'Some privacy please, Mr Black?'

Em blushed through veiled concern but it was not in her to beg.

'Of course, please I forget myself! As though privy to your most pressing circumstances!'

And Joseph joined the suspicious rabble at the door placating them audibly and all the while destroying me in this girl's eyes.

'Oh Mary is a good girl. She knows that he is not wholly hers. But here look! The very girl to put down your worries, Mary, our Mary! Dear Mary, we have guests I think you too long in preparing and now you are not prepared!'

'What can this be?'

She pushed passed the crowd, my heart stopped as she stopped before us.

'Well then Master Freddy! Oh this will not do you poor thing, you must be Emmeline? I would say some of my elderflower and honey will put colour back in them cheeks, you look exhausted, my Lady.'

'And you are the eponymous Mary, dear sweet girl.'

'Oh I am just Mary, my Lady, that is all.'

'Yes, well, you could not be more succinct.'

Emmeline painfully realized that my reason for preoccupation also involved this girl. Hideously marked, a peasant if I was honest, no more insult could I have bestowed. Glad enough though that she was schooled enough to not give me up.

'Run along then girl and, yes, you are right, the lady could do with some refreshment, and your staring, truthfully, is disconcerting! Please desist.'

Shocked at my bitter manner she held her breath and lowered her eyes.

'Of course, please excuse me, I shall fetch it immediately.'

I heard a sob but that was all. If I could have spared a moment's sympathy it would have been for me! Ridiculous girl! What did she think or presume? And Em! I took her hand irritated that she pulled away.

'Freddy, I will be brief and plain. I apologize firstly for my impertinence but no choice was left me.'

'Em, please?'

I went to press her hand and yet again she withdrew.

'Frederick, I only come by your whereabouts through Phillip. He himself would not hear a word on coming here, and felt you forgo your right to the news I bring. I fear he has given you up but still I have more pressing news to impart. Frederick, you must listen man!'

Almost shrill she pulled away from me and placed her hands on her lap.

'Em, I do not understand your coldness or indeed Phillip's.'

'You do not? Still I must not be selfish and feel an obligation to tell you that your father has sent word that he might see you. I fear I may be too late for he lays dying. Frederick! If only you had remained at home! Again I think of myself, I am sorry, Frederick, I come here with this news and to offer you carriage home. That is all, my only reason for I do not enjoy being here. But tell me, Frederick, would you have it different? For I am the sole person alive prepared to bring you this news.'

Joseph listening with overly dramatic intent called,

'Mary! Come on girl, this is a rare occasion, is it not? To serve such an illustrious guest, indeed it is rare to find such a female!'

He bowed before her and took her hand, unflinching she returned.

'Mr Black, I do not stay, and wish no refreshment, I am no innocent. Frederick, if you come, you come now.'

'Allow me to answer in your stead, Frederick, for he would only be too delighted, Emmeline. For sure this new communication from his father holds promise. Ay? What do you say, Frederick? You do little to hide your excitement, man! Ha! I believe I join you but will say that our expectancies are quite different.'

'Frederick!'

'Em, I am sorry, let us go, and let me assure you that it is for you that I do so.'

'Dear Lord, spare her at least your pity, man! Are you not worth more, Emmeline?'

'Much more, Mr Black, though feel you too attentive of my pride. I must be careful you do not injure it with such bold words.'

I took her arm and paced quickly to the door.

'Mary, our guests are leaving, I cannot think what keeps you, girl! Will you not wish them safe journey? Mary!'

But no answer came, all achieved to perfect effect but still I could feel no charity towards the girl! Audacious! I thought. To put herself forward so and take such liberties in such off-hand manner! The sobbing was most unnecessary! Desperate to not be embarrassed further, I ushered Em to the waiting carriage and she made no secret of the fact that she was in no way interested in further revelations to be had here.

'I say, Frederick?' Joseph waylaid our hastened escape. 'Disappointment is always valid and never contrived by another, venture within, and I am sure you shall find recourse.

I say this – ' He shouted as the horses made off, 'That I may retrieve myself from yet another tiresome end! And Frederick, save us, but I do believe you shall have reason yet to return. What a laborious business this proves!'

Still I remained unaffected, too enveloped by thoughts of a handsome fortune that would be mine on my father's death. Perhaps then pending death had softened this monster? Though what begets a monster? Still no time for such introspection I would pay further addresses to Emmeline for if nothing else her appearance had fortified a resolve that a bit of distance from The Hangman's Hitch might be no bad thing.

'Em, dear sweet girl, pray why so distant? I am aware that you may be shocked to find me at recreation in such a place but am I not allowed?'

'Your choice, Frederick, but you cannot help reliving your contempt for the place and Phillip, I believe Phillip knows more than he says. Why else his extreme reaction?'

'But Em, I have business there you know this.'

'I know you will not desist in this connection, Fredrick, not that your business there is pressing. I am sure it seems to me that you badger them more than they do you. And before you injure me further, the girl Mary, is it? I require no weak attempt at justification.'

She looked away pained and I too required no more pertinent soul-searching so did the same until I felt it time to enquire further of my father's news.

'You have all the information that I have. I have given instruction to the driver that you be let out there, nothing else needs be said, surely? Frederick! I cannot believe you have no shame and dare to look confused! God knows I was warned that I owed you nothing and now I wish I had been more sensible!'

'Sensible! Sensible, Em!' I could contain my fury no longer. 'Let it be said that you are this above all else! Perhaps this jaunt of yours will do more for your reputation than all your careful plotting! Still take care, that in her wake, you do not befall a similar tragedy to your departed confidante Sophia!'

Fully aware that I was wrong to speak so, but I cared not, not any more. People such as the Sopersworths would very shortly be beneath my condescension and riches that they had never seen the like of at my disposal.

'I hope all goes well for you, Frederick, I truly do for there is nothing more to be gained from this alliance. Driver, please hurry!'

'Yes, please do, I find no beauty in the scenery and long wish this over!'

Neither did she blush nor scold at a thoroughly reprehensible assault. I might have admired her more at that time for her strength, pride, and courage but as had been made plain to me too often, I had no time nor capacity to appreciate such qualities. First comes the vanity in seeing them in yourself, of that I was habitually deluded, but your liking of someone is born of similarities even if in a small way and there can be no deception here. I looked at her profile for one last time and bitterly felt that I had not and would not miss it. Very aware of who I was, surely Joseph had promised this? I felt it and that he had delivered.

'Funny,' I remarked as we drew up at the gates of my father's house. 'The Hangman's Hitch was, perhaps, not all bad. No, I am quite sure, right now, that was purely what surrounded me and was reflected back at me. Charity? Why should they? Especially of spirit, no indeed. I believed the place would be a better one if a better person was to travel there. And you, Em, well you shall rally of that I am sure. Perhaps, if you are lucky, rid yourself of that expression for it is more akin to a sour old maid, girl! But at this moment suits you!'

I leaped from the carriage and looked no more. Not even a cry of grief from a young girl hindered my progress. I cared not to hear, and they pulled away.

Chapter 34

Here was wealth! I thought, here was where I belonged. Amongst riches untouched for sheer superfluity and tales of how it was begotten. I even amused myself with the notion that perhaps one such as Black had helped in its acquisition. Perhaps? It comforted me that it had survived such a battery, if indeed there had been one.

'Where is my father?' I sobbed loudly, surprised at the emotion so readily to hand.

I banged on the door and continued to wail and plea an audience. All very unnecessary but still I enjoyed it.

'Lord, man, I feel 'tis an age I have beaten this door! Abraham, please take me to he who lays dying, please God he still lives?'

The old sage, who was Abraham, had seen me conspire and collude from as little as five, and never disguised his disdain for me. Funny that my father thought it acceptable, even that he would beat me sometimes but bitter regret would be his, I thought, and he would relive each beating and it would hurt him more than ever me.

'Well?'

'Master Frederick, I would say 'tis good to see you but grave tidings and affairs have dogged your progress back here. We have heard much of your trials and company kept, unfortunately we have felt repercussions from some of your choices, but still 'tis not my place to say.'

He held the door and I pushed past him resentful that my dramatics had had no effect. How could a man, nay peasant, appear so superior? Why did I cringe at his stare?

Inside, as ever, I felt it cold. My mother had kept a royal distance till she died five years gone. I had never known her or my father's love, no, more resentment that I sometimes begged it. Strangely I enjoyed being once again surrounded by those with no expectation of me, it was incredibly liberating.

'The drawing room is cold, Brahms, you will see to it.'

'Of course, Sir.'

His silly smile that played about his lips was for sure bravado. That my father had seen sense and would leave all to me was obvious and no few changes would be administered here.

'And my father? He is aware that I am here?'

'He is, Sir, but is resting, and shall see you after dinner. Shall I have a place set for you, Sir?'

'Well of course, you stupid old fool! Insubordination, you will not be so ready to be remiss in your attentions when I am master to all this. Now be gone man and have the fire built, I wish to be alone with my grief.'

He went to leave.

'And my dogs?'

'You are not aware then, Sir?'

'Well no, I am not, man! Why do you think I ask, to appear a simpleton? Perhaps like your son, Brahms, yes?'

'I am sorry to say, Sir, that indeed the dogs are dead. A spate of animal mutilations followed a most unpleasant visit. I thought you aware? It was a most upsetting time for many households. Resentment can produce such evils, do you not find so, Sir?'

'No more, Brahms! I have heard enough please be gone!'

He went to leave again.

'Wait, did they catch the monsters who did this?'

'No, Sir, though it was obvious to all who perpetrated it. Was the shame, Sir, that prevented it being made more public.'

'Shame?'

But he was gone, and I a little sickened as any man who loses a good animal cried a little into my hands and thought if evidence of true grief was ever needed for my father he would find it here, though not for he.

Dinner was announced at seven and I sat at an empty table with an overly exaggerated service.

'Sara?' I asked as she bought me the first course,

'What was it that done for my father and how long has he ailed?'

'"Tis not my place, Sir, 'tis family matters, and I am under strict instruction to just serve you and not enter into such things. If it pleases you, Sir?'

'Please yourself though you might think to secure my loyalty for things will soon be different here, girl, be gone, and take this food with you. I do not dine and shall not be kept from my father's side by the servants.'

Exasperated I pushed past her and headed for my father's bed chambers. Such secrecy and formality was rather unnecessary I thought, he had asked for me!

Before me lay an old man barely breathing, not more than fifty but still exhaustion put him at twice that. Grey with lips tinged blue. Much letting had happened and the blood stained sheets made my heart leap briefly, not from grief but from the wish that he already be gone. I settled beside him not wishing to announce my presence, feeling this would produce better effect.

'Father,' I whispered gently taking his hand.

'There being no other who would call me so I presume that is Fredrick.'

The wasted face of a man in agony seemed animated by my presence, but then hatred also had this effect. I took courage and laughed,

'Yes, Father of course it is I, I am your only son. It is good to see you can still enjoy a sarcastic wit. But father I came here as soon as I could as I only received word today that you wished to see me. Please let us make right our wrongs. I cannot bare to be parted from you thinking things bad between us.'

'And yet, I could. In fact, I draw you here today to exact a pleasure that will make my passing more comfortable. You look confused, Fredrick, I must explain. Not long since, after I had given you up, I was visited by a young woman, a wretch, bearing child. With her several unsavoury sorts. I only admitted them for more hunger of your demise. You see, Freddy, allow me to finish, 'tis a dying man's indulgence surely. I never had respect for you and was embarrassment not shock that had me turn you away when your cowardice threatened the family name. You would be dead by now and more dear to me in that state than you have ever been.'

'Father! You are weak and sadly I feel delusional. Stop this madness, come we must forget it all and make amends.'

'I shall continue. Mary, yes that was her name. Came here with baby saying it yours and oh, I remember that she did plead your case so sweetly. I must laugh Frederick for she was a damned ugly one! Hah! I could not bear the audacity but for want of laughing sent your whore of Babylon from here with your spawn, if it be so? I believe Brahms had her beaten and those that followed her! So no, 'tis you who are deluded on all counts, dear son, not I. What do you say to that, my Frederick, ay?'

'I have nothing more to say or plead, dear father,'

I stood above him shaking with rage at these revelations, wanting to stop his gaping mouth struggle for breath.

'Now one last pleasure, to say that you will receive not a penny on my death, which will be shortly, not a penny! Brahms, Brahms! Take him from me!'

I grabbed his scrawny neck and then struck him again and again, blood burst from his wizened frame and I kept striking him until it felt like he popped. He lay there motionless, horror struck and dead, the family claret soaked my shirt and face, shaking I knew I must escape! To The Hitch! I thought, God hope none had heard but none came. Each creaking board had me reeling but I found shirt and tails in his chest, dressed quickly, and covered him with the sheet. I escaped through the servants' quarters and to the yard where I found a mount and made faster away than looked decent. Shocked bystanders stood aside and even some called my name, but I was chasing a feeling of exhilaration, no time to check how I appeared. By the time this feeling was exhausted I found myself not far from Cleveton and not far now from the ends. My ends. I decided to go about the place, I was aware of a back road that would serve better and so settled on it. It seemed as though this dark night, with no stars nor moon, deftly led me, and with no strength, will, or thought. I believe I glimpsed Heaven in a moment of emptiness. Perhaps we only ever do live it briefly and is why we chase it forever, and given the chance I would do so again.

As the sound of Cleveton being put to bed faded, I found myself once again on the familiar track that led back to where beginnings were made, ends would be met. But I was so tired, so very tired. I feared nothing more than another labour to extract myself from the very comfortable judgement passed on me long before I even realized it. The overwhelming blackness of the night seemed to cosset me, each step took faith so where I trod mattered not with no capacity to fear. Was that then why most went to the gallows hooded? A small charity for those damned to far worse than life had offered up. Perhaps.

Then there it was as though built by a man who raised his own gibbet. The only thing on earth that could inspire this was so unearthly yet was as real as he who sat outside lit by a tiny lantern with a rope.

Not a word did I speak as I approached. One last breath of what this night had offered me, one last check that all was settled.

'No hood?'

I choked.

'No audience.'

About Donna Maria McCarthy

The youngest of seven, six of which are boys! I grew up in a rural Oxfordshire community until the age of eleven when my family came to settle in Southampton.

My influences and go to reads are Charles Dickens, in particular *A Tale Of Two Cities*, Hillary Mantel, *Wolf Hall*, Anne Rice, *Interview with the Vampire* . . . The list could go on but these represent a broad spectrum.

I am also inspired by this great country of ours and it's society which has evolved through many bloody wars and a rich sometimes infamous history . . . From ruling the waves to loss and austerity, eventually realising that to be a world leader in the 21st Century nothing more was needed than acceptance, diversity, understanding and abundant talent – which as a nation we do really rather well.

ENJOYED
THIS BOOK? WE'VE GOT LOTS MORE!

Britain's Next
BESTSELLER

DISCOVER NEW INDEPENDENT BOOKS & HELP AUTHORS GET A PUBLISHING DEAL.

DECIDE WHAT BOOKS WE PUBLISH NEXT & MAKE AN AUTHOR'S DREAM COME TRUE.

Visit **www.britainsnextbestseller.co.uk** to view book trailers, read book extracts, pre-order new titles and get exclusive Britain's Next Bestseller Supporter perks.

FOLLOW US:

 BNBSbooks    @bnbsbooks   bnbsbooks

BRITAINSNEXTBESTSELLER.CO.UK